PRAISE FOR THE

"A traditional mystery comp
secrets and the self-serving manipulations of others . . . A good read
with urban grit and a spicy climax." —*The Hamilton Spectator*

"A mystery that fits the bill." —*National Post*

"The novel's short, punchy chapters whisk the story along to a thrilling climax, while the characters' relationships and rivalries provide a
strong emotional anchor." —*Quill & Quire*

"This is truly a fast-moving, action-packed thriller . . . Great story
with strong plot!" —Nightreader's Read and Blog

"The modest but resourceful Casey is a perfect heroine for our times,
a combination of thought and action."
—Lou Allin, Crime Writers of Canada

A Casey Holland Mystery

Beneath the Bleak NEW MOON

Debra Purdy Kong

TouchWood
Editions

TouchWood Editions
touchwoodeditions.com

LIBRARY AND ARCHIVES CANADA CATALOGUING IN PUBLICATION
Kong, Debra Purdy, 1955–
Beneath the bleak new moon / Debra Purdy Kong.

(A Casey Holland mystery)
Also issued in electronic format.
ISBN 978-1-77151-027-1

I. Title. II. Series: Kong, Debra Purdy, 1955– Casey
Holland mystery.

PS8571.O694B45 2013   C813'.54   C2013-901758-5

Editor: Frances Thorsen
Proofreader: Cailey Cavallin
Design: Pete Kohut
Cover image: Speeding cars: Notorious91, istockphoto.com
Texture overlay: Dimitris Kritsotakis, stock.xchng
Author photo: Jerald Walliser

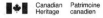

We gratefully acknowledge the financial support for our publishing activities
from the Government of Canada through the Canada Book Fund, Canada
Council for the Arts, and the province of British Columbia through the
British Columbia Arts Council and the Book Publishing Tax Credit.

This book was produced using FSC®-certified, acid-free paper,
processed chlorine free and printed with vegetable-based inks.

1 2 3 4 5 17 16 15 14 13

For my incredibly smart and creative daughter, Elida, who has already accomplished so much.

ONE

CASEY LOOKED THROUGH THE BUS window at the clear night sky, grateful for the new moon rather than a full one. New moons meant fresh starts. Full moons meant extra work for security personnel. Tonight, her shift had been peaceful—until the stink of cigarette smoke signaled trouble.

With Halloween only four days away, problems had already erupted on Mainland Public Transport buses. Firecrackers, drunken passengers, and fights had prompted Stan to assign more security staff. Tonight's misbehaving riders—the reason Casey had been assigned the M7 bus—were the teenaged twin girls at the back. The driver's report indicated that they began riding the M7 two months ago. Shortly afterward, passengers started filing complaints about one of the girls smoking on the bus.

Casey stood and soon spotted the culprit. The smoker's bright pink hair complemented her sister's purple, gelled spikes. Aside from their different hair colors, Purple's chubbier face made it easy to distinguish her from her twin. Purple scarfed down french fries, while her sister took a long drag on a cigarette.

The driver, Adrianna, said the girls boarded the northbound bus at Granville Street and Seventieth Avenue at 3:30 PM, three days a week, and exited at Granville and Sixteenth. Four and a half hours later, they always made a return trip, carrying three bags of food and a lot of attitude. Adrianna believed they worked at a nearby restaurant because she had heard the girls gripe about the kitchen staff. She also verified that the pink-haired sister usually lit up after wolfing down food. Adrianna's repeated requests to put out the cigarette had inevitably resulted in a tirade of verbal abuse. Taking a calming breath, Casey started down the aisle of Mainland Public Transport's newest, and much needed, acquisition. Although secondhand, the recorded announcements for upcoming stops, computerized ticket machines, and wide platforms instead of narrow, riveted steps were a big improvement over the older buses. Tonight, most of the passengers were adults, although there were a few younger teens and a couple of seniors.

"Hello, ladies. I'm with MPT security." Casey displayed her ID. "Would you put out the—"

The purple-haired girl started to gag. As she clutched her throat, her knee nudged Casey. Oh lord, the girl was choking. Prepared to use the Heimlich maneuver, Casey reached for the girl, until partially chewed fries shot out of her mouth, hit Casey's leather jacket, and landed on her running shoe. Totally grossed out, Casey shook off the moist glob. As Pink erupted with laughter, smoke shot out of her nose and mouth. Purple also bellowed with laughter but then began to wheeze. She removed an inhaler from her pocket and drew in deeply.

Casey gripped the back of the seat and waited for the class acts to finish. Which moron had said that girls were sugar and spice and everything nice? Casey had met more than her share of girls driven by spit and vinegar. She held her ID close to their faces.

"As I was saying, I need you to put out the cigarette." She kept her voice calm but firm. "The sign clearly states that smoking isn't allowed." Casey pointed to the NO SMOKING OR LITTERING sign above the windshield.

Pink regarded her with contempt. "A pretend cop with a little plastic card. How pathetic is that?"

Chatting passengers grew silent. Some looked up from their electronic devices and newspapers. Casey removed her notebook from an inside pocket and jotted down the date and time. She was going to enjoy throwing these two out. "I need to see your passes, please."

"What for?" the chubby sister asked. "We've showed them a million times."

Which was how Adrianna knew that these two were seventeen-year-old grade twelve students. "Because I need your names."

Amusement betrayed Pink's defiant tone. "You first."

"Casey, and you?"

Pink turned away.

"I'm Paige," the chubby girl mumbled.

Casey turned to the sister. "What about you?"

The girl rolled her eyes. "Lara."

"Last name?"

"Forget it."

"Well, Lara, my card gives me the right to stop this bus and ask you to leave if you keep breaking rules."

Truthfully, Mainland Public Transport couldn't afford to lose paying customers; not when Gwyn had invested so much time and money to acquire south Vancouver routes and purchase this big shiny bus. MPT might lose the twins' business, but there were far more complainants who'd go back to using TransLink's huge fleet if something wasn't done fast.

Smoke billowed out of Lara's nostrils. "If you kick us off, I'll have your ass fired, bitch."

"You can try." Casey noticed grease seeping onto the seat through the bottom of their bags. "I'm not the one breaking the rules, and you should know there's a twenty-dollar fine if you're caught littering three times. Rules and regulations are posted on the partition behind the driver's seat."

"We can't afford any damn fine," Paige said. Her sweater cuffs were frayed and there was a hole at the shoulder. Lara's torn jean jacket looked three sizes too big. Still, these two had money for cigarettes, hair products, and makeup. Why did some people think the rules didn't apply to them?

"Last chance, Lara. Put that cigarette out, or I'll have the bus stopped."

Lara started to reply when the sound of powerful car engines distracted her. Casey couldn't see anything on Granville. In her eleven years with Mainland, she'd seen plenty of speed freaks, but street racing had become more common over recent months. Cars were louder, faster; drivers more reckless. People used to race in the wee hours of the morning, but lately they'd started much earlier. Some of these idiots even recorded their races and posted them on the Net.

The vehicles sped closer. Casey crossed the aisle and peered out the window. Two northbound black sports cars were zigzagging in and out of traffic. Granville was a busy six-lane thoroughfare. Were those guys completely nuts?

"Shit, look at him go!" Lara poked her head out the window and hollered at them to go faster.

Casey pulled out her cell phone and marched toward the front of the bus. She was about to call 911 when she heard Adrianna on her phone, describing the racing vehicles. One of the racers' brakes screeched as he tried to keep from rear-ending a van. His opponent passed him in the fast lane and cut in front of the van. The van blasted its horn and slowed. The racer behind the van darted into the curb lane.

Casey's hands curled into fists. What the hell were these morons doing? As bus passengers stood for a better view, Casey reached for the microphone near Adrianna.

"Everyone sit down, please."

Only half of the passengers complied. Adrianna slowed for the yellow light at the Forty-First Avenue intersection. The racers had almost reached the intersection but weren't slowing down. Casey opened a window. Anxiety made her stomach clench. The light turned red.

Forty-First's green light came on, and a woman in a pink track suit jogged west into the intersection. The racers had slowed but weren't stopping. Casey's breathing quickened. The jogger kept her head lowered, as if oblivious to traffic. Surely she could hear the engines, unless she was wearing headphones and had the music cranked up. Despite the street lights and vehicle headlights, it was too dark to tell for certain.

"Oh my heaven!" a passenger yelled. "They'll hit her!"

The racer in the curb lane made a sharp right turn onto Forty-First and headed east. The other racer—now at the front of the pack—skidded. The brakes on his sports car squealed.

Casey stuck her head out the window and waved frantically. "Hey, watch out! Hey!"

Passengers also began yelling and waving. The jogger raised her head as the braking vehicle slid through the intersection at an angle.

Passengers gasped. The jogger tried to veer out of the way, but the racer struck her with a horrific thud and she was airborne. The sports car stopped. People on the street and in the bus screamed. Some swore. Casey clamped her hands over her mouth and forgot to breathe. The woman hit the asphalt face down and rolled three times before stopping on her back. Moans and shouts of outrage erupted throughout the bus and on the street. The vehicle took off, continuing north, and soon merged with the parade of red tail lights.

"Someone get the make and license plate!" Casey shouted. She turned to Adrianna whose mouth was open, her eyes wide with shock. Adrianna still held the cell phone against her ear, but she wasn't saying anything. "Adrianna, are you talking to 911?"

She didn't respond. A woman behind Casey was sobbing.

"Adrianna!" Casey gripped her colleague's shoulders. "I need your help!"

Color rushed to Adrianna's face. "Yeah. They're still on the line."

"Tell them we need an ambulance." With her heart slamming against her chest, Casey grabbed the first aid kit from the cupboard behind Adrianna's seat.

"Casey, if you're treating her, dispatch will need the woman's vitals." Adrianna handed her the phone.

"Thanks." Casey charged out of the bus.

The dry late-October air cooled her flushed cheeks. She was about to enter the intersection when the southbound light changed to green, yet none of the vehicles at the front of the line moved. Drivers had stepped out to either assist the jogger or call for help. One young woman cried as she paced back and forth in front of a silver Echo.

Keeping her hand raised and her kit in plain view, Casey ran toward the people gathering around the jogger. Traffic in all three northbound lanes had also come to a standstill. Farther down the line, vehicles had begun to honk and some were making U-turns.

A woman shouted, "I saw him hit her!"

Casey threaded her way among the spectators until she reached the jogger. A white-haired man was checking the jogger's pulse. Blood poured from the poor woman's forehead and nose and streamed down her face. Between the streams, her cheekbones were scraped raw.

"Are you a doctor?" Casey asked.

"Afraid not." His worried eyes blinked at her. "I sure hope you are."

"No, but I have first aid."

"That will help. Her pulse is weak and she's unconscious, I think."

"Is she breathing?" Casey asked.

"Yes."

She relayed the information to the dispatcher. "This area needs to be secured, so we won't be hit." Casey spotted three large men with beards and black, wavy hair. "Hey, could you guys direct traffic around us? This lady can't be moved till the ambulance arrives." The men looked at one another, then nodded and moved toward the vehicles.

Casey put the phone down, unzipped the kit, and tore open a packet containing latex gloves. As she put the gloves on, she swept strands of blood-soaked hair from the jogger's face. She scanned the woman's body, noting that her left leg was bent at an awkward angle, pushing her hip off the ground.

Casey leaned toward the victim. "Hello! Can you hear me?"

No response.

"That maniac ran the red light," the man said.

"I know." Casey pulled her own shoulder-length curls back and leaned close to the victim's face. A wisp of warm air grazed her cheek. Glancing at the man, she said, "Will you keep her head and neck still while I check her out? I'll get you some gloves."

"Of course." The man loosened his tie and popped the top button on his shirt. The lower half of his light gray suit jacket was splotched with blood.

"I'm Casey, by the way."

"Rod."

After he put on the gloves, Casey showed him how to keep the woman's head steady should she wake up and try to move. She fetched a flashlight from the kit and offered it to an older teen standing nearby. "Will you hold this for me?"

"Sure." He took the flashlight from her.

"Does your watch have a second hand?" Casey asked him.

"No."

"Then shine the light on mine."

As he did so, she monitored the victim's breathing rate. When she was done, a familiar voice said, "Has she croaked?"

Casey glanced up at the twins. "No." But she was breathing too slowly.

"Her face is gross." Paige's mouth twisted in revulsion.

"Unless you girls are first aid experts, get the hell out of here." Casey glared at them, then checked the woman's pulse points. They were weak. She looked at the kid holding her flashlight. "I have to check for injuries. Follow my hands."

Starting with the woman's right arm, she moved quickly and firmly over arms, torso, hips, and legs. The left leg could be broken. The kneecap didn't feel right either.

"I think I hear sirens," Rod said. "She's bleeding pretty badly."

"Head wounds do that." Casey lifted a plastic bag from the kit and gave it to the teen. "There's a blanket inside. Drape it over her." She removed a thick gauze pad from the package, then pressed it to the woman's forehead. "That's quite a cut. She must have landed on something sharp."

"I saw a flattened can on the road," Rod said.

Casey cringed at the image of jagged tin slicing through skin. Blood seeped out from under the pad. The sirens grew louder.

"I can't believe people would race on a street like this," a woman blurted. "What in heaven's name were they thinking?"

"It's not just them," someone answered. "No one slows down or bothers to check for pedestrians. Someone's getting hit every week."

One of the sirens stopped. Moments later, an officer emerged through the parting crowd. Casey looked at the cop with the thick, gray mustache and relief washed over her. Casey used to see a lot of Constable Denver Davies when they were in a couple of criminology courses together. She'd also met him occasionally on the job, whenever he was patrolling the same area she was working.

"Hey, Denver."

"Casey?" He knelt by the victim. "What brings you here?"

"I'm on the M7 tonight. Saw the victim jogging west on Forty-First. She entered the intersection just after the light turned green, but a sporty black vehicle ran the red light and hit her. She went flying through the air, hit the ground, and rolled."

A second patrol car arrived. "I'm surprised the fire department hasn't shown up yet," Denver said. "They usually beat us."

"I wish they had." She would have gladly let them take over. "The ambulance should be here any minute."

"How bad is she?"

"She's breathing and has a pulse, but I don't know." Casey didn't have a good feeling about this.

"Want me to take over?" he asked.

"No, it's okay, but could you get me another pad from the kit?" As he did so, Casey shifted her weight. The rough asphalt made her knees ache. She sat on the road, crossed her legs, and, despite the sweat on her lower back, shivered in the cool night air.

"Any idea who she is?" Denver asked.

"I didn't find any ID on her."

"Hey, Double D," a younger cop said as he approached. Casey didn't have to see Denver's face to know that he was probably swallowing back a nasty retort. Denver was a bit on the flabby side, unfortunately in the wrong places. "No sign of a black anything racing down Granville or side streets," the young cop said.

"Un-friggin'-believable," Casey muttered.

"Who are you?" the cop asked her.

"She's Casey Holland," Denver answered. "An experienced security officer with MPT." He turned to Casey. "This is Liam MacKenna, with the Hit and Run Team in Traffic."

Casey nodded to MacKenna, who ignored her as he looked at the victim, then turned to the spectators. "Anyone see what happened?"

"Two cars were racing north on Granville," Casey replied. "Weaving in and out like maniacs, cutting people off. I couldn't see the plates."

"One was a Lexus, which turned right onto Forty-First," Rod said. "I don't know the make of the hit-and-run vehicle."

"Freakin' chance racers." MacKenna turned to Denver. "Have you talked to witnesses yet?"

"I just got here."

Casey wanted to ask MacKenna what he meant by chance racers, but a car horn blasted and one of the civilians she'd asked to help with traffic was now yelling at a driver.

"Hey, Double D," MacKenna said. "Can you organize traffic control before someone else gets mowed down?" Without waiting for a response, MacKenna spoke into his radio, while Denver met up with two more officers. "Okay, I want everyone on the sidewalk," MacKenna said to the spectators. "You people are trampling on a crime scene and blocking traffic." He herded them toward the curb.

When Denver returned, Casey said, "I've never seen MacKenna before. Rookie?"

"No. He has a whole five years. Been brown-nosing his way up the ladder like a monkey on speed."

Denver had been a patrol officer for fifteen years. He once told her he wasn't the ambitious type, and that the criminology classes were simply to keep up. She had no idea if he felt he had to, or whether someone had told him to, but she'd always sensed that Denver's story was more complicated than he wanted her to know.

"You said one of the vehicles was a Lexus." Denver moved closer to Rod and opened his notebook. "Can you tell me anything else about the vehicle?"

"Not really. The windows weren't tinted or anything."

"I got a glimpse of the Lexus driver," said the teenager with the flashlight. "He was white and looked about my age."

"Where were you when you saw him?" Denver asked.

"Standing on the corner." He pointed to the northeast corner. "I was walking south, waiting for the light to change."

"Then you would have seen the jogger?" Casey asked.

"She passed right in front of me," the teenager answered. "I heard people yelling at her to watch out, but she was wearing earphones."

Casey glanced at the road. She hadn't noticed an iPod or anything.

"What else can you tell me about the driver?" Denver asked the teen.

"Clean-shaven, wore glasses, and he looked kind of scared, but I only saw him for, like, three seconds."

"Was he alone?" Denver asked.

"I think so."

The second gauze pad had soaked through. "Where in hell is that ambulance?" Casey muttered.

"I saw the passenger in the car that hit her," a shaky female voice said.

Casey looked up at a middle-aged woman fumbling with the ends of a blue wool scarf.

"Ma'am?" Denver stepped closer to her.

The woman stared at the victim. Her lips trembled and she removed her glasses to wipe her eyes. Denver moved to block her view. "I appreciate how difficult this is, but anything you can tell us would be helpful."

Casey heard the kindness in his voice. All those years with VPD, and Denver still had compassion.

"I was in the northbound curb lane." She paused. "I probably should have looked at their license plates, but those cars made me so nervous, the way they were zipping in and out of lanes like that." She slipped her hands into her coat pockets. "When the car stopped after hitting that poor lady, I saw a young man in the passenger seat."

"Can you describe him?" Denver asked.

"I'm pretty sure he wore a gold hoop earring, like mine." Her fingertips fluttered against the small gold circle dangling from her ear. "And a red bandanna."

"Did you see anything else?"

"Just his profile." She hesitated. "His mouth was open, like he was shouting or screaming. And he wasn't a big man. At least I think it was a man. I suppose it could have been a woman."

Casey's hopes sagged. Would they ever be able to identify these guys?

As Denver wrote down the woman's contact information, the ambulance finally pulled up and the paramedics took over. Casey's knees creaked as she stood, and her butt was freezing. While she removed the bloodstained gloves, she described what she knew of the victim's medical condition.

Rod also peeled off his gloves. "Is there someplace I could put these?"

"Sure." She held out an empty bag. "Thanks for your help."

He nodded and looked at the jogger. "Your arrival was a blessing. Maybe she'll make it."

"That would be good." Although Casey still had a bad feeling about this.

Once Denver had finished talking to Rod, he stepped closer to Casey. "Are you working this route all week?"

"Yes. Mondays, Wednesdays, and Fridays." The twins' riding schedule.

Denver watched his colleagues direct traffic. "Another pair of eyes would help. I heard a couple days ago that several races are planned over coming weeks. Maybe this disaster will slow things down. Who knows?"

Casey didn't ask who had told him this. Denver placed professionalism above friendship, and since she was a civilian in VPD's eyes, she headed back to the M7 bus, which was parked at the stop just past Forty-First Avenue. Officers had cordoned off the intersection and were rerouting traffic, so this part of Granville now seemed eerily quiet. It wasn't supposed to be like this at eight-thirty on a Wednesday night.

As Casey boarded the bus, Adrianna said, "Will she be okay?"

"I don't know." Casey noticed that half of the passengers were gone. "Have the police talked to you?"

"Just finished with them a minute ago. I'm free to go."

"Finally." Lara threw a crumpled bag on the floor. "Let's get moving."

The twins had taken seats near the front, probably for a better view of the carnage. Casey looked at the third, full bag oozing on the seat between them.

"We'll go after you've picked up your garbage and wiped off the grease your bags left on both seats."

Lara's hate-filled eyes were fixed on Casey.

"Just do it, Lara," Paige said, handing her a wad of paper napkins from the remaining full bag. "We're really late."

Lara jumped up and stomped toward the back.

"You've got blood on your jeans," Paige remarked to Casey.

Casey spotted dark smears above the knees and felt a little queasy. As she slid into the seat behind the twins, she watched the ambulance leave. Denver and other officers were placing markers on the road next to bits of debris. The crowd on the sidewalk had started to disperse, and MacKenna was taking a closer look at skid marks.

Casey looked up at the night sky and tried to spot the dark new moon. In short minutes, it felt as if the whole world had become bleaker and more somber. So much for fresh starts.

TWO

SOMETIMES, THE MOST HEARTFELT PRAYERS weren't enough. And sometimes, all the medical talent in the world couldn't mend a body ripped apart inside. Casey had known this long before Wednesday night, yet news of the jogger's death still filled her with grief, helplessness, and fury. Images of that poor woman flying through the air had haunted her sleep for the past three nights.

Casey picked up the *Vancouver Contrarian* and read, *More Street Racing Carnage* in black bold letters. Beneath the heading: *On October twenty-seventh, street racers struck and killed twenty-nine-year-old Beatrice Dunning, a Vancouver high school science teacher.*

Casey tossed the paper onto the living room floor. There was no need to read the article a fourth time. She knew it by heart; hell, she'd lived it. The trip to Vancouver General Hospital later that night . . . meeting the grief-stricken parents and learning from Denver—who'd also come by—that Beatrice had died in the ambulance. The moment Chuck Dunning started thanking her for trying to save his daughter, Casey lost it and collapsed into a tearful embrace with both parents.

She folded the *Province* and the *Vancouver Sun* newspapers. Both had printed factual stories. The smaller, edgier *Contrarian*, however, had been publishing a gripping series on street racing by journalist Danielle Carpenter. Carpenter had written about the emotional toll racing took on the families, friends, and colleagues of those killed, or severely injured, by racers who believed they were invincible.

Casey picked up the *Contrarian* again and found herself reading another piece by Carpenter, this one in the editorial section. *Over two hundred young people have died in high-speed crashes in British Columbia in recent years. Innocent bystanders have also been killed: people walking by the road, standing on curbs, waiting at bus stops;*

children riding bicycles. Skulls have been crushed and limbs severed, simply because of the need for speed.

Casey pictured Beatrice's bloodied face.

The police and the public must do more to catch those with too much horsepower and too few brains. Parents need to stop buying their kids expensive cars and expensive lawyers. If they refuse, then perhaps parents should share a cell with their kids. Judges must stop handing down pathetically light sentences.

Casey paced around the living room. To stop street racing would be like trying to stop a tornado in its tracks. Once these guys started up, one could see it coming, anticipate its path and destruction, but how could anyone prevent the maelstrom from playing itself out when everything was happening so fast? As far as Casey knew, the police still had no leads on the hit-and-run vehicle. Maybe they never would.

Lou entered the room, carrying a large cardboard box marked HALLOWEEN. Summer followed with two more boxes. Cheyenne trotted after her, tail wagging, carrying a plastic orange pail in her mouth.

"We've left decorating too late," Summer said, gathering her dark hair—still damp from swim practice—in a ponytail. "We'll be lucky to finish before the party. This year, we should start on Christmas right after Remembrance Day, to cheer this room up."

"Not a bad idea," Lou said.

Casey barely glanced at the walls, well aware that this big old room of Rhonda's sure needed something. Dark wall paneling, an ancient burgundy sofa, and wall-to-wall red shag carpet hardly lifted one's spirits. The dreary room reminded Casey of Rhonda's absence.

As Summer took the pail from her golden retriever, Casey wondered how badly the girl missed her mother right now. Rhonda loved this holiday . . . all holidays. For a while, Summer had acted out and threatened to leave home, but once she'd re-established contact with Rhonda, she'd settled down. Casey was relieved that Rhonda had decided to stay as involved as possible in her daughter's life, though the arrangement was far from perfect. Frustration was beginning to set in, as Rhonda repeatedly told Casey to ensure that Summer did her chores and homework. Then she had the gall to follow up with phone calls to see if Casey was staying on top of things.

"Everything okay?" Lou asked Casey, his face pensive.

"Yeah, fine." Or it would be once she stopped being so maudlin. She'd been grateful that he'd stayed over last night. A comforting hug after another nightmare had calmed her down.

"Are you sure?" Lou wandered toward her. The worry in his gray eyes contradicted his happy face T-shirt.

Casey liked that he was only a little taller than her, and that she didn't have to reach too far to touch his hair. "I've been reading the papers again."

Lou placed his hands on her shoulders and kissed her cheek. "Want to help us make this room even spookier?"

She appreciated the attempt to cheer her up, but she'd rather get out of here. "Actually, I should pick up some groceries, then start the housework."

She didn't look forward to the cleaning part. Becoming Summer's legal guardian was a big enough responsibility, but when Rhonda had also asked her to become caretaker for this big old house, Casey knew that a lot of her free time would be lost. Summer preferred to use this room and the large kitchen at the back rather than hang out in Casey's third-floor apartment. Although Summer kept the kitchen clean, for the most part, Casey was the one who washed the floor and cleaned the fridge. She also did most of the yard work.

Mercifully, the two tenants occupying the second-floor studio suites paid their rent on time and were rarely home, which meant little work in that respect. Still, with a job plus school, she'd been tired a lot these past eighteen months. Rhonda wouldn't be eligible for parole for another eight and a half years, a reality Casey didn't want to think about.

"Remember how late we were last year with Christmas?" Summer opened her box. "We didn't even set up the village."

"I'll help you," Lou said. "It'll be fun."

"You truly are a holiday junkie," Casey remarked.

"I like to celebrate stuff, like the fact that we've been going out one year, five months, and twenty-two days."

Casey looked at him. "Have you been crossing the days off a calendar?"

"I figured it out last week, just for fun." Lou lifted a life-sized, glow-in-the-dark skeleton out of the box. He laughed as Cheyenne barked at the skeleton, then sniffed it all over. "We're going to miss you tonight," Lou said to Casey. "With your seniority, you shouldn't have to work till 2:00 AM on a Saturday night."

Casey said nothing. What could she say? Lou knew she'd never really cared for Halloween silliness. She'd only agreed to this one because Summer had asked for a party and Lou had volunteered to host it. From there, things had evolved into inviting a few of his buddies over as well.

"How many friends are coming tonight?" Casey asked Summer.

"Six, and maybe one more." She removed a row of paper witches from the box. "His name's Jacob."

A guy friend? This was new. Until recently, Summer had come home from school complaining about how disgusting boys were.

"Is he a classmate?" Casey asked.

"Yeah, in math and science." She pulled Cheyenne's inquisitive snout out of the Halloween box. "We sort of hang out."

Sort of? What did that mean, or should she ask? "Make sure Jacob's parents know there will be plenty of adults around, and that the kids will only be drinking pop," Casey said. "If his parents need to talk to me, you can give them my cell and landline numbers."

"I'll call him later."

Lou rummaged through a box. "Do you have any corn syrup and red food coloring? I need to make blood."

Disgusting. "I'll put them on my grocery list." Her cell phone rang.

When she answered, a quiet male voice said, "Miss Holland, this is Chuck Dunning, Beatrice's father."

"Oh." Her breath caught in her throat. "Hi." Casey stepped into the hallway. She'd given Mr. Dunning her business card and said he could contact her if he needed anything.

"I've, uh, that is, my wife and I have made funeral arrangements." When his voice cracked, Casey's cheeks grew warm. She sat on the bottom step of the staircase by the front door. "We were hoping you could come to the service."

It was a kind gesture, but she hadn't known Beatrice. Attending would seem intrusive. "That's nice of you. When is it?"

"Tuesday at eleven." As he gave her the name of the church, the despair in his voice made her want to cry. "We'd really appreciate it if you could come. After all, you helped try to save my little girl." He choked on the last word.

Casey's eyes filled with tears.

"I'm sorry," he said finally. "It's just that . . . Well, this is so . . ."

"I understand." Casey rested her elbow on her knee and placed her hand on her forehead. "I'll be there."

"Thank you."

As he disconnected, a chorus of "Whooooh" followed by Summer and Lou's laughter in the living room jolted Casey. She wiped her eyes, plastered on a smile, and returned to the Halloween merriment.

THREE

THE HEELS ON CASEY'S PUMPS sank into the cemetery's soggy grass. Standing in one spot for so long hadn't been a great idea, but she'd been afraid to fidget, to show how uneasy and out of place she felt. A large group had gathered at Beatrice Dunning's grave. Boots, gloves, hats, and umbrellas obscured her view of the many wreaths surrounding the polished casket. It was just as well. Funeral wreaths and caskets depressed her, as did the sparse maple trees carefully interspersed among tidy rows of plaques. She had assumed the interment would be for family and close friends; however, as she'd paid her respects to the Dunnings after the service, Mrs. Dunning had gripped Casey's hands and said, "See you at the cemetery." Not a request or command, but an assumption; one that would have been rude to contradict.

In front of Casey, Beatrice's female students clung to each other and wept, while the boys stood apart with their heads lowered, hands rising furtively to wipe their eyes. Other guests dabbed noses or struggled to keep umbrellas upright in the occasional gust of wind. In the past few minutes, the rainfall had fizzled into a light sprinkle, yet umbrellas stayed up. Casey didn't blame people for wanting a partial shield from so much grief. Today, she'd learned that a stranger's funeral wasn't much easier to bear than one for someone she'd known.

Casey spotted a short South Asian woman staring at her. This same person had sat in the pew across from her in the church. Three times, Casey had caught the woman watching her. The first time, she'd smiled at Casey and nodded. Later, she simply stared as if to say, who are you and why are you here? Despite the dark lipstick and black eyeliner, this woman barely looked twenty, too young to be a teacher, too old to be one of Beatrice's current biology students. Perhaps a former student?

Tiring of the woman's stare, Casey looked away and focused on the few orange and yellow leaves still clinging to the branches of an enormous maple tree by the cemetery's fence. Behind the tree trunk, someone dressed in black was watching the funeral. The individual was petite enough to be female, yet something about the wide stance and the way their hands were shoved in their pockets made Casey think this was a man.

Was he a curious bystander? One of Beatrice's students? Or was he someone with a guilty conscience? TV and radio newscasters had announced the date and time of the service. Casey's heart beat a little faster.

The minister asked everyone to pray. Casey lowered her head as far as she could without losing sight of the man by the tree. When he headed for the gate leading out of the cemetery, she shifted her weight back and forth until her heels were free. Glancing over her shoulder, Casey took a small step back. She hadn't noticed any police watching the crowd, but this was a large crowd. They could be film-ing the mourners. If they were here, were they watching the guy leave? She moved slowly to avoid drawing too much attention and didn't see anyone else follow him. After clearing the group, Casey hurried after the bystander. The guy walked at a fast clip. Casey started to jog.

She tried not to make much noise, but he glanced over his shoul-der, hesitated, then kept going. Casey ran until she caught up with him. When he stopped, she noticed the gold hoop piercing his right earlobe. Oh, hell. The witness had mentioned a gold hoop worn by the passenger in the hit-and-run vehicle.

"Hi," she said, trying to appear friendly. "I saw you watching the funeral and just wanted to make sure you were okay."

Confusion creased his brow. The guy was Asian, possibly Chinese, late teens or early twenties, and his fingers twitched. "I . . . uh . . ." His voice faltered.

"Did you know Beatrice?"

"N-no English."

His gorgeous leather jacket, gold watch, and large jade ring suggested wealth. The kid resumed walking, but at a faster pace. If he hopped into a car, she wanted the plate number. When he glanced over his shoulder and saw her following, he bolted. Casey took off after him, wishing the police were as interested in this kid as she was. Her job had given her plenty of practice chasing suspects in heels and tight skirts, but speed and stamina were always obstacles. The guy darted across an intersection as the light turned red. One motorist blasted the car horn, but the kid kept going. By the time the light changed in Casey's favor, he had reached the next intersection, turned left, and vanished.

"You handled that pretty badly," someone said from behind Casey.

Casey turned around to find the South Asian woman smirking. Was she a cop? "Excuse me?"

"You lost him." The pink crystal stud in her nose sparkled against her brown skin.

"Who are you?" Casey asked. "And why are you following me?"

"I'm Danielle Carpenter."

Whoa. This was a surprise. "You write for the *Vancouver Contrarian*." Given the maturity of her articles, Casey had assumed the reporter was older.

Danielle's smile revealed perfect teeth. "You've read my work?"

"Yeah, it's really good."

"Thanks, and you're Casey Holland."

"How do you know my—"

"I overheard the Dunnings introduce you to people. I also know what you do for a living, and how you tried to save Beatrice's life."

Casey started to walk back to the cemetery. Beatrice's friends and relatives, red-eyed and sniffling, had thanked Casey for her heroism—a word that made her want to sink through the floor. Whatever she'd done, it obviously wasn't enough.

"What did you want with that guy?" Danielle asked.

"To see if he knew Beatrice. He'd been watching the funeral from a distance."

"Damn, I wish I'd seen him."

"You might have, if you hadn't been so busy looking at me."

"I was waiting for a chance to talk to you," Danielle replied. "What did the guy say?"

"That he doesn't speak English."

"But you didn't believe him, or you wouldn't have kept following. So, what's up?"

Part of Casey wanted to discuss his nervous manner and speculate about his presence, but she didn't want to wind up in print with her opinions taken out of context. "I don't know."

"Come on, something about him bothered you."

"No, I was just curious."

"You were there when Beatrice was hit, so you must have heard talk about the racers. Do you think he's connected?"

"No idea."

"But you were wondering?"

"The thought occurred to me."

"Racers are cowards at heart, Casey. I doubt any of them would take the time to actually show up at a victim's funeral. All these punks care about is the next race, though they might go underground for a few weeks."

Casey opened the cemetery gate.

"Had you realized that Beatrice was too far gone while you were doing first aid?"

Lou and Denver were the only ones who knew she had feared the worst. "How long have you been with the *Contrarian*, Danielle?"

"I'm not with them," she answered. "I'm freelancing."

"Oh."

"I submitted articles to the big papers on spec, but they wanted wimpy, watered-down shit, and it shouldn't be when people are losing their lives." Danielle's voice rose. "Everyone pretends street racers are dumb kids who will outgrow the need for speed, and a lot do, especially after one too many close calls. But there are also hardcore freaks who don't care who they hurt as long as they win, and they need to keep winning over and over again."

"You're preaching to the converted."

"Sorry." Danielle shrugged. "It just pisses me off." She watched the mourners begin to leave. "Have you seen other races while you've been riding buses?"

"Nothing like what happened Wednesday night." Casey walked slowly, in no hurry to catch up with the mourners. "One of your articles mentioned a sharp increase in racing over the past year, but you never explained why."

"New drivers are on the scene, as are some rich assholes who've been placing huge bets on races. It's just another facet of a subculture that's worth billions. Hell, even corporations cash in by selling new products to the racers who gave them the ideas in the first place. And don't get me started on the auto shows selling high-performance parts."

The vehemence in Danielle's voice prompted Casey to change the subject. "Are you going to the reception?"

"No. What about you?"

"No." Casey hadn't been invited, which was fine. She needed to put all this sadness behind her.

"Did Beatrice say anything to you while you were helping her?"

"No." Enough questions. She didn't want to be interviewed. "With all the articles you've been writing, aren't you worried that street racers will decide you're too nosy?"

"Hell, I want to give them something to worry about, and I'm just getting started," Danielle replied. "You see, I know who killed Beatrice."

FOUR

DANIELLE CARPENTER WAS EITHER A headline-seeking liar or playing games. Either way, Casey wasn't impressed. "Let me get this straight. You actually know who ran her down?"

"More or less."

"What does that mean?"

Danielle switched her large, vinyl bag from her right to left shoulder. The picture on the side was of a woman hang-gliding. The caption beneath said BORN TO FLY. "The racers could be part of a group who've been chance racing."

Liam MacKenna had used the same word at the accident scene. Casey had wanted to ask what chance racing was, but the guy had been too busy interviewing witnesses. "What's chance racing?"

"It's when drivers race in high-traffic areas. Sometimes it starts spontaneously with two jerks revving engines at a stoplight. Now that gambling's part of it, most races are planned in advance. The thing is, the drivers have ramped up the danger by racing early at night and on heavily used thoroughfares."

Casey shivered as the damp November air penetrated her clothing. Mourners were driving away. "Whatever happened to plain, ordinary drag racing?"

"It's still around, along with hat racing, which is all about distance."

"Hat racing?"

"It's when guys race right across the city or to a designated point in the burbs, usually late at night."

"Do you know who these chance racers are?"

"One called himself Eagle, but I think they're using numbers instead of names online, now."

"The police could track them down."

"Before how many more people die?" Danielle shot back. "I told

VPD about these guys weeks ago, but all the stupid asses cared about was the name of my source, which I wouldn't give."

If she'd been uncooperative and blunt, Casey understood why things hadn't gone well. She stopped at Beatrice's grave. White roses covered the shiny casket. She prayed for Beatrice, and for justice.

Once Casey started to move on, she said, "Do you think Wednesday's race was spontaneous or planned?"

"I didn't hear about any prize money on it and the cars' descriptions weren't familiar, so they were either just two guys at a stoplight or wannabes, or maybe even hardcore racers trying out new cars," Danielle answered. "Those guys are obsessed with driving bigger, better, faster. Half of them are rich kids whose parents are dumb enough to buy them luxury vehicles. The other half hold down two or three jobs to raise the cash for parts to build souped-up cars."

"How much prize money is offered?"

"Thousands per race, and I hear the purse keeps growing."

"How many hardcore racers are in this group of chance racers?"

"Five on the A team, a few more on the B team, and a bunch of wannabes."

"Quite the hierarchy." The Dunnings' limousine pulled away. Casey felt bad for not saying goodbye.

"Someone named Leo was organizing races, but I haven't seen his name in a while," Danielle said. "He's probably using a number too."

"What does your source say about this tragedy?"

"He claims he doesn't know what's going on, but I think he's lying. Anyway, I tracked down a witness who said the passenger in the hit-and-run car wore a gold earring and red bandanna. Was the guy you tried to talk to wearing a gold earring?"

Casey hesitated.

"Shit, he was, wasn't he?" Danielle grabbed Casey's arm. "Tell me."

"Lots of guys wear gold earrings, and let go of my arm."

As Danielle did so, she said, "I need a detailed description."

Casey recalled the kid's wide cheekbones and suspicious expression.

"Please, Casey."

This girl was far too intense. Casey stepped back to distance herself from all that angst. "He could just be an innocent bystander."

"Come on, think about it. A kid with a gold earring happens to show up at the funeral, then runs away when you try to talk to him. Do you honestly believe it's a coincidence?"

Casey wished she hadn't let that kid get away. A dozen vehicles followed the limousine along the narrow, curving road out of the cemetery. Casey looked over her shoulder. The groundskeepers would soon be tucking Beatrice in for good, and she didn't want to be around when they started. Casey picked up her pace.

"My ride's gone," Danielle said. "Can I get a lift?"

"Where do you need to go?"

"The main library on Georgia, but anywhere within a few blocks is fine."

Casey unlocked the passenger door to her old Tercel. "More research?"

"Yep. My laptop crashed and I can't afford to fix it." Danielle looked the car over. "I take it MPT doesn't pay well. No union?"

"Not yet." It was a sore point with some employees. "And I don't like spending money on cars. I plan to drive this one into the ground."

"Then your shoes must be grazing the asphalt."

Casey inserted the key in the ignition. "Do you have a car?"

"I'm saving up and looking for something that reflects me."

"Bold and saucy, then."

Danielle laughed and unzipped her plum ski jacket. She glanced at the backseat. "Do you live in your car?"

"I occasionally do surveillance work. The sleeping bag and pillow come in handy."

Danielle rummaged through her enormous bag until she removed a plastic container and folded paper towel. "Want half of an egg salad sandwich?"

"No, thanks."

"I've got granola bars and the best homemade pecan squares you've ever tasted. My mom's a fabulous baker."

"Lucky you." Casey missed Rhonda's scrumptious cakes, cookies, and muffins. "Do you live at home?"

"For now. My girlfriend wants me to move in, but I'd rather have a steady job first."

No car, no computer, and living at home. Hmm. "When did you graduate from journalism school?"

Danielle pulled the lid off the container. "A few months ago."

"I take it the *Vancouver Contrarian* doesn't pay well either?"

Danielle barked out a laugh before biting into her sandwich. Casey rolled down her window and tried not to gag on the smell of hard-boiled egg. She cruised down the narrow, winding road and saw another funeral in progress.

"There's going to be another race soon," Danielle said.

"How do you know?"

"Upcoming races are posted in coded language for the gamblers. The info's up only a couple of days, then deleted. I cracked the code because my source blurted something out."

"Did you tell the police?"

"Of course."

"I thought you said the racers might go underground."

"Maybe not. If the hardcore racers weren't involved with Beatrice's death, they may want to try another race in a different part of the city. The prize money is too enticing and the need for speed too addictive." Danielle unwrapped a pecan square. "The group gave itself a name. I never wrote about it because I don't want them, or the gamblers, to realize how much I know."

"What is it?"

Danielle's dark eyes gave her a long look. "Roadkill."

FIVE

AS THE M7 BUS PULLED up, Casey shivered in the chilly November air. The southbound Granville and Broadway stop was crowded with folks waiting to board. Teenagers scampered inside, while a couple of seniors cautiously stepped onto the platform, their gnarled hands gripping the rail. Tucking the latest issue of the *Contrarian* under her arm, Casey boarded last and paused when she saw Adrianna's tense expression.

"Are you okay?" she asked.

"I'm cramping up a bit."

Uh-oh. Adrianna was only in her fifth month of pregnancy. "You want me to take the wheel? My license is still valid."

"Thanks, but it's not that bad, and I've called for a replacement. He'll meet us at the Thirty-Third Avenue stop." Adrianna checked her mirrors and merged back into Granville Street's southbound traffic. "My husband will be there too."

"Are you sure you don't want me to take over?"

"I'm fine, really. There's been no pain for ten minutes, and if I focus on driving, I won't worry so much." Adrianna attempted a smile. "By the way, those snotty twins were in horrible moods when they boarded this afternoon."

"Did they break any rules?"

"No, but they were swearing a lot and complaining about school."

Casey found two unoccupied seats, one behind the other. It was just after eight and the bus was two-thirds full. Most of the passengers looked exhausted and glum. She sat behind the first empty seat. The huge volume of transit users along this corridor was the main reason both MPT and TransLink buses serviced this route. Boutiques, bistros, art galleries, and other retail outlets contributed to the congestion, but after Sixteenth Avenue, when the area became more residential and Granville Street widened, traffic moved a little faster.

If the twins were on schedule, they would be boarding shortly. Casey flipped through her paper and found Danielle's byline on page three. She'd written about the people whose lives Beatrice had touched and her legacy as a teacher. Casey slumped back in her seat as sadness again swept over her.

The M7 stopped for the twins, who stomped down the aisle with their usual bags of food. The tantalizing smell of french fries made Casey's stomach rumble. Tonight's chicken salad supper hadn't been filling.

Pink-haired Lara scowled when she noticed Casey. "Oh look, it's Deputy Dog, the overpaid babysitter."

"Have a seat, girls, before you fall."

The only free seat was in front of Casey. As they plunked down, she smiled.

"Shouldn't you have a better job at your age?" Paige opened her food bag and retrieved a handful of long, thick fries.

"I like my work," Casey replied. "Do you like yours?"

"How do you know we work?" Lara asked, her eyes narrowing.

"Because you stick to a schedule and always bring the same food on board. It's logical to assume you work in a restaurant."

"It's not really a restaurant when they only serve burgers," Paige remarked.

Lara lifted a double-patty burger with lettuce and tomato. Creamy mayonnaise oozed out of the bun and plopped onto the wrapper. Casey inhaled deeply. Lord, it smelled good. Over the past three months she'd stepped up her quest to eat less fatty food. Tonight she was regretting it.

Nearing Granville and Thirty-Third, Adrianna slowed the bus. When they stopped, she stood and winced.

Casey hurried up to her. "Are you okay?"

"Another cramp . . . intense."

Adrianna's husband filled the doorway and helped Adrianna outside. Casey had met him at a couple of office parties but couldn't remember his name. She was about to wish Adrianna good luck when the sight of the replacement driver constricted her throat.

"Hi, babe, how you doin'?"

Casey held back a nasty reply. What the hell gave Greg the right to call her that? They'd been divorced for over three years, and she'd hardly seen him in months. "Medical leave's over, huh?"

"Back's better since the surgery." His gaze swooped up and down her body. "You look great."

As if his opinion mattered. Greg, however, had gained a ton of flab around the middle. His face was rounder and the blossoming second chin did nothing for his appearance. What had happened to the slim, muscular, fifteen-hundred-meter runner she used to admire? She headed back to her seat.

Paige turned and swallowed her food. "Why did you look at that guy like he's a giant worm? He treat you like shit or something?"

Female radar always amazed Casey. All that intuition and women still made bad choices in men. Greg was a classic example.

"So is he, like, some loser ex-boyfriend?" Lara asked.

"Why are you two so interested?"

"Just curious," Paige answered.

"He's still hot for ya," Lara remarked. "I can tell from the body language."

The remark made Casey cringe. She sat down and immersed herself in the editorial page of the *Contrarian*. A number of letters supported Danielle's condemnation of street racers, and some recounted their own near misses with maniacs on the road.

"There's the spot where that jogger got smucked," Paige remarked.

Casey looked up and saw the roadside memorial of flowers and cards fastened to a light standard. She had told Denver about her encounter with the Asian kid. She'd also mentioned Danielle's revelation about a racer called Eagle, an organizer known as Leo, and the group called Roadkill. Denver didn't volunteer much information in return. She hadn't expected him to.

Lara turned around. "I guess you couldn't save that jogger, huh?" The girl had a talent for baiting people.

"She died in the ambulance."

"Maybe we could find out who hit her," Lara replied.

"Sure, you go ahead and do that." Casey focused on the *Contrarian*.

"No, really," Paige said, swallowing her food. "We know kids who are into racing."

Casey turned a page. She would love to get some names, but letting the gruesome twosome know this wouldn't be smart.

"One of them is a Chinese guy from Richmond," Lara added.

Richmond was known for its large Asian population, and the city was just on the other side of the Arthur Laing Bridge at the end of Granville Street. Still . . . "That narrows the field down to a few thousand kids," Casey said.

"We know kids who hang with the Chinese kid's sisters," Lara replied. "We could get a name."

"Tell the police, not me."

"We don't talk to cops," Paige said.

Casey tried not to smile. "Why is that?" She watched the twins scrunch their empty bags. "What did you two do?"

"We just don't," Paige replied, turning away.

"There's an empty seat at the back," Lara said. "Let's go."

When the twins stood, Casey said, "Take your garbage with you." She nodded toward the greasy crumpled bags on the seat.

Lara looked like she'd just been asked to dip her hand in horse poop. Glaring at Casey, she grabbed the bags. "Bitch."

Ditto, Casey thought as she thumbed through her paper again. A minute later, she smelled cigarette smoke. She smacked the newspaper on the seat, opened her notebook, and jotted down the time before approaching the girls.

"This is the second time I've told you not to smoke in here. Put that cigarette out right now, Lara." A nearby conversation stopped.

"Chill," Lara said. "We're out of here in two minutes."

"Put it out now, or we'll be contacting your parents about a fine or suspending you from riding our buses for a month."

Lara blew smoke in Casey's face. Casey yanked the cigarette out of the girl's mouth and mashed it into the floor.

Beneath the makeup, Lara's face reddened. "No one else cares, so why are you making a big deal out of this?"

"They do care. I'm here because of passenger complaints. Doesn't it occur to you that someone with asthma, cancer, or emphysema could be on this bus?" She felt the M7 slow to a stop. "Why can't you think of anyone besides yourselves?"

Lara jumped up. "You are the biggest bit—"

"Knock it off!" Greg's voice ricocheted around the bus as he marched toward them.

Casey fumed. Why was he interfering with her job?

"You two." Greg pointed at the twins. "Out!"

The girls stayed put.

"I've got this, Greg," Casey said.

Ignoring her, he said, "This bus doesn't move until you girls leave."

"But our stop's three blocks away," Paige replied. "And the cigarette's out."

"I don't give a damn."

Lara snatched the crumpled bags. Paige wrapped her arms around the full one.

"My mom will have your asses fired!" Lara stomped to the exit.

"Sure, little girl." Greg followed them down the aisle.

Casey didn't know which made her angrier: Greg's interference or the twins' insolence. She waited until the girls had exited before she moved closer to Greg.

"Stupid kids are ruder every damn day," he muttered.

Casey took a deep breath. "You had no right to butt in."

He merged back into traffic. "I was just trying to help."

"Well don't." She didn't need his macho crap back in her life.

"I heard about your promotion to second-in-command a while back," he said. "Congrats."

"Thanks. It means I know what I'm doing."

She started to walk away when he said, "Uh, can I talk to you a minute? It's about the house."

Not *the* house, her house. The one she grew up in, the one she and Greg had shared until she'd learned about his affair with Tina and moved out. The memories had been too painful to stay. Besides, she'd wanted to show their colleagues that she wasn't a vindictive, bitter ex-wife. Apart from not needing the cash, she wasn't sure why she hadn't sold the place. Yet keeping the house had become a good investment. Greg paid his rent on time and took care of the property, or so he'd told her. She hadn't seen the place since she'd moved out.

"We shouldn't be discussing personal matters—"

"Money's been tight." Greg kept his gaze on the road. "Tina's pregnant again."

A second baby? No surprise there. Greg had always wanted three or four kids fairly fast.

"The thing is, she quit her job," he went on. "I was wondering if we could have a temporary reduction in rent until I can put a few more paychecks together."

Was he for real? "Greg, I haven't increased the rent since we began this arrangement."

"I appreciate that." His Adam's apple moved up and down. "It's just that I heard your dad owned a fancy house on Marine Drive and had a fair bit of cash, and that your mom had a condo in Yaletown. That had to be worth some big bucks, so you must be doing okay, right?"

Un-friggin'-believable. "I had to pay off Mother's many debts. Living within her means was never her strong suit, though I guess the grapevine didn't tell you that part. But belated thanks for the sympathy card." Given that Greg and Mother had never met and Mother's name rarely came up during their marriage, Casey had been shocked that he'd sent her a card at all.

"You're welcome." He checked the side mirrors.

"As for the cash and the Marine Drive place, there's a complicated legal dispute about who owns what, so I won't see a penny anytime soon, if ever, by the time the lawyers are done."

"Sorry to hear that."

She just bet he was.

"Look, I wouldn't ask for the reduction if there was another choice," he said. "We've maxed out our credit with the banks, and our families are broke."

Then why didn't he rent a cheaper place in the suburbs? Why should she take a financial hit because of Tina's pregnancy?

"Will you at least think about it?" he asked.

No way in hell, but why start an argument now? "All right."

She'd turn him down later, when she felt like it. Casey returned to her seat, wondering if she was a touch vindictive after all.

SIX

"GREG HAD THE GALL TO ask for a reduction in rent. Can you believe that?" Casey slumped against her sofa and sighed. It was only 10:00 PM, but she was exhausted and frustrated by her shift on the M7 bus.

"He had no bloody right to ask," Lou said, his arm firmly around her shoulder.

"Have you seen him since he's been back?" she asked.

"Yeah. This afternoon, from a distance. As soon as Greg spotted me, he took off." Lou shrugged. "Probably still thinks I'm the one who told you about Tina."

Casey had never told Greg which driver blabbed about his affair. Although she'd tried to make it clear that Lou wasn't the one, Greg didn't believe her. It was actually another driver who'd ratted Greg out and then quit the company the same day he spilled the news.

"I always hated how Greg started referring to you as *my wife* rather than by your name," Lou said. "He knew it, too. Told me he did it on purpose."

"Really?"

"After you split up, the asshole said he knew I had a thing for you, and that he needed to keep reminding me who you were married to. I told him he couldn't have expected the marriage to last, seeing as how he'd broken his vows." Lou scratched the stubble on his face. "That's when he threw the first punch."

"I always wondered how it started, and I do remember the huge shiner you gave him." She also remembered that Lou and Greg's friendship ended right after the fight.

"I bet he regrets losing you," Lou said.

"What makes you say that?"

"One of the guys kidded him about his weight." He watched

Casey's guinea pig, Ralphie, scamper around the cage on the book-shelf opposite the sofa. "Greg said the old ball and chain was making him fat." Lou turned to her. "He never talked about you that way."

"I wasn't a great cook."

"You've gotten better." Lou smiled and gave her shoulder a squeeze. "Anyhow, the jerk's only been back a week and he's already trying to grab overtime shifts. That's money out of my pocket, which pisses me off when I'm trying to save."

Lou rarely discussed finances, but Casey knew he wasn't a big spender. "What are you saving for?"

"My own house someday." He kissed the back of her hand. "Meanwhile, what do you think about us living together? I mean, me moving in here."

Casey's mouth fell open. "This is a surprise."

"I know, but the timing feels right, and I'd pay half of everything. I could be settled in by Christmas." His eyes were cautious, hopeful. "What do you think?"

She was thinking, what was the rush? "Are you unhappy with the way things are?"

"Well, our shifts are crazy and we don't see each other at all some days, and we've been together nearly a year and a half." His expression became intense. "Don't you think it's time we took our relationship to the next level?"

Casey wasn't convinced that relationships worked in levels, but her heart and stomach fluttered with a mix of delight and trepida-tion. "I think it's a good idea. But this still feels like it sprang out of nowhere."

"I'm blurting it out like a moron, but it's been on my mind for a couple of months." Lou stroked the back of her hand with his thumb. "Truth is, I was planning to bring it up over a romantic dinner this weekend, but my mouth got ahead of me."

Because they were talking about Greg? She glanced at Lou's old ABBA T-shirt. Living with Lou would mean regularly listening to his god-awful disco collection. There'd be lots of adjustments, big and little.

After two quick knocks on the door, Summer stepped in, followed by Cheyenne. She looked from Casey to Lou, then back to Casey. "What's with you two?"

"What do you mean?" Casey asked.

"Lou looks worried, and your face is all red and your eyes are kind of weird."

"I mentioned moving in." Lou waved his hand in front of Casey's face. "I think she's going into shock. Maybe we should lay her down and throw a blanket over her."

Casey smacked his thigh. "You caught me off guard, that's all."

"That would be fantabulous!" Summer's eyes shone.

Casey knew she'd approve. Lou was the only male role model in Summer's life, and she treated him like a beloved older brother. "Did you get your homework done?"

"Yeah, Jacob helped me. He's good at science."

Casey hadn't met the boy yet, but Summer was always on the phone with him or chatting online. She'd have to learn more about the kid.

"When are you moving in?" Summer asked Lou.

He glanced at Casey. "After the shock wears off."

"What's the big deal?" Summer replied. "You're here practically every night."

Four nights out of seven, on average, Casey thought, but it wasn't the same as living together. Living together was huge. While Lou might have been thinking about this step for a while, she hadn't. On the other hand, she couldn't think of a good reason why he shouldn't. Lou was the best man she'd ever known.

"You are moving in, right?" Summer asked Lou.

"Yes, he is." Casey nodded emphatically. "By Christmas."

"Cool."

As Summer left, Lou stroked Casey's back. "Are you okay? Heart rate back down?"

She smiled. "I'm fine."

"You looked like you were about to hyperventilate."

"I wasn't." At least she hoped not. "Are you sure you want to live with me? I'm still not a great cook and I'm a bit of a slob, and there will be lots of chores."

"Casey," he said, gripping her hands. "I'm looking forward to it. Every bit of it."

"There will be stressful days and probably not enough quality time. We'll also have to figure out where to fit all your furniture." Glancing at his T-shirt, she tried not to think about the music. "What if I mess up, Lou?"

"No one gets through life without messing up now and then. We'll work it out, Casey."

"I once thought I could work things out with Greg."

"He was a control freak who wouldn't let you travel, or go to school, or build a career that paid better than his."

She knew Lou was the opposite. Things could still fall apart, though, and then she'd lose the best friend she'd ever had. Was it really worth the risk?

"I'd better head home." He gulped the last of his beer and then stood. "Got another 6:00 AM shift."

Lou's pensive expression filled her with guilt. Had she hurt his feelings because she wasn't jumping up and down with excitement? He deserved a better response.

Casey followed him to the door. As he opened it, she said, "Start bringing your stuff over."

Doubt flickered in his eyes. "Are you sure?"

"Absolutely." She put her arms around him.

Lou kissed her tenderly. "We're good together. You know that, right?"

"That's the one thing I do know."

After Lou left, Casey shut the door and wandered around the living room. Were they good enough to last a lifetime, though? That's what moving in meant, didn't it? Permanence. Yet he hadn't proposed. Probably because he needed to take things one step at a time; maybe opt out if he decided she wasn't really committed to their relationship after all. And that would be her fault. Had she ever let Lou know that she hoped they'd last forever? Did she have hope? She wanted to.

Casey looked at her pine coffee table and bookcase, her rocking chair with the comfy black cushion, the sunflower footstool. She looked at her suede sofa, the color of dark jade. It might work with Lou's garish plaid brown and yellow furniture.

The phone rang. Casey was surprised to hear Danielle Carpenter's voice. "I just found out that Eagle's connected to the Regency Fitness Center in Richmond, though I'm not sure if he's a member or an employee," Danielle said. "Word is he's there on Saturdays, so I'm going to check it out. I could use help scoping the place inside and out. Will you come with me?"

Was she nuts? "Sorry, but Saturdays are chaotic around here."

"It wouldn't be all day. My friend Ginny can help for most of it, but I could sure use your surveillance skills."

"Danielle, this is a police matter. We shouldn't get involved."

"I told the Richmond RCMP everything, but they don't have the time or manpower to stake out fitness centers all day."

Casey moved to the bay window overlooking the front yard of this corner lot. "Even if Eagle shows up, how will you recognize a guy you've never met?"

"By his car. I told you, these guys drive hot, flashy machines. Action in the parking lot could be more interesting than anything happening inside. If we hear a souped-up engine, all we have to do is get a plate number."

A car sped past the front of the house, a common occurrence on this residential street. Casey herself had done it a million times. She peered out the window but couldn't see much past the fence and the weeping willow tree. The vehicle turned right and disappeared.

"You want Beatrice's killer caught, don't you?" Danielle went on. "These guys are racing around town, doing whatever the hell they want, and now they've killed someone. Haven't you had enough?"

The guilt trip annoyed her. "The police will catch them."

"Maybe, but not fast enough. My source says they're racing again soon, and don't you think the cops could use some help chasing down leads?"

"When's the race?"

"I don't know, which reminds me, how are you with word puzzles?"

"Lousy. Why?"

"Because on the forums they've started using some kind of strange code to communicate, and I can't figure it out."

"My boyfriend's good with puzzles; I'll ask if he can help. Have you forwarded the code to the Vancouver Police?"

"Yeah, and I haven't heard squat. If I pay for your workout, will you come? Please?"

Casey rubbed her forehead. "Let me think about it."

"Okay, but I'm going no matter what. I'll call you tomorrow."

Danielle sounded obsessed. Was she that worried about innocent people, or was she desperate to make a name for herself as a journalist? She was right about one thing: Roadkill had to be stopped.

Ralphie stood on his hind legs, pressed his tiny paws against the wire mesh, and started to whistle. For a guinea pig, he was awfully punctual about his evening snack.

After she fed him a piece of carrot, she looked up Denver's home and cell numbers in her address book. They had worked on a couple of class projects together, and he'd been generous about making himself available. She tried his cell phone.

When he answered, Casey said, "Are you at work?"

"On a break. MacKenna and I are grabbing some food. What can I do for you?"

"I just got a call from Danielle Carpenter, the reporter I told you about."

"What did she want?"

"Danielle thinks a racer known as Eagle is connected to the Regency Fitness Center in Richmond. She wants me to help her with some parking lot surveillance on Saturday."

"Talk her out of it. Danielle Carpenter has no business there."

"I tried, but she's determined."

"Carpenter's a head case," MacKenna said, loudly enough for Casey to hear.

"She's an angry kid on a vendetta," Denver said.

Casey frowned. "You guys know her?"

"We've met," Denver replied. "I didn't tell you before because it wasn't relevant. I didn't think you two would be in contact again."

"What do you mean by 'vendetta'?"

"I take it she didn't tell you about her brother?"

"No."

"Ben Carpenter was killed while street racing three years ago, and his passenger was seriously injured."

"That explains a lot."

"MacKenna was first on the scene after the crash. Here, he'll tell you."

A short pause and then MacKenna said, "Carpenter wasn't wearing a seatbelt. The kid went right through the windshield, landed on his head, and snapped his neck."

Casey closed her eyes. "Oh."

"His buddy went through the window too. Sustained major head injuries," MacKenna added. "Claims he doesn't remember anything about that night, but I have my doubts."

"Lots of people lose their memory after severe crashes."

"I think this kid's evasiveness is more than memory loss. Their car was sideswiped, probably by the guy they were racing, which would explain why Carpenter lost control. I'm still trying to find out who they were racing that night."

"Was Ben Carpenter part of Roadkill?"

The line was silent for a moment. "How do you know about them?"

"Danielle told me."

"Roadkill didn't exist then, but Carpenter had a rep for reckless-ness. It looks like baby sister has the same trait."

"Put Denver back on." When he did so, Casey said, "I could try talking Danielle out of this stakeout again, but I don't think it will work."

Denver muttered something she couldn't quite decipher. "This isn't the best idea I've ever had, but maybe you should go along and make sure Danielle doesn't do something stupid. She needs to understand that if she digs too deep, she could get hurt. There are people who want to keep racing going and they won't tolerate meddling."

"Can't she be stopped legally?"

"Sitting in a car watching people isn't illegal, depending on where she's parked and how she conducts herself. That young woman doesn't have a whole lot of respect for us, so I doubt she'll listen to me."

He was right. Casey knew all too well about quests for justice. The traumatic death of a family member wasn't easy to make peace with, and certainly not when major questions were left unanswered.

"While you're there," Denver said, "try and find out who her source is. We need to talk to that individual."

Another reason for encouraging her to go. "Okay, but I think Danielle is as good at withholding information as she is at acquiring it."

"You've handled strong-willed people and tough situations before, and that girl needs some levelheaded guidance. Let me know what happens, and take care."

Casey put the phone down and propped her feet on the footstool. She'd take care all right, she was good at that. But how would she convince a headstrong woman on a vendetta to do the same?

SEVEN

CASEY RUBBED HER GLOVED HANDS together and shivered, a chill seeping through her old, rust-ravaged Tercel. She'd been staking out the Regency Fitness Center's parking lot for nearly an hour and had had enough. Gas was too expensive to keep the heater on, and she had to open the window a bit to keep the windshield from fogging up. Surveillance never had been her favorite thing; in November it really sucked.

Squinting through the rainy windshield, she watched a couple of people leave the building. She'd backed into the corner of the center's L-shaped parking lot so she could see the entrance and every stall. So far nothing exciting had happened. She doubted anything would. Given the number of middle-aged patrons driving SUVs in and out, the place seemed more likely to attract Eagle's mom than Eagle. None of the engines were powerful either, and she hadn't seen a black Lexus. Denver had told her they still weren't able to identify the vehicle that hit Beatrice Dunning, which was disappointing. It had been dark and the racers moving fast, but surely someone must have seen something.

A tall, husky guy in a bomber jacket and black track pants emerged and hurried along the front of the building only to disappear around the corner. Thirty minutes ago, she'd seen a young woman, also in black track pants, head the same way and return fifteen minutes later. Since there was no parking on that side of the building, employees probably took smoke breaks there.

Desperate to warm up and stretch, Casey stepped out of the car. Danielle wasn't due back for a few minutes, so why not do something useful? Casey flipped up her jacket hood and sauntered past the double oak doors, glancing through a vertical window beside each door. There was no sign of Danielle in the lobby. She continued on until the sound of a large car engine caught her attention.

A shiny, gray Dodge Neon turned into the lot and cruised past each stall as if looking for someone. The Dodge turned the corner and disappeared from view. Seconds later, the vehicle reappeared. It was dark outside, and the bright headlights prevented Casey from seeing the driver or the plates. A moment later, the vehicle left the premises. Whatever, or whomever, the driver had been looking for apparently wasn't here.

Casey turned the corner and found the employee leaning against the wall, beneath the roof's overhang, taking a drag on a cigarette. When he saw her, he stood a little straighter. Floodlights gave her a clear look at his wary expression. He couldn't be more than twenty, perhaps even still in high school.

"Hi," she said.

The kid nodded. "How you doin'?"

"Not bad." She noticed a dozen cigarette butts crushed into the gravel footpath. Soggy grass bordered the path. "Nice spot for a break. You could use a table with an umbrella, though."

"And a mini-bar." He smiled, adjusting his glasses.

"Definitely." She grinned as she glanced at his name tag, which said HARVEY. "I have a friend who's looking for a job. Do you know if this place is taking applications?"

"I dunno. Try the front desk."

"Thanks." Evergreens concealed most of the wooden fence separating this property from a car dealership. "Is the Regency a good place to work?"

"Pretty much. Decent benefits, nice staff." Another grin.

"Cool. The center was recommended by a friend of a friend who I think works here. His name is Eagle."

No more grins. Just a flicker of alarm, then a quick check of his watch. "Don't know the name." Harvey took another drag on his cigarette, then blew a long stream of smoke from his mouth.

He sure as hell did know it. "Maybe I got the wrong place. Nice talking to you."

As Casey continued down the side of the building, she could

almost feel his gaze on her back. Did Harvey lie about knowing Eagle because of the racing thing, or was Eagle simply bad news? Turning the corner, she followed a footpath along the back wall.

Several yards ahead, a small waterfall spilled into a pond surrounded by three small maple trees and a pattern of stones. Beyond the pond, tall, thick bushes bordered the fence. In daylight this would be a tranquil view for patrons. Picture windows exposed a dozen people on treadmills and stationary bikes. A couple of women glared at Casey, but most patrons ignored her. There was still no sign of Danielle. Casey turned the corner.

The fourth side of the building brought Casey back to the parking lot and the flashy purple Camry Danielle had noticed earlier in the day. She'd told Casey to watch for the driver, but he hadn't appeared. She checked her watch. Danielle was late. Enough waiting. Casey hauled the gym bag out of her car and headed for the entrance.

Inside, the lobby looked more like a legal office than a fitness center. The smell of cedar was appealing, as was Diana Krall singing "The Look of Love" through hidden speakers. The navy carpet felt soft under her feet. Halogen lights illuminated a long counter manned by two young Asian women.

Casey started to approach them when Danielle emerged from a room on the left side of the counter. A sign propped by the door invited guests to frequent the juice bar. Danielle's short curls were still damp.

"You're late," Casey murmured.

"Sorry. Checking leads, but nobody knows Eagle, or so they say. I looked for a kid with a gold earring, but the only ones wearing gold around here are the soccer moms. Any luck at your end?"

"I talked to one of the staff outside: a kid named Harvey, who shut down when I mentioned Eagle's name."

"Good. That means we're close." Danielle plunked a twenty dollar bill in Casey's hand. "Enjoy your workout, and keep the rest for your gas and time."

Guilt swept over Casey. Danielle couldn't afford this. "I'd rather pay my own way."

"No. I told you this was on me and I keep my word."

"Thanks." Casey handed her the car keys.

Danielle strolled toward the young receptionists. "Hi there. My friend wants to work out. And could I get some information on memberships? This place is awesome."

While one clerk took Casey's money, her colleague opened a glossy brochure and began a lackluster sales pitch. When the girl was done, Danielle said, "I'll take this home and think it over." She started to leave, then stopped. "By the way, do you know Eagle? He's a friend of a friend of mine, and I heard he works here."

The receptionist began straightening brochures. "No one named Eagle works here."

Her colleague looked down and appeared to be studying the scheduling book.

"Guess I heard wrong." Danielle turned to Casey. "I'll show you where the change rooms are." As she led Casey away, she whispered, "They know him."

"Agreed. By the way, I saw a Dodge Neon with some major horsepower enter the lot, cruise down the side, then turn and leave."

Danielle's eyes lit up. "Was it gray?"

"Yeah, why?"

"One of Roadkill's A-team members drives a metallic gray Neon." She gripped Casey's arm. "This place is the key." She scanned the lot as if anticipating the vehicle's return.

"If he comes back, try to stay out of sight," Casey said. "Whatever you do, don't follow him."

Danielle laughed. "As if I could keep up in your old rust bucket."

→   →   →

AS CASEY FINISHED dressing, someone announced that the fitness center would be closing in ten minutes. She stepped out of the change room to find the receptionists counting cash and flipping through receipts. They were joined by a woman whose oval face and tiny nose matched theirs. The woman's neck was draped with three gold chains of different lengths. Gold earrings, bracelets, and a wristwatch complemented her black blouse.

She spoke Cantonese to the girls, then noticed Casey and smiled. "Would you like a membership brochure?"

"My friend picked one up, thanks." Casey stepped outside.

"Your heater's crappy," Danielle said, as Casey slid behind the wheel. "Don't you have a window defogger?"

"There isn't usually enough hot air in here to need one."

Danielle stuck out her tongue and rummaged through her enormous bag. "I forgot to give you a cinnamon bun with your name on it, and I mean that literally. My mom made it."

She handed Casey a plastic-wrapped bun. Casey grinned at her mashed and smeary name. She'd always had a weakness for sweet and yeasty baked goods. "This is great. Thank her for me."

"It'll keep you busy while we wait to see who drives off in the Camry with the stovepipes."

"Stovepipes?"

"The two tailpipes. I want to see the driver's face."

"You wrote down the license plate. Can't you just give it to the police?" Biting into the doughy bun, Casey savored the taste of plump raisins, cinnamon, and brown sugar.

"Sure, right after my source tells me who it belongs to."

Casey chewed slowly. "What if he doesn't want to tell you?"

"Then I'll use leverage."

"Such as?"

"I think he's betting on races. When I asked him to help me find out who struck Beatrice Dunning, he said he'd lose money if people got suspicious."

"What does he do for a living?"

"Washes dishes at his parents' restaurant for minimum wage."

"Which restaurant?"

"Doesn't matter."

It did to Denver. Casey listened to the rain tap the roof and windshield. "Could your source be the one who posts schedules of upcoming races?"

"Nah, coming up with codes isn't his thing." Danielle watched the entrance. "Three more people are leaving. Turn on your windshield wipers."

One of them was a patron heading for a Jeep Cherokee, which left two cars in the lot. Casey spotted Harvey, now wearing a backward baseball cap. Since they'd be leaving shortly, she reluctantly wrapped the rest of her cinnamon bun.

"Look! The guy with the ball cap's getting into the Camry," Danielle said. "I saw him inside from a distance but didn't get a chance to talk to him."

"That's Harvey." Casey listened to the Camry's engine rev up. "Wow."

"With an engine like that, he's definitely into racing. Maybe he's called Eagle in the racing world."

The other vehicle was a Honda Civic driven by a young woman.

"That's the juice bar girl," Danielle said, watching her. "No guts in her engine."

The Camry followed the Civic out of the lot. As Harvey cruised past them, he glanced their way. He'd just cleared the lot when a silver Jaguar drove in and eased up to the entrance. Tinted windows shielded the driver's identity.

"Expensive wheels," Danielle remarked. "Bet it's the owner."

The Regency's entrance opened and the two receptionists stepped out, followed by the woman with the gold chains. While the woman locked the building, the girls climbed into the backseat. The woman stared at Casey and Danielle as she headed for the passenger's side.

"We should go." Casey eased the car forward.

"Once I find out where Harvey lives, we can start some serious surveillance. If all goes well, he'll lead us straight to Roadkill members."

We? Was she serious? "Why don't you save yourself a lot of time and trouble and give the plate number and your source's name to the police."

"You still don't get it," Danielle replied. "If the cops really cared about street racing, they would have caught most of the racers by now. Someone has to clean the streets, Casey."

"Danielle, you're taking this too personally."

"It should be personal to everyone. People are dying because racers break laws and greedy assholes encourage them to do it. Why the hell aren't more people outraged?"

Casey understood her vehemence. Grief did that to people, but this girl was heading down a dangerous path. "I heard about your brother."

The fury in Danielle seemed to deflate. "Who told you?"

"A VPD officer named Denver Davies. He's a friend of mine and a decent man."

Danielle nodded. "I know him."

"He told me." Casey paused. "Denver's concerned that you're getting in over your head. Apparently some of these gamblers are nasty guys who wouldn't hesitate to shut you down any way possible."

Danielle looked away from her. "You think I don't know that? My source is connected. He's watching out for me."

"Twenty-four-seven?" When Danielle didn't respond, Casey said, "I'm worried that your need for justice is causing you to take unnecessary risks."

"I know what I'm—"

"Listen to me," Casey interrupted. "I took big risks once to find answers about my father's death, and my actions nearly killed someone I love."

"But you felt there was no other way, right?" Danielle replied. "After Ben died, races kept going and now more people are dead. The rush is addictive, Casey. The best high racers can get, and they won't stop on their own. Someone has to shut them down."

"Acting without thinking won't help the problem."

"I *am* thinking," Danielle shot back, "*and* learning more every damn day. Now that I've got a lead on one racer, I'll find others. I also have a source who lets a little more slip out each time I push him. I'm close to nailing these guys, I know it."

Casey sighed. That was the whole bloody problem.

EIGHT

JUDGING FROM THE SCOWLS ON the twins' faces as they boarded the bus, Casey knew this ride wouldn't be fun.

"She's here," pink-haired Lara said to her sister as they took the seat in front of Casey.

Greg glared at the twins. His gaze drifted to Casey, who gave him a warning look. He turned around. The twins opened bags of food and began scarfing down fries. Why hadn't they chosen a seat farther away from her? There were plenty of empty seats on this quiet Monday night.

Paige practically unhinged her jaw to get her mouth around a mayo-dripping burger. Lord, this pair would need quadruple bypasses before their fiftieth birthday. While they ate, the twins engaged in a silent conversation through glances and head nods until Lara turned around and said, "Did you hear about the street race tomorrow tonight?" Her tone was a little too smug.

"No." Casey focused on the preschoolers shoving each other across the aisle. The woman sitting behind them—presumably the mother—told them to knock it off, which they did, for about five seconds.

"Two of the guys who'll be racing are called Hellhound and Eagle," Paige said as she munched her food.

"They live in Richmond," Lara added.

Before she could stop herself, Casey turned to the twins, who smirked at her.

"A friend told us that Eagle was racing when that jogger got mowed down," Paige added.

Holy crap, did these princesses actually have a serious lead? "How does your friend know this?"

"Like we said the other day," Paige remarked, "they're connected to Eagle's sisters."

Casey made a point of looking unimpressed. "Tell the police, not me."

"I told you, we don't talk to cops," Lara shot back.

"You never said why." As their smug expressions vanished, Casey couldn't help smiling. "How many run-ins have you had with them?"

"Too many." Paige stuffed two more fries in her mouth.

Lara smacked her sister's pudgy arm and said to Casey, "There's a race on Knight Street tomorrow. We could find out which one is Eagle's car."

Casey knew the street well. Knight was long and wide, a natural speedway.

"Hellhound drives a purple Camry," Lara added.

Oh sweet lord, Harvey's car. Their info was spot on. Better play it cool. "I know," Casey said. "I talked to Hellhound a couple of days ago at his workplace and watched him drive away. His Camry is quite the machine. Have you seen it?"

Lara's smile faded. "I bet he told you squat about the race."

"Why would he? I'm not a racer, and obviously they need to keep a low profile."

"We could find out who else will be there," Lara said.

"We could find out all sorts of shit the cops won't know," Paige said. "You want to help nail the driver who hit that jogger, right?"

Casey studied the girls. "Why would you two go to all that trouble?"

"Simple," Paige answered. "We give you information and you leave us alone. No fines or lectures or other crap."

The offer didn't surprise her. Although the bargain would never happen, Casey sure as hell wished there was a way to gain access to the twins' contacts. Beatrice died ten days ago. When Casey last spoke with Denver, there'd been no new leads.

"I'm not convinced you two can come through."

Paige and Lara exchanged frustrated glances.

"We know that Eagle's mom owns a fitness center in Richmond called the Regency," Lara said. "Follow her and you'll find him."

Casey brushed imaginary dust off her jeans and tried not to react to this revelation. If the twins were telling the truth, the rich-looking woman she'd seen climbing into the Jaguar on Saturday could be Eagle's mother, and the receptionists his sisters. It explained their guarded reaction when Danielle mentioned his name.

"You'll have to do better," Casey remarked. "I've already been to the Regency and met the mom and sisters."

"Bullshit!" Paige blurted.

"The place caters to people my age and older, which is probably why the sisters looked so bored behind the counter." Casey smiled as the twins turned back around. With any luck, they'd keep quiet for the rest of the ride.

Did Danielle know about tomorrow's race? If Casey told her, Danielle would want to know her source, but mentioning the twins wasn't an option. Danielle would want to interrogate them, and putting those three together could be an explosive combination. Besides, what if they were lying about the date and/or location?

After the excursion to the Regency two days ago, the only contact she'd had from Danielle was a link to the forum containing coded info about the next race. If Danielle learned that Eagle's mother owned the Regency, she'd want to follow her. There was no proof that the Asian woman and receptionists were truly related to Eagle. Still, it was worth mentioning to Denver.

As the bus passed the Granville and Forty-First stop, Casey looked at the tributes for Beatrice. Every time she saw the flower-covered light standard, the sadness returned. Someone pulled the cord as a roaring car caught up to the M7. Casey rushed to the nearest empty seat across the aisle, opened the window, and peered at a pair of blazing headlights weaving in and out of traffic. She inhaled sharply and her stomach clenched. Was it a Roadkill driver, or just another maniac?

Greg slowed the bus as the black vehicle zoomed past. Casey looked to see if other racers were approaching, but none were. Passengers grew silent. The anxiety was almost palpable.

"It's a Volvo C70 coupe," she heard Greg say on his cell phone.

He then gave the year the car was made. The guy always had been a bit of a car nut.

Casey hurried to the front of the bus but couldn't see the vehicle. The sound of screeching brakes made her gasp.

"Hold on," Greg said into the phone. "Something's happening."

Casey gripped the pole behind his chair. She thought she heard an agonized scream. Oh god, this couldn't be happening again.

"Greg, stop the bus. I need to get off."

"I'll see if I can get closer."

Casey fetched the first aid kit as Greg eased the M7 forward until he caught up to stopped traffic. He opened the doors while he told the dispatcher that there may have been a collision. Casey bolted south down Granville. Her lungs felt raw in the night air and her throat was bone dry. One and a half blocks ahead, a car horn blasted, then another. Casey kept running. She heard shouts.

Southbound traffic wasn't moving at the Granville and Forty-Ninth intersection. A couple of vehicles had been abandoned. Some people were crying, others shouting. A few simply stood in the middle of the intersection, their expressions shocked and horrified. Casey couldn't see what everyone was staring at, but a woman's high-pitched wail told her more than enough. As she maneuvered her way through spectators, a woman said, "A whole family! I can't believe it."

A man in front of Casey shouted, "Step back, please!"

More horns blasted from east and westbound drivers who were too far away to see what was happening. Casey surged forward and finally broke through the cluster of spectators.

"Oh, no."

A woman and child were sprawled on the asphalt. The girl looked maybe ten years old. Blood soaked her white tights and seeped onto a sheet of music trapped under her right leg. A man and a woman performed first aid on the child, while a gray-haired lady wailed over the motionless woman.

"Can I help?" Casey bent near the man. "I have first aid training."

"We're doctors," the man replied without looking up. "The other victim's deceased. If you've got something to cover the body, do so."

As Casey opened the kit, she noticed three people directing traffic. She approached the dead woman whose eyes were open, her mouth slightly parted. Blood pooled around her head. An elderly man squatted next to the keening woman and rocked back and forth on his heels. His hands covered his face and his shoulders shook. Casey carefully placed a blanket over the victim's head and body while distant sirens grew louder.

"If you want to help," one of the doctors shouted at Casey, "get the crowd back to make room for the ambulance!"

Two Asian men in their twenties burst through the spectators. They saw the little girl and halted. One of them lifted the blanket off the body, then moaned. The other blurted something in Japanese.

"Okay, people!" Casey shouted. "We need to clear the area for emergency vehicles. Can everyone move to the sidewalk, please?"

As people started to comply, Casey approached the Japanese man who was watching the doctors work on the child. The other man tried to comfort the distraught seniors.

"Excuse me. Do you speak English?"

He barely nodded.

"Do you know the little girl?"

"My niece . . . Crystal."

Casey took a deep breath. "And the woman on the ground?"

Tears glistened in his eyes. "My sister, Anna-lee."

The mother. Casey figured the grieving seniors were the grandparents. Her heart had been pounding since she left the bus. Queasiness was settling in, accompanied by a surreal lightheaded feeling. A fire truck arrived. The young Japanese men helped the elders to their feet. Casey retreated to the curb on shaky legs.

"How could anyone do that?" a male voice said next to her. "The guy's insane."

Casey saw a teenaged boy clinging to a girl about the same age. The girl dabbed her eyes. "We should go, Jeff."

"Did you see it happen?" Casey asked them.

"Hell, yeah," Jeff answered. "The freak sideswiped that Kia." He pointed to the damaged car by the curb.

"Is the Kia's driver okay?"

"Think so. He's the one waving his arms and yakking." He pointed to a man standing near the Kia.

"Did the hit-and-run driver strike the pedestrians, then hit the Kia? Or did he hit the Kia first, then veer into the pedestrians?"

"He hit those people first, then took off," Jeff replied. "That's when he sideswiped the Kia."

"I heard screeching brakes," Casey said. "The driver must have tried to avoid the pedestrians."

"No! He braked to avoid a pickup." The girl choked back tears. "The asshole hit them on purpose!"

Casey wasn't sure she'd heard right. "What?"

"He went straight for them, man," Jeff said, barely able to contain his emotion. "Like he was targeting them."

"Are you sure?"

"Damn right. I know what I saw."

Nausea roiled in Casey's stomach. "Which way did he go?"

"West. Down Forty-Ninth."

"Did either of you get a look at the driver?"

"The windows were tinted," Jeff answered.

The ambulance arrived, followed by two police vehicles.

"We heard him shouting," the girl said, sniffling.

"Shouting?"

"Like he was on a rollercoaster." She wiped her tear-streaked face. "Excited, ya know? He had to be high, or a total psycho."

Casey tried to breathe, but it felt as if someone had kicked her in the ribs. Her mind reeled. "Stay here, okay?" she said to the couple. "The police will want to talk to you."

Denver and Liam marched toward the center of the intersection.

Denver took over traffic detail, while MacKenna spoke with the doctors. As Casey walked toward Denver her legs felt even weaker, as if she'd been wading through mud.

When Denver noticed her, he said, "Don't tell me you saw this one, too?"

"I heard it. Got here a couple of minutes later."

Denver shook his head and watched the traffic.

"It was a black Volvo, and I was just talking to two witnesses . . ." She gulped down air. "The hit-and-run driver also sideswiped that Kia." She pointed to the car. "The driver's the one waving his arms around."

Denver's facial muscles tightened as MacKenna joined them. "Another week, another freakin' horror show."

"This one's different," Casey replied. "The racer was alone and didn't even try to avoid the pedestrians. The witness I talked to swears that the driver deliberately struck those people." Her voice trembled as she spoke. "This was cold-blooded murder."

NINE

CARRYING A BASKET OF CLEAN laundry, Casey trudged up the stairs to her third-floor suite and tried not to think about that poor child, Crystal, and her mom lying in the intersection. Lou had heard about it last night and come over after his shift. All night long, her emotions had alternated between grief for the family and rage at the driver. She was grateful Lou had chosen to hang around this morning.

"Maybe we should install a mini washer and dryer in your apartment so we won't have to trek down to the basement all the time. I'll pay for it," Lou said, following her up the stairs with the second basket. "Do you think Rhonda would mind?"

"She said I could change whatever I wanted in this suite." But where would they put a washer and dryer?

"Have you told her I'm moving in?"

"Yep." Casey opened the door. "Her exact words were 'it's about time.'"

Rhonda adored Lou as much as Summer did. After Casey left Greg and moved in here, Lou had started coming by fairly often, as a friend. Rhonda had always claimed he'd been in love with Casey from the get-go and, after her divorce, had encouraged Casey to go out with him. It took a bullet in Lou's chest to open her eyes.

Casey dropped her basket by the coffee table and slumped onto the sofa. Lou plunked his basket next to hers and turned full circle. "Where should we put my couch?"

In the nearest dumpster if it were up to her, but saying so out loud would be rude. A week had passed since Lou suggested moving in, and she hadn't yet come up with a plan to make room for his furniture. Even if he brought only half of it, her apartment would still be cramped.

"What if you sell some of your stuff and make a few bucks?" Casey said. "Or we could store some of it in the basement."

"We could store your things just as easily and give this room a new look."

Oh, crap. "You've only brought over one small box so far. It's kind of hard to picture how the room will look in plaid."

"I don't want to overwhelm you with a truckload of stuff," Lou replied. "I know how scary this is."

Scary didn't begin to cover it. "I'll be fine." Casey wrapped her arms around him.

He kissed her and then checked his watch. "My shift starts soon, and Summer won't be home from school for a while, so get some rest, okay? You were tossing and turning all night."

"I will." She was too restless right now. As Casey began folding towels, Lou left for work. She was glancing about the room, wondering what she could possibly banish to the basement, when the phone rang.

"Did you hear what happened last night?" Danielle asked.

"Heard the screams, saw the victims."

"Oh my god. Talk about lightning striking twice."

"I work afternoon shifts on a Granville Street bus these days." Casey leaned back against the sofa. "Thankfully, doctors were on the scene before me."

"Did you see the car that hit them?"

"For a split second. It was a Volvo."

"Word is the little girl will live. She's only ten, for shit's sake."

Casey rubbed her eyes. "Her name's Crystal." Denver had called to tell her that the girl had several broken bones and had undergone surgery to stop internal bleeding.

"I know. The mother is Anna-lee Fujioka." Danielle paused. "It seems she and the grandparents were walking Crystal home from piano lessons when the Volvo struck. Anna-lee tried to shield Crystal. Some think it was a targeted hit involving drugs."

Denver had said the family wasn't known to police. "Does anyone in Roadkill drive a Volvo?"

"Volvos aren't Roadkill's style, and I doubt there's a connection anyway. The jerk wasn't racing anyone. I also heard that the car was stolen and torched in Queen Elizabeth Park."

Casey had learned the same thing from news coverage. Queen Elizabeth Park was at Cambie and Thirty-Third, just a few minutes from the scene of the crime. A large part of the park was situated on a hill. Roads and parking lots weren't plainly visible from the street, especially after dark. Had the driver planned to leave the vehicle in the park, or was it a random decision? Either way, he'd taken a big risk. There was a restaurant on the hill that stayed open fairly late, and he could have been seen.

"Are you certain there's no connection? It's the same time and place." Casey began pairing up socks. "Not to mention the same recklessness."

"Roadkill lives to race and collect prize money and bragging rights. Killing people would draw too much attention. This was just some copycat psycho, probably high on drugs and pissed off at the world."

"Or a frustrated wannabe who's been rejected by the group too many times."

"Roadkill members are racers, Casey, not car thieves. These guys' identities are wrapped up in their vehicles. It's a huge pride thing. Stealing someone else's wheels to race would be like taking their sister to a dance."

"Have you talked to your source about it?"

"He says he doesn't know what's going on, but there might be another way to find out, seeing as how I learned something cool about the Regency Fitness Center." Danielle spoke faster. "Guess who owns it? No, don't. I'll tell you. It's owned by a woman named Mary Wing. Wing as in Eagle, get it? Eagle is probably her son."

"Maybe." Apparently the twins were right.

"The girls we saw climbing into that Jaguar with the older lady could be Eagle's sisters," Danielle added. "Eagle might even have been the driver."

"If that's true, he would have recognized me from the funeral."

"Good, let him freak a little. By the way, I found a last name for

Harvey, who drives the purple Camry. It's Haberkorn, and I know where he lives too."

Also known as Hellhound, according to the twins. "You're pretty resourceful."

"It wasn't hard. I borrowed my dad's car and followed Harvey home from the Regency last night. I had only been watching the place for an hour when he took off again. He met a guy at a garage not far from his house."

Casey didn't like the sound of this. "Are you sure you weren't spotted?"

"Totally. They headed for the pub next door, so I went in and managed a good look."

Casey dropped a pair of socks. "For god's sake, Danielle. That was way too dangerous."

"Relax, it was fine. They had a short, intense discussion, then Harvey's friend went back to the garage, where his car was parked, and guess what?"

"Do I want to know?"

"He drives the gray Dodge Neon! This is it, Casey. I've now got the plate numbers of two racers. It's all coming together."

"But you don't know for sure that they're part of Roadkill."

"Even if they're not, they could lead me to them. The racing community's not that big."

Bloody wonderful! There'd be no stopping her now. "Have you told the police any of this? After two deaths, I'm pretty damn sure they'll take you seriously."

"I will after the next race, which my source says is on Knight Street tonight, so your boyfriend doesn't have to worry about deciphering Roadkill's code."

The twins' information was good again. "You aren't going, are you?"

"I sure as hell am. I want to record the start of a race, showing vehicles, faces, and license plates." Danielle let out a huff of air. "If we both recorded the action, I'd have a better shot at getting all of them."

"I don't have a camcorder."

"A cell phone might do, if you got close enough."

"Are you completely out of your mind?"

"How many times do I have to say it? Ben died three years ago, and the stupid cops still don't know who ran him off the road."

"Wait a sec." Casey sat upright. "I heard that your brother was sideswiped by the person he was racing. It was an accident, wasn't it?"

"No, it wasn't." Danielle paused. "After the crash, I went to see Richie in the hospital."

"The passenger?"

"Yeah. He was Ben's best friend. Richie was doped up and mumbling something about getting hit on purpose. By the time he was alert enough to talk, his memory was gone. The cops claim they never got any leads, but I think Liam MacKenna's been protecting his friends."

"You know him?"

"MacKenna was the one who came to the house and told us about Ben."

It made sense. He'd been at the crash scene. "What do you mean by MacKenna protecting his friends?"

"My source said that MacKenna used to drag race, legally and illegally. I'm not sure what he's up to."

Did Denver know this? "So, MacKenna might still have contacts in the racing world?"

"More than contacts—buddies. I heard his racing days ended when he crashed and burned, and I mean that literally. MacKenna's car flipped and caught fire. Guess he traded a risky sport for a risky job."

And now he was working for the Hit and Run Team. "He struck me as a man who had no patience for street racing."

"Maybe it's just an act. Anyway, I'd bet my last buck that someone in Roadkill knows who was on the road with Ben that night. Word is that a couple of them were racing back then, which means capturing these guys on tape would give me enough leverage to get one of them to talk."

"You're assuming too much, Danielle."

"Here's a fact: the race is at 2:30 AM, probably to avoid extra patrols earlier in the evening. If you watch Harvey's place while I stake out the Wings', then we'll have a good chance of following them right to the start location."

"Not if they're in a hurry to get there," Casey replied. "Listen, the police already know about the race. There's no need for us to go."

"I'm going anyway, with or without you."

Damn. Denver would want her to keep Danielle from doing something stupid, and letting her go alone didn't feel right. "When do you want me at Harvey's place?"

"Early, in case they change their minds about the time. Anyway, I'll call you tonight with the address. Gotta run."

There had to be a better way to stop Roadkill. As Casey folded a towel, her empty stomach rumbled. Man, she was starving. What she wouldn't give for scrumptious, fatty food right now. The image of a double-patty cheeseburger oozing mayo and ketchup, plus thick wedges of fries, made her salivate, and then she thought of the twins' ubiquitous food bags.

It might not be a bad idea to learn a little more about them, as well as their connection to street racing. Their information was certainly good; too good. Besides, if their behavior worsened, she would need to contact their parents. Since the twins weren't likely to volunteer contact info, maybe she could locate a phone number or address from their employer. The twins had to work near the Granville and Sixteenth bus stop, where the M7 picked them up in the evening. It was only a twenty-minute drive from here.

Casey looked at her laptop, where a partially finished essay about the impact of religious beliefs on criminal justice policies over the past hundred years was waiting to be finished. It could wait a little longer. She'd already written her report about last night's shift and emailed it to Stan, who'd been forced to finally join the computer age. Casey retrieved her purse and car keys.

→   →   →

TWENTY-FIVE MINUTES LATER, she was circling residential blocks near Granville in search of a parking spot. The many retail outlets between Broadway and Sixteenth Avenue, and the reserved street parking for local residents, made parking scarce for visitors. Yet hopping a bus would have taken twice as long.

After she finally found a spot, Casey stepped out of the car and hurried down Fourteenth Avenue until she reached Granville. She looked at the southbound bus stop just past the Sixteenth Avenue intersection. Beyond that, retail outlets disappeared for several blocks.

Waiting for the light to change, she scanned single-story, elegantly decorated windows advertising hair salons, art galleries, and boutiques. The variety of outlets reminded her of Commercial Drive near her own neighborhood, except Granville was, for the most part, more upscale. A few blocks away, the Shaughnessy area's mansions sat on some of the city's richest real estate. It was odd that the twins would work in this part of town.

She strolled down Fifteenth Avenue, a short street that ended at the Granville Bowling Club and the Vancouver Lawn Tennis and Badminton Clubs. It wasn't long before she spotted the word MONTY'S painted in white on a dark brown awning a few doors ahead. She walked closer and studied the mock Tudor wood-framed building. The menu on the door listed a variety of burgers, milkshakes, and "The World's Best Fries."

Inside, she inhaled the aroma of deep-fried potatoes. Throughout the room, enormous plates of fries and burgers covered nearly every surface. Thank god her rumbling stomach couldn't be heard over "Jailhouse Rock," which was playing on the jukebox. Gray Formica tabletops and chrome chairs with red vinyl seats provided a cheerful fifties atmosphere. Maybe that was why the place was packed. Or maybe some people still preferred high-fat food to the West Coast staples of salads, seafood, wraps, and pasta.

Casey sat down at the last available stool at the counter as a sixty-something waitress in a pink poodle skirt and white puffy sleeves appeared. An image of Lara and Paige in these outfits made Casey grin.

"Hi there, I'm Betty." The waitress handed Casey a single laminated page. "What would you like to drink?"

"Coffee and a glass of water, please."

"Sure thing."

As Betty scooted off with remarkable speed, Casey browsed the menu and decided on a Swiss cheese and mushroom burger. When Betty returned, Casey placed her order and then said, "Will Lara and Paige be working later today?"

Skin puckered between Betty's brows. "It's their day off."

"I don't know them well, but we've chatted on the bus a few times." Casey put on her best smile. "The bags of food they bring on board smell so good that I had to come here."

"Glad you did," Betty answered. "My husband and I own this place, and we love new customers."

Betty fastened the order to one of several clips hanging above the serving window. While Casey rehearsed the lie she was about to tell Betty, she watched two older cooks scurrying back and forth in the kitchen.

When Betty placed an oversized mug in front of her, Casey thanked her, then said, "I found Paige's student ID on the bus last night. Do you know how I can reach her to give the card back? I imagine she needs it right away."

"That girl's always losing something. Been like that all her life." She swept coins into her pocket and placed dirty dishes below the counter. "You can leave it here. They'll be in tomorrow."

"I take it you've known the twins a long time?"

"Since they were born." Betty wiped drops of ketchup and mayo off the counter. "Their mom and I have been friends for more years than I can remember."

Which explained why the girls worked here. "The thing is, Paige will need her ID to get on the bus. If you have her phone number, I could call her."

"Their phone's broken," Betty said as she worked. "And the girls don't have cell phones."

Casey had noticed. It was rare for girls their age to never bring electronic gadgets on the bus. "I'll be in their area after lunch. I'll drop it off at their school's office."

"That will work."

Casey sipped the coffee. Lord, it was good. "I see the twins every Monday, Wednesday, and Friday. They must be reliable workers."

"They have to be." Betty placed ketchup and vinegar bottles in front of Casey.

"Yeah well, it's tough to save for university."

"It's tough to live. Thank heaven they can help their mom with the bills."

A customer at the far end of the counter waved Betty over.

So, the family didn't have money to throw around. She couldn't ask Betty for the twins' last name when she was supposed to have Paige's ID. There was another way, though. She was considering the pros and cons of her plan when Betty presented a mountain of fries and a thick, juicy burger oozing mushrooms and melted cheese.

"Wow. That was fast."

"We aim to please. Enjoy your lunch, sweetie."

"Thanks."

Casey picked up the burger and took a bite. It was every bit as good as she'd imagined.

TEN

CASEY SHIVERED AND SHIFTED HER feet to keep warm on this cold, foggy night. The M7 bus was fifteen minutes late, which probably meant Greg was driving. At MPT, he had a dubious reputation as the driver who couldn't stay on schedule.

Although Adrianna's pains had disappeared and the baby was fine, she was on medical leave for a month. Greg had become her regular replacement, and Casey was already fed up with his stupid hangdog expression. At least he hadn't asked her about rent reduction again, nor had she given an answer. Discussing personal stuff while riding wasn't appropriate, and she didn't want to see him outside of work. She'd leave him a note when she got around to it.

The M7 finally lumbered up Granville and pulled over at the Broadway stop. Casey followed the last passenger on board. The puffy sacs under Greg's eyes were darker than normal and his expression more pathetic.

He handed her a folded sheet of paper. "We're moving out. Sorry to do it here, but this is the only time I see you."

Whoa, this was a surprise, but a welcome one. As she read the note, Greg merged back into traffic. They'd be out by December thirty-first, seven weeks from now.

"Asking for a reduction in rent was stupid," he said. "I shouldn't have let Tina talk me into it."

She should have guessed it was Tina's idea. Casey had occasionally spotted Tina picking Greg up from work. The woman was usually applying lipstick, brushing her hair, or yakking on the phone while she waited in their big SUV.

"Have you found a place?" Casey asked.

"Not yet. A friend in Abbotsford told me about a vacancy in his building. I'm checking it out on the weekend."

Abbotsford was in the Fraser Valley, over an hour's drive from Vancouver, on a good day. Casey tried not to smile. "How does Tina feel about this?"

"Like she's about to be dragged through the gates of hell. Says Abbotsford's too far away from her parents, but really she's just too lazy to pack."

That was a nasty thing to say. "Good luck."

Casey stayed near the front of the bus, but not close enough for Greg to keep chatting with her. The M7 eased up to the Sixteenth Avenue stop; Casey spotted the twins. She stood and moved toward the entrance, knowing this encounter wouldn't be friendly.

Lara boarded first and scowled at Casey. "Why were you at the diner, and what was that bull about Paige losing her ID?"

Casey had figured that Betty would mention her visit. Paige stood next to her sister, a full, greasy bag in each hand. Casey nodded toward the bags. "The food you always bring smells so good that I had to try the place."

"How did you find it?" Paige asked.

"There aren't many burger joints near that bus stop." She braced herself for the third lie in two days. "I did find an ID on the floor after you two left and thought it was yours, Paige. After I left the diner, I took a closer look and realized it belonged to someone named Patty. Speaking of IDs, can I see both of yours, please?"

"What the hell for?" Paige asked.

"Part of my job is to make sure they're current, and I've never checked yours."

Lara snorted and rolled her eyes.

"Do it, ladies," Greg said, "or out you go."

The girls yanked their cards from their pockets and shoved them in Casey's face. Their last name was Wiecz. Too bad student cards didn't come with addresses.

"Thanks very much. Have a seat, girls."

Casey sat across from the twins. While they ate, she rummaged through her handbag for the article she was supposed to read for tomorrow's class. She was halfway through when a familiar face boarded the bus at the Forty-First Avenue stop, just past the intersection where Beatrice had been struck.

Danielle searched faces and smiled when she spotted Casey. Lord, what was she doing here? Danielle had called again at suppertime yesterday to say that the race had been canceled because too many people knew about it. Danielle's source had accused her of leaking info, which could be true.

When Danielle slid in beside her, Casey said, "How did you find me?"

"You told me when and where you worked, remember?"

Right. Big mistake.

Danielle placed her large black bag on the floor and peered at the article. "What are you reading?"

"Something for criminology class." She noticed the twins watching her with a mix of contempt and curiosity.

"How far are you from your degree?"

"Eons. I only have eighteen credits so far."

"At least you won't be stuck on buses all your life."

"It's not so bad. The hours are flexible, my supervisor's great, and I get to help people." Unless she took over Stan's job one day, though, there was little chance to move up in Mainland's small, cash-strapped company.

"What will you do with your degree?" Danielle asked.

"No clue." She'd thought about it now and then, but nothing had really sparked her interest. Without looking directly at the twins, Casey knew they were listening. The girls were unusually quiet, their heads turned toward her and Danielle. "I'm not sure why you're here, but I really can't chat while I'm working."

"This won't take long."

Casey looked out the window as they passed the newest memorial at Granville and Forty-Ninth. Granville was becoming the saddest street in the city. Flowers, cards, and a half-dozen small stuffed animals covered more lamp standards.

"No one in the racing scene believes Roadkill members had anything to do with Anna-lee Fujioko's death," Danielle murmured. "They're trying to rationalize the first as an accident. Some of those bastards actually blame Beatrice Dunning for running across an intersection without paying attention."

"The Fujioko family's offering a twenty-five-thousand-dollar reward for info on the driver," Casey said.

"I hope it works." Danielle kept her head lowered, as if unable to look at the tributes. "My source says there's a big debate about whether to hold off racing till things cool down, but I doubt they will. There's too much at stake." Danielle glanced at the twins before turning back to Casey. "Liam MacKenna might be racing again."

"You're kidding. Who told you this?"

"My source. I asked for proof, but all he'd say is that MacKenna's back in the scene and out to raise some shit."

Casey peeked at the twins, who were still working on those burgers. Since they were behaving, she decided to pursue this a little further. "Why would MacKenna want to race when it ended so badly last time, and especially now?"

"Who knows? Maybe a cop's life is too boring and he needs the risk."

"Or maybe he's not racing at all, just making his presence known so Roadkill won't pull more stupid stunts."

Danielle examined the chipping purple polish on her nails. "I went to the Wings' place last night and saw a guy about my age take off in a gold Mitsubishi." Danielle's eyes shone. "He was wearing a red bandanna on his head and a gold earring in his right ear."

Casey's shoulders tensed up. "And his face?"

"Clean-shaven, young." Danielle gripped Casey's arm. "He's Eagle, I know it. You were talking to Eagle at the cemetery. He was there when Beatrice was hit. I think Roadkill was racing that night after all."

Casey saw the twins glance her way. "Why would Eagle be a passenger, though? Wouldn't he be racing his own car?"

"Yeah, that was weird." Danielle let go of Casey's arm. "I followed the guy to a mansion in Shaughnessy and found out that it's owned by a family named Mueller."

"You've already checked them out?"

"I'm starting to. Eagle left twenty minutes later with a blond chick, who he took to a movie," Danielle added. "I also found a forum run by someone calling himself Speed Demon. I think there's another race tonight, so I need to watch Eagle's place again. I'm really close to catching these freaks."

Casey remembered all too well how it felt to be close to finding answers, to be convinced that all it would take was a little more digging.

"I need someone to watch Harvey Haberkorn's house while I watch the Wings' place," Danielle said. "Please?"

Casey spotted Lara practically leaning into the aisle, presumably to eavesdrop. "You don't know for sure there's another race, right?"

"Actually, I do." Danielle leaned closer to her. "Harvey writes a blog under the name Hellhound. By what he says, I'm convinced that he's on the A team."

Casey noticed the twins drinking cans of pop. They didn't usually bring drinks on board.

Danielle also turned to the twins, who returned her stare. "Why do you keep glancing at those girls, and why are they so interested in you?"

"I can't go into that. Did Harvey mention the hit and runs on his blog?"

"No, which is suspicious, seeing as how everyone else on the Net is talking about them." Danielle glanced at the twins. "I've posted comments to Hellhound hoping he'll respond. I'm pretending to be an Alberta racer."

Lara pulled a cigarette out of her pocket and smirked at Casey. Casey kept her expression impassive as she said, "I told Denver about Harvey and the Wings. They already knew a fair bit."

"Yet the races still go on."

"I think the police know more than they're saying, Danielle. If something's going down tonight, odds are they know about it. There's no reason for us to be there."

"Hey, Deputy Dog," Lara called out. "Who's your friend?"

Casey cringed. The last thing she needed was a scene.

"Maybe she's the deputy's deputy." Paige stuffed wrappers into her bag, then wiped her greasy hand on the back of the seat. "A doggy wannabe."

"Wow, you meet the nicest people here," Danielle remarked to Casey. "I can't imagine why you'd ever want to leave security work."

"I don't interfere with your job," Casey murmured. "Don't interfere with mine."

"Only if you promise to help with surveillance."

"You have a car now?"

"My dad's."

"He doesn't mind?"

"He rarely goes out since Ben died." Danielle looked out the window. Two more blocks passed before she said, "Dad used to coach Ben's soccer team, run marathons, and even ski."

The M7 approached the twins' stop. Lara pulled out a lighter and winked at Casey. Man, that girl was begging for a confrontation. "Was Ben the active type too?"

"Totally," Danielle answered, with the flicker of a smile. "He never stopped moving. Used to take me skateboarding, kayaking, you name it."

The recorded voice announced the next stop. Lara stood, snatched the empty bags, and threw Casey a nasty sneer as she slipped the cigarette between her lips. Paige held the full bag as she slid to the edge of the seat, then stopped a moment to fiddle with something. Greg eased the bus to the stop. When he opened the doors, Paige jumped up and hurried after her sister.

"Uh, Casey?" Danielle said, nodding toward the empty seat. "They left a mess."

Casey spotted a brown puddle on the seat, a pop can on its side. The puddle was seeping into a three-inch cut in the padded vinyl.

"That's it! Danielle, I need you to move." Casey stood as Greg started to pull out. "Stop the bus!" She headed for the back exit.

Greg braked, then turned in his chair. "What are you doing?"

"They've slashed the seat and spilled pop everywhere," she called out. "Don't bother waiting, I'll catch the next bus."

Noting the time, Casey stepped onto the sidewalk. As soon as she had a moment, she'd record the incident in her notebook. The girls needed to be held accountable. By the time she reached the intersection, the twins had already crossed Granville and Seventieth Avenue and were heading west down Seventieth on the north side of the street. The yellow light turned red. Crap. She stepped back and started down the south side of Seventieth.

"Better start running, or you'll lose them," Danielle said, joining her.

"You shouldn't be here."

"I still need an answer about the stakeout." She looked down Seventieth. "What are you planning to do with the delinquents?"

"Find out where they live so we can contact the parents."

"You have jurisdiction to do that?"

Probably not, but Danielle didn't need to know that. "The family doesn't have a working phone, so Stan will need an address."

The damp night cooled her flaming cheeks and penetrated her open jacket. The farther Casey walked the less angry she became and the less confident she felt about approaching the house. All she wanted to do was jot down the address without anyone noticing.

The twins were a full block ahead. She hurried past a side street called Cornish. By the time she reached a second street, the girls were turning right at the next block. Casey jogged across the street and followed the twins onto a short, narrow road. Bungalows occupied the right side of the street. Clusters of weeds and bushes hid the rail tracks on the left.

The twins entered a property midway down the road. Casey jogged ahead and reached a broken gate just as the girls stepped inside a single-story clapboard house that had seen better days. Lights inside illuminated two green sheets covering the picture window. A bare bulb shone next to a door with peeling paint.

"Wait here," Casey said. "I can't see the house number."

She tried to be quiet, but gravel crunched beneath her feet as she approached the door. The sheets parted and someone peered out. Casey stopped. When the face disappeared, Casey memorized the house number. She started to leave when the door opened and Paige stepped onto the stoop.

"What the hell?"

"I need your address, and you were too far ahead to ask." Not that Paige would have told her.

"Who's there?" Lara poked her head out the door. When she saw Casey her eyes blazed. "You bitch!"

"My supervisor will need your address. You two have broken rules four times and have now vandalized private property. Your parents will have to be notified regarding possible fines."

"You can't." Paige sounded anxious. "Look, we promise we won't do it again."

"I've already given you more than enough chances."

"We're not paying any fine," Lara blurted.

An obese woman with disheveled hair shoved between the girls and stepped onto the stoop. Her head shook slightly, as did the beer can she was holding. "What in holy shit's goin' on?" It sounded as if her larynx was lined with sandpaper.

"Nothing," Paige replied.

"They ain't social workers, are they?" the woman asked.

"Just people from work," Paige replied. "Go finish supper, Mom. We'll be right in."

Casey noticed that Lara hadn't said a word in her mother's presence. The second the mother had appeared, Lara had lowered her head. She hugged herself and kept her feet pressed together, as if attempting to make herself inconspicuous.

"Stop yakking and get your butts inside. Lara, light me a smoke," the mother said.

Lara followed her back into the house, while Paige glared at Casey. "Get off our property." She too headed back inside and shut the door.

"Wow." Danielle gave a low whistle and trailed Casey out of

the yard. "They may be rude little shits, but part of me feels sorry for them. I could see their mom shaking from here, like she's going through withdrawal or something. Do you know if there's a father?"

"No idea." Somehow, she doubted it.

"If you're off duty now, we should head for Richmond right away."

For reasons Casey didn't quite understand, helping Danielle for a short while didn't sound so bad. If she could learn who Danielle's source was, Denver would be pleased. Besides, Lou was busy moving in some of his belongings tonight, and Summer had her friend Jacob over. It wasn't as if she'd be greatly missed. "I can only help for a couple of hours."

"Where's your car?" Danielle asked.

"Near Broadway and Granville."

"Can you record on your phone?"

"Yeah, but I'm not sure how much will be visible in the dark."

"Don't worry about it. Sooner or later, one of those guys will make a big mistake," Danielle said. "And I want to be there when it happens."

If the street racers made a big mistake, Casey didn't want to be anywhere near them when it happened.

ELEVEN

CASEY FLEXED HER COLD GLOVED fingers and shifted her weight behind the steering wheel. With any luck, Danielle's plan wouldn't be a complete waste of time. Recording faces and license plates at the start of a race while trying not to attract attention would be interesting, if not dangerous. Casey doubted she could pull it off. And keeping up with Harvey Haberkorn's Camry in this old Tercel wasn't going to happen, if he even bothered leaving his house tonight.

Casey had been parked in front of the Haberkorn residence for a half hour and was tempted to go home, until she remembered telling Denver she'd do what she could to keep Danielle out of trouble. She kind of liked the junior journalist and wasn't about to let Danielle get hurt searching for answers.

For the umpteenth time, Casey studied the Haberkorns' modest two-story home for signs of movement. Sheer drapes covered the large picture window in an illuminated room that seemed unoccupied. Two smaller windows above the double-car garage had been dark since she arrived. Harvey's purple Camry was parked on the street, in front of the house. Presumably, the garage and driveway were reserved for his parents' vehicles.

Casey hoped she could go home soon. It was nearly ten. She should check in to make sure Jacob had left. When she called an hour ago, Summer and he were still doing homework. Even though Lou had met Jacob at the Halloween party, all he'd said was that Jacob was an interesting kid. Summer had described him as artistic, smart, and not a total "jerk-face." Since neither was a glowing endorsement, Casey really wanted to meet Jacob.

A vehicle cruised toward her. She'd seen only two cars come and go since she'd been here, as well as a man walking his dog. A black Lexus turned into the Haberkorns' driveway. Was it the same Lexus that had been racing the night Beatrice Dunning was killed?

Casey grabbed her binoculars and zeroed in on the plate number. The vehicle eased into the garage. A man stepped out, carrying a briefcase. Garage lights revealed a bald head fringed with gray; not the right age for a street racer. Had Harvey used his dad's car that night? The man entered the house. A light went on in one of the rooms above the garage.

A tap on her window made Casey flinch. She spotted a long mouth set in a heavily lined face. Wisps of hair stuck out from under a hat. She rolled her window down a little.

"Is everything okay?" the man asked. "You've been here a while." He shone a flashlight on her backseat. "I'm from neighborhood watch."

"I'm fine, thanks. A friend asked me to meet her in front of Harvey's house, but she hasn't shown up and I'm trying to find out where she is." Casey tapped her Bluetooth.

"You can't stay here long. People will call the police."

A call came in. "Eagle's making his move!" Danielle shouted in her ear. "He lives ten minutes from Harvey. If a gold Mitsubishi shows up, duck."

The man wandered off about the same time the front door of the Haberkorns' house opened. "Wait a sec," Casey said. Floodlights sprang on, giving her a clear view of Harvey, who was wearing the glasses and ball cap she'd seen on Saturday. "Harvey's heading out too."

"Stay with him, and don't let him see you."

Right, sure. No frigging problem. Casey leaned over until the handbrake dug into her ribs. When the Camry pulled away, she started after it. Man, the kid drove fast.

After a couple of minutes, Danielle yelled, "Where are you?"

"I don't know, and stop shouting." She followed Harvey onto a busy commercial street lined with strip malls. The Camry was in the slow lane, four cars ahead of her. "Where's your guy?"

"Half a block ahead of me, heading west," Danielle answered. "I don't know the street name."

"Oh man, he's making a left-hand turn at the speed of light,"

Casey said, hearing Harvey's tires screech. Did the guy know she was following?

"Don't lose him!"

"Then shut up and let me concentrate."

The steady stream of traffic made turning left impossible. She was going to lose the Camry. From above her came the loud rumble of a low-flying jet preparing to land at nearby Vancouver International Airport. Traffic swooshed past her as the light turned yellow. Since she was in the middle of the intersection, Casey floored it.

"Shit, I can't see the Camry . . . Wait." She sped through another yellow light at the next block.

"Eagle's pulled into a place called Winnie's Donuts," Danielle said.

"Harvey's turning right at the next street." Casey zipped into the right lane, unaware she'd cut someone off until she heard a horn blast. "Sorry, buddy."

"Whoa, the Camry just showed up too!" Danielle said.

"Where's the donut place?"

As Danielle gave her a street name, Casey spotted a neon donut perched on a roof. The shop was located on a corner lot with several parking stalls at the front of the building as well as four down the side. A black BMW was parked in one of the side stalls, the Camry and Mitsubishi in front. The upper half of each of the shop's walls was clear glass, making it easy to see patrons, and for them to see the street.

After Casey parallel parked in front of the shop's entrance, she spotted Harvey and a short guy with black hair inside, standing at the counter, their backs to the entrance. The short guy had to be Eagle. An elderly couple sat at a table by the entrance. Another guy with hair the color of straw sat in a corner of the shop, watching Eagle and Harvey.

Someone darted in front of her car and for two panicky seconds Casey forgot to breathe, until she recognized Danielle. Casey unlocked the passenger door.

"Where's your car?" she asked, as Danielle climbed inside.

"Across from you."

Casey spotted a white Ford Taurus with a dented fender.

"I can't tell what's going on." Danielle stared at the donut shop. "I'm going in."

"Don't you dare. If Eagle was driving that Jaguar at the fitness center, he probably saw both of us."

"But wouldn't you love a coffee and donut?"

Casey took the binoculars from Danielle, who'd nearly sat on them when she climbed in. "You've probably got enough treats in that huge bag to open your own bakery. You can see plenty with these."

"Thanks." Danielle zeroed in on the group, then handed the binoculars back to Casey. "See if Eagle is the guy you talked to outside the cemetery. He's sitting down, facing us."

Casey focused on the group and recognized him right away. "Yeah, he's the one."

"I knew it! This is great."

Casey's eyes widened at the sight of a shiny Dodge Neon cruising into the shop's lot.

"Oh my god!" Danielle's dark eyes sparkled. "That's the car you saw at the Regency, isn't it?"

"Looks like it. So, have we stumbled onto a pre-race craving for fat and sugar?"

"Probably a last-minute meeting about the route." As a powerful red Subaru Imprezza roared into the lot, Danielle grabbed the binoculars from Casey. Every head in the shop turned and looked. "Awesome! I think the A team's fifth and final member just arrived."

"What on god's earth has he got under that hood, a rocket engine?"

"Could be nitrous oxide. It gives engines a real boost for a bit. It's dangerous shit." Danielle studied the Imprezza. "Some morons have even tried jet fuel. It's like driving around with a firebomb waiting to explode."

A man with cropped hair, a goatee, and a mustache stepped out of the Neon. As he headed inside, he looked over his shoulder at the South Asian guy emerging from the Imprezza.

Danielle grinned. "We need everyone's plate number."

She started to open the door when Casey clamped her hand on Danielle's arm. "Stay here. I'll do it." She stepped out of the car before Danielle could respond.

Hoping to appear relaxed and unhurried, Casey strolled down the sidewalk, then bent down and pretended to tie her shoe. She jotted down the Imprezza's and Neon's plate numbers, then stood and continued on. After she'd put some distance between herself and the shop, she turned and started to head back, when Danielle, now wearing a bright green tuque, stepped out of the car. Damn it! Why wouldn't that stupid girl listen? Casey picked up the pace. By the time she reached the Tercel, Danielle was already inside, talking to the clerk behind the counter.

"Idiot!" Casey slid behind the wheel and grabbed the binoculars. Danielle was wandering through the place while searching for something in that giant bag of hers.

The man with the goatee turned in his chair to look at Danielle as she disappeared down a hallway. Great. *Just great.* At least the others were too focused on their conversation to notice her. They were leaning forward in their chairs, ignoring their beverages and donuts. No one looked happy, including Goatee Man, who'd turned his attention back to the guys.

A blue Mazda pulled into the lot. Despite its expensive appearance, the vehicle didn't sound as powerful as the others. A big guy stepped out. Tall. Dark curls. Familiar.

"Oh, crap." Casey lowered the binoculars. What was Liam MacKenna doing here, and in street clothes?

She phoned Danielle, who answered with a sharp, "What?"

"Liam MacKenna just walked in."

"Why am I not surprised? Can you see him?"

"He's approaching the racers. Are you in the bathroom?"

"Yeah. If I open the door and look down the hall I can see their table."

"Don't. MacKenna could turn around any second."

Casey lowered the binoculars and was startled by a chubby guy walking past her car toward the shop. He glanced over his shoulder in her direction. Was he part of the Roadkill gang? She hadn't heard a souped-up engine.

"Casey, what's happening?" Danielle asked.

"An Asian guy just walked by my car and saw me using the binoculars. He's entering the shop."

"Nice work, Sherlock. What does he drive?"

"I don't know. I didn't hear a car pull up."

"What's he look like?"

"Chubby face, average height, black bomber jacket." She heard Danielle mutter an obscenity. "Do you know him?"

"Maybe."

Casey looked at the shop. The clerk seemed to be looking for someone. "Did you place an order?"

"Yeah."

"The Asian kid's heading for the Roadkill guys. Oh wait, now he's heading down the hall, and MacKenna's following."

"I'll slip out while they're taking a leak."

"Keep the line open." Fifteen seconds later, there was still no sign of Danielle. "I thought you were leaving. Where the hell are you?"

"MacKenna and the kid are arguing in the men's room. I can't make out all the words."

"I don't care. Get out of there now!"

"I need to know what they're saying."

"Get out, or I swear to god I'll come in there and drag you out. Blow your nose as you leave so they can't get a good look at your face." Danielle disconnected the line. "Damn it!"

Finally, Danielle re-emerged from the hallway, sneezing and wiping her nose. Her plum ski jacket was draped over her arm, and Goatee Man was watching her again. The others, however, were still having an intense discussion.

Danielle paid for her purchase, while Goatee Man strutted up to the counter and spoke to her. Danielle smiled and said something. Oh hell, now what was she up to? The guy handed Danielle what looked like a business card, then ambled back to the table. MacKenna reappeared. Casey held her breath as Danielle spotted him, picked up her purchase, and hurried out the door. MacKenna stayed at the counter and watched her leave but didn't follow, thank god. "What were you bloody thinking?" Casey yelled, as Danielle slid into her seat. "MacKenna's watching you, and so's the guy with the goatee."

"His name's Dominic, although he likes to be called Dom."

"How bloody sweet. Oh, shit! MacKenna's coming outside."

"We should leave."

Casey started the engine and watched MacKenna climb into his car. "He's ignoring us."

"Interesting that he knew Roadkill would be here," Danielle remarked.

"He didn't talk long," Casey replied. "Didn't even sit down."

MacKenna started to leave but stopped. In the rearview mirror, Casey saw his face turned toward them. The last thing she wanted was a reprimand. She held her breath and waited until MacKenna finally drove off. She was a little surprised that he hadn't approached them. Maybe the cop hadn't wanted to be seen talking to them. She shut off the engine.

"How can MacKenna own a cool car like that on a cop's salary?" Danielle asked.

"Don't start." Casey watched her bite into a shiny maple-glazed donut. "What did you and this Dom character talk about?"

Danielle swallowed. "He asked me out like I thought he would, seeing as how he was ogling every pair of boobs in the pub the other day. All I had to do was take my coat off and, sure enough, he came over." She laughed. "We're meeting at the River's End Pub on Friday night, the same place he and Harvey went to. Dom works at the garage next door."

"I don't like this. What if he recognized you from the pub and wants to know what you're after?"

"Guess I'll find out."

Casey rolled her eyes. "Learning who ran your brother off the road won't change anything, Danielle. Even if the culprit's caught and punished, it won't stop the grief. That only happens with time and professional help. Trust me, I know."

Casey hadn't had counseling until she'd been diagnosed with depression months after Dad's death. Mother's fatal car crash hadn't triggered the same response, yet different emotions popped up now and then, usually while Casey was trying to fall sleep.

"Is justice too much to ask?" Danielle finished off her donut.

"That depends on your approach." Casey lifted the binoculars. "The Asian kid's coming back down the hall. He's approaching the table."

Danielle snatched the binoculars from her. "Oh, shit."

"You do know him, don't you?"

"It's Richie."

"As in the guy who was with your brother when he crashed?"

"Yeah." Danielle's voice was subdued as she watched the shop. "He's leaving." She handed the binoculars to Casey and grabbed a copy of the *Contrarian* from her bag. She held the open newspaper in front of her face.

"Why don't you want him to see you?"

"He'd be pissed."

"Why?"

Danielle didn't reply. Casey watched Richie cross the street behind her car and head for the intersection.

"Did you get the plate numbers?" Danielle asked.

"Not for the BMW."

"We need it. My gut says it belongs to the kid with the straw-colored hair."

Casey sighed. "First you have to promise to stay here this time, and I bloody mean it."

"Totally. No worries."

Flipping her jacket hood up once more, Casey stepped out of the car and glanced at the guys. All were eating and drinking now, apparently more relaxed. Casey stayed on the sidewalk as she passed the

BMW. Danielle was right. It had to belong to the straw-haired kid. This vehicle was far too flashy to belong to the older patrons. Better make this fast. Once more, she pretended to tie her shoelace as she memorized the number.

Casey started back but faltered at the sight of Richie running toward her car. What the hell? Afraid of attracting Roadkill's attention, Casey walked to the corner as casually as possible. It wasn't easy, what with the adrenaline rush making her legs want to run so badly they were almost twitching. When Richie flung the driver's door open and climbed inside her Tercel, she forgot about Roadkill and bolted for the car. The engine started.

"Hey!" Casey yelled.

The Tercel jolted forward, crossed the centerline, and immediately veered back to the curb. Mercifully, there were no oncoming vehicles.

Danielle sprang out of the car. "Are you out of your freaking mind?"

Richie clambered out. "Y-you are!" His head swayed a little from side to side.

"Scaring me won't work, Richie."

He flapped his arms up and down. "You'll get k-killed, stupid!"

"Say hi to your parents for me," Danielle shot back. "Tell them where we bumped into each other tonight, and why."

"Screw you, Danni!" Richie stomped back down the street, waving his hands and talking to himself in Korean.

"I pulled the key out of the ignition," Danielle said, plunking it in Casey's hand.

"What the hell was that about?"

"He's mad at me for coming here, but he won't do anything. Richie knows that if he goes too far, I'll tell his parents some interesting things about how he spends his free time."

"Such as?"

"Let's go." Danielle glanced at the donut shop. "We're attracting attention."

Casey saw the members of Roadkill watching them. She hurried inside the car. "Your brother's friend is still into the racing scene?"

Danielle swept her hand over her cropped black hair. "Yes."

Casey thought about that for a few seconds. "He's your source, isn't he, Danielle?"

"I can't tell you that."

"I'm not moving until you do." More silence. "I'm right, aren't I?"

When Danielle said nothing, Casey smiled. Even if she was wrong, he was one more person for Denver to check out. Instinct told her she was bang on. Why would a guy who'd lost a friend and suffered life-changing injuries stay involved with racers?

Casey jumped when someone tapped the passenger-side window. Oh good lord, it was the straw-haired guy. She couldn't quite determine his ethnicity, but black, almond-shaped eyes and a narrow, pointed nose suggested a multi-racial background.

Danielle gave Casey a wary glance, before rolling down the window.

"I saw that guy try to jack your car," he said. "Are you okay?"

"Yeah," Danielle replied. "The guy's an old friend who still treats me like a kid. He's mad because I'm out late." She smiled. "Is he a friend of yours?"

"I've seen him around. He hangs out at the donut shop a lot. Well, have a good night."

"You too," Danielle replied.

The rest of Roadkill still appeared to be interested in them. So much for not being recognized on stakeouts. Casey watched the guy enter the shop and wondered if he'd gotten what he'd come for.

TWELVE

"SORRY, CASEY, BUT I HAVE no choice." Stan rolled his chair back from his desk. "You're suspended until the complaint's been investigated. But don't worry; you're still on the payroll. The girls are the ones who vandalized the bus and broke the rules. They'll be held accountable."

Casey crossed her arms. In six years of security work, no one had filed a complaint about her. "Unbelievable."

"Listen, kiddo, I'm on your side."

"Sorry, Stan. It's just so frustrating."

"I know." He reached for the OLD FART, BIG HEART mug Casey had given him last Christmas. "I understand why you thought the girls wouldn't give you their address, but couldn't you have looked it up?"

"Following the twins seemed faster."

"I thought you were working on your patience."

"I was—am—but stuff happens." She'd built a solid reputation at Mainland through quick action. There was no room for hesitancy. No one complained about her impatience when she captured suspects. When things went wrong, though, the issue sometimes came up.

"How did you know their phone doesn't work?" Stan sipped his coffee.

Casey picked up her own mug. No point in evading the issue; Stan knew her too well. "I had lunch at the diner where the twins work. One of the servers knows the family well, and she told me."

"Why did you choose that place to eat?"

"The burgers and fries they bring on board always smell fantastic, so I had to try it."

He gave her a long look. "How did the family's phone come up in conversation?"

"I figured we'd need their number sooner or later, so I asked the server about contacting the family."

"And she told you just like that?"

"Well, no." Casey fidgeted in her chair.

Stan scratched his trim gray beard. "Let's hear it."

She told him the story she'd made up about finding Paige's student ID. When he gave her another one of those penetrating stares, she focused on his paisley tie and hideous purple and white striped shirt. "I wanted to learn more about the girls because I needed to know where they were coming from."

"Why is that?"

Casey sighed. "Here's the deal. The twins wanted to give me information about the racer who killed Beatrice Dunning, provided I let them keep breaking rules." She cringed when Stan plunked his mug down. "Of course, I didn't make the deal, but the info the girls gave me turned out to be true. Somehow, they have a connection to the racers, and I wanted to learn more about them."

"I've seen your need for justice before, Casey. You get emotionally involved, try to fix things, and then mistakes happen."

"It's not my quest for justice this time. It's Danielle's. I'm trying to watch out for her."

Since she'd noted in her report that Danielle was a witness, she'd had to tell Stan who Danielle was and what she'd been doing on the M7. Casey wasn't surprised to learn that Mrs. Wiecz had filed a complaint about Danielle too, unaware she wasn't an MPT employee.

"You forgot to put Danielle's phone number in the report," he said. "I'll need to call her."

Casey gave him the number. "I guess Marie will be taking my place?"

"Yep."

She stood and wandered to the window that overlooked staff parking and the yard. Two diesel engines roared to life. Since Marie rode the M7 on Saturdays and knew the twins, Casey supposed it was inevitable. Her number one rival was bloody well taking over.

Casey turned to Stan. "Does she know about my suspension?"

"She's been fishing for info, but I told her you needed to spend more evenings with Summer."

Marie wasn't stupid. She'd figure it out and then she'd make sure everyone at Mainland knew. Casey sighed. She might not like the demon twins, but she hated leaving assignments unfinished, especially under these circumstances.

"What happens next?" she asked, returning to the chair.

"Gwyn's set up a meeting with Mrs. Wiecz and her daughters for late this afternoon."

Mainland's president was a decent enough man, but Gwyn perpetually worried about the bottom line and public image. "Do I get to be at that meeting?"

"Gwyn wants to hear their side of the story alone, although he'll probably want to talk to you after that. He might want you to meet with the family to work this out." Stan took another sip of coffee. "Adrianna and Greg will vouch for you."

"The twins could accuse us of conspiring against them," Casey said. "Will I need a lawyer?"

"I'm sure it won't come to that, so don't sweat it, okay? You've got a stellar track record, and I have tons of passenger complaints about Lara's smoking."

Yet there was only so much Stan could do. Gwyn had final say on who stayed and who went at Mainland. Casey ran her hand over the rivets and tiny gouges on Stan's old mahogany desk. His desk and ancient chair were the only things left in the room that really suited him. The PC he'd grudgingly agreed to learn to use certainly didn't, nor did the dwarf jade bonsai his wife had bought him for stress relief.

What other changes were coming? Mainland's technological upgrade had eliminated two clerical positions and reduced the hours of others. Would Gwyn get rid of her as well? Even if she wasn't fired, the incident would be in her personnel file.

Stan stood and headed for the door. "After you're reinstated, I'm not sure I'll put you back on the M7."

"Why?" Did he think she'd screw up again?

"There could be bad blood on the twins' part, and your presence might fan the flames. I don't want to risk more trouble."

Why hadn't he fought harder to keep her from being suspended in the first place? "Please, let me see it through. I can't run away from this."

Stan let out a long puff of air. "I'll think about it."

When he opened the door, Casey knew the discussion was over, except for one more question. "When will I find out how the meeting went?"

"Don't know. Tomorrow's Remembrance Day, and I'll be at the ceremony, so maybe tonight or Saturday."

"I understand." The wait might kill her.

Casey returned to her desk, propped her elbows in front of her keyboard, and massaged her temples, until she realized it wasn't helping. She opened the drawer and peered at a bottle of Advil, a few coins, and two packs of gum. It was little to show for nearly six years in security. Her gaze drifted to the eight Employee of the Month certificates on the wall above the filing cabinets. Five had been awarded to her, but the last one was from two years ago. What had she done since that was so wonderful?

She looked at the three empty desks occupying the security department's small space. Stan's assistant, Amy, normally occupied the desk next to Casey, but recent cutbacks had reduced her hours as well.

Casey began re-reading her report, paying close to attention detail and ensuring she'd included facts rather than opinions. Would these words be enough to exonerate her? Could she have added anything to justify her actions? Her cell phone rang.

"Big news." Danielle sounded excited. "Remember the house in Shaughnessy that I saw Eagle visit?"

"Where his girlfriend lives?"

"Yeah. It seems she has a twenty-year-old brother named Morris. Both he and Eagle go to SFU. Maybe you've taken classes with them and didn't even know it."

"Not unless they're criminology students. How did you find this out?"

"That's what resourceful journalists do," she replied. "You won't believe this, but the kid who came out and asked if we were okay last night was Morris Mueller. He owns the black BMW. Cool, huh? I've identified all of Roadkill's hardcore members except the guy in the red Subaru."

"Let the police do it. They'll want to talk to the racers and Richie."

Casey had planned to call Denver when she got home last night, but Summer had still been up and struggling with math homework. By the time Casey had finished telling Lou what had happened at Winnie's Donuts, she'd had no energy left to repeat everything to Denver.

"I think the cops should put a scare into Richie," Danielle said, "but I don't want him arrested. Don't tell them about the gambling."

"Why not?"

Danielle paused. "He's been like a brother for as long as I can remember. I want to try to get through to him first."

"He's connected to street racers, Danielle, one of whom mowed down Beatrice Dunning."

"You think I don't know that?" The irritation in Danielle's voice quickly faded. "Just let me talk to Richie. When he realizes how much I've learned, he might agree to walk away before he gets in any deeper."

"Exactly how deep is that?"

"I'll tell you after I see Dominic Mancuso tomorrow. Maybe by then I'll have found a way to approach Eagle without scaring him off. Did you see how miserable the guy looked the whole time he was at the donut shop? I think Beatrice's death is still gnawing on his conscience."

"I didn't really notice. Too busy taking down license plate numbers and trying to keep you out of trouble. Speaking of which, the police should approach Eagle, not you."

"The second they do, his parents will probably hire some big-time lawyer. Can you help with more surveillance? Mom's making a new batch of cinnamon buns."

"It won't work," Casey replied. "Roadkill members know my car and most of them will recognize us."

"We could wear disguises and borrow cars. You must have a friend who'll lend you one."

"I wouldn't ask. Call me tomorrow."

She hung up, feeling more than a little uneasy. Somebody needed to convince Danielle not to pursue Roadkill, but who would she listen to? Meanwhile, Casey needed to keep busy. Schoolwork would help, and she'd now have time to rearrange her closet and drawers to make room for Lou's things.

He still hadn't brought much over, and they hadn't yet sorted out the furniture issue. Talking over her concerns about living together hadn't eased her worry. Each new day brought on more doubt. What if they saw flaws in each other they hadn't noticed before—flaws they found intolerable? What if Lou just up and left? Decided she wasn't good enough to build a future with? What would she do? What would his departure do to Summer? He was the only male role model in her life . . . Oh lord, where had the air in here gone?

Casey shut off her PC, grabbed her coat, and hurried out the door. Each breath grew more shallow and more rapid. She jogged down the two sets of stairs. By the time she reached the ground floor, she was close to hyperventilating.

Casey looked down the corridor at the lunch room on her right, the ladies' locker room farther down on the left. She kept a change of clothes and shoes in there, an umbrella, makeup, a couple of sci-fi paperbacks. Nothing she needed. Nothing that mattered.

She crossed the hall, pushed the glass doors open, and let the cold November air fill her lungs. Beneath the dark clouds, Casey closed her eyes and began to feel better. She had a good future with Lou, and her suspension would be lifted. Everything would turn out just fine.

Casey started for her car, when a petite blonde strutted toward her. The blonde's hands were shoved in the pockets of a pink coat trimmed with fake, white fur. The woman looked familiar, yet Casey couldn't quite place her. The woman stopped a few feet away and stared. Casey noticed she had dark roots and wore pink lip gloss that matched the color of her coat. Furtive, pale blue eyes looked translucent beneath the cobalt eye shadow.

"Casey?"

"Yes."

"I'm Tina Berger, Greg's wife."

Crap. "Hello."

"Greg said he changed his mind about asking you to reduce the rent. Is that true?"

"Yes."

"I want to put the request back on the table. See, I love that house, and if we had the money, we'd buy it from you. But I've had to leave my job, and we're having another baby. I don't know what to do."

So, she wanted the first wife to solve her financial problems? Casey opened the Tercel's door. "Does Greg know you're here?"

"He will." Tina's pink lips pouted. "I'm only asking for short-term help. Our little boy just started preschool and he's so shy that changing schools would devastate him."

Casey slid into her car. Using the kid to gain sympathy was beyond tacky. "Sorry, but you're already paying about four hundred bucks less a month than the going rate."

Tina glared at her. "You hate me because you think I'm a home wrecker."

"Actually, I'm quite relieved that he's with you and not me." She closed the door and then rolled down the window.

"I don't want our kids to be shuffled around every two years like I was." Tina's voice rose. "Don't do that to my children."

"Tina, your family life is not my concern. In fact, it has nothing to do with me."

"Greg was right." Tina stepped back. "You *are* a self-absorbed bitch!"

Casey started the engine. "And *you* are a total waste of time!" She shoved the gear into reverse.

"Just try and evict us!" Tina yelled. "We have rights, you know!"

"I'm *not* evicting anyone! Greg changed his mind about asking for a rent reduction and gave notice instead. *Obviously* he didn't tell you." She enjoyed the shock on Tina's face. The woman opened her mouth to speak, but nothing came out. "He promised you'd be gone by December thirty-first, and he had better keep his word."

As Casey backed up, she saw Tina march to their big SUV. If money was tight, why weren't they driving something older and smaller? The roar of a souped-up engine caught Casey's attention. She turned in time to see a dark, sporty vehicle race past Mainland's entrance and disappear.

THIRTEEN

CASEY CLIMBED ONTO A CHAIR and began wiping down the baking-supplies cupboard in the downstairs kitchen. The cupboard hadn't been cleaned since Winifred's mercifully short stay last year. The only other good thing to have come from that visit was Winifred abandoning her attempt to gain legal custody of Summer. Too bad Summer hadn't inherited her grandmother's need for cleanliness. Much as the girl loved to bake, she spilled everything and had gotten lazy with the cleanups.

Casey's cell phone rang. She retrieved it from her pocket and answered, "Hello?"

"Hey, kiddo, how are you doing?" Stan asked.

"Hanging in there." She hadn't talked to him in two days, not since he'd told her she was suspended. "How did Thursday's meeting go?"

"The Wieczs never showed."

She got down from the chair. "That doesn't help."

"Gwyn tried the number the mother gave, but the phone's still out. One of the twins called from the diner yesterday and left a message saying there'd been a medical emergency with their mom, but that she's okay now. Gwyn will try to reschedule on Monday."

Casey's spirits sank. Rumors about her absence would be flying at work.

"I've been trying to get hold of Danielle Carpenter," he went on, "but she hasn't returned my calls."

She hadn't heard from Danielle in a couple of days either. "I'll see if I can get a hold of her."

"The sooner the better. I really need a statement from her to give Gwyn."

"Please let me know when the meeting takes place."

"Count on it. Take it easy."

She'd been trying, but it wasn't going well. Casey shoved the phone in her pocket and turned back toward the cupboard, when she heard the familiar sound of Lou's pickup crunching the gravel in back. Thank heaven. She could use a supportive shoulder. Casey opened the door as Lou removed two fairly large boxes from the passenger seat.

"Need some help?" she called out.

"I'm good, thanks." He traipsed through the backyard and up the steps. "I brought my lava lamps."

Oh, no. Lou owned ten of them: red, blue, purple, green, yellow; large and small. She never understood his fascination with watching icky globs float up and down and slowly break apart into smaller globs, only to merge again. She hadn't spent the night at his apartment since she'd become Summer's guardian and had almost forgotten how Lou liked to plug in the lamps while they were in bed. She'd never had the heart to tell him that she found them more quirky than romantic.

"I'm not sure there's enough space for all those lamps in the bedroom," she said.

He placed the boxes on the kitchen table. "We could put some in the living room, and I brought my disco collection over. It'd be cool to listen to them with the lamps on, just like old times." He kissed her, then stepped back. "What's wrong? You're smiling funny."

This wasn't the time to confess that disco and lava weren't her idea of romance. "I just talked to Stan." She told him about the canceled meeting. "I resent teenaged punks who hold far too much power over my future."

"It will work out, Casey. Stan would never let you go."

She hugged him. "Thank you." No one at Mainland was indispensable, though. "He hasn't been able to reach Danielle, and she had a date with Dominic Mancuso last night. I'm a little worried."

"You're letting things get to you." He kept his arms around her. "It's almost noon. Maybe she's busy running errands."

"Maybe." Casey picked up her cleaning cloth and climbed back on the chair.

"Where should I put the lamps?" he asked.

The tool shed sprang to mind. "How about the downstairs living room? Christmas isn't far off, and we'll be spending more time there anyway. It'll be fun having them glowing with the tree's lights."

"Don't you want them in our bedroom tonight?"

She kept her back to him. "Not really."

"Okay." He paused. "You should tell me what else you don't want upstairs, and, while I think of it, what about ground rules?"

"Ground rules?" She stopped wiping a shelf and looked over her shoulder. Was he being sarcastic?

"Yeah, I need to know about stuff like remote controls and toilet paper rolls."

"You're rhyming."

"Not intentionally." Lou smiled. "I just don't want you getting mad if I hog the remote or put the toilet paper roll on wrong."

"I won't."

"Just post the rules, boss, so I know what they are."

"Lou, I don't want to be the boss."

"It was a joke."

"Sorry. Little slow on the uptake." She turned back to the shelf.

"Actually, I think you're still a little freaked out about me moving in, aren't you?"

Casey paused and then stepped down from the chair, tossing the cloth on the counter. "Not freaked out, just afraid that I'll disappoint you."

"We'll have good days and bad days." Lou started to frown. "Do you think I'll only stay as long as we're having fun?"

"Something like that. What if things turn lousy and stay that way a long time?"

"Then we'll work on ways to make them better."

Casey sat down. "When I was with Greg I thought that too."

"Greg wasn't committed to your marriage. He bailed way too fast." Lou reached for her hands. "We've known each other over ten years. I was there when you got married and when your marriage fell apart. I was there when your parents died. I've seen you angry, depressed, and upset. I've seen you doubt yourself more times than I can count. Why would I leave over a rough patch?"

She attempted a smile. "All the big moments, huh?"

He stroked her hair. "I know you're the fastest flosser in the universe and that you only snore when your nose is stuffed up. What more is there to know?"

"That I'm probably not a great person to live with if unemployed."

"I also know you're a worrier." His reassuring arms engulfed her. "Maybe we should grab something to eat."

"Actually, I want to hang around. Summer's bringing Jacob over shortly, so I'll finally get a chance to meet him. I'm a little surprised she hasn't introduced us yet." She noticed Lou's smirk. "You never told me much about him after the Halloween party."

"There wasn't much to tell." Lou grinned as he picked up the boxes.

"Is there something I should know?"

"Not really."

"Your face says otherwise. What's up?"

"He likes jewelry."

"What kind and how much?"

"You'll find out. Why don't you give Danielle a call while you wait?" Lou carried his lamps down the hall.

Casey took his advice, but the call went to voice mail. Was Danielle still with Mancuso? How far would that girl go to get information? Casey picked up the cloth and returned to cleaning.

The front door opened and she heard Summer's voice. Cheyenne, who'd been napping in the living room, gave a couple of excited barks. Casey stepped down from the chair as footsteps headed toward the kitchen. Summer entered the room, followed by Cheyenne.

"Is Jacob with you?" Casey asked.

"In the living room. I'm just getting us a snack."

Lou returned and said, "I'm going to grab another box. Wait for me and we'll meet him together."

He was grinning again. Good lord, what was wrong with the boy?

Casey turned to Summer, who was rummaging through the fridge. "What have you two planned for today?"

"Jacob's helping me build the Christmas village. It'll be fantabulous."

"A Christmas village already?"

"You said I could start after Remembrance Day."

"Right." She'd forgotten.

Summer placed cheese, bologna, and crackers on plates, then grabbed two cans of pop, before heading back down the hall. Casey was tempted to follow, but since Lou clearly wanted to accompany her, maybe it would be better to show some restraint.

Once he returned, he put the box down, then took her hand and led her down the hall. In the living room, Casey found a short, scrawny kid sporting a tall mohawk that she was pretty sure was horribly out of fashion, not to mention stupid. All ten lava lamps were on, and the kid seemed mesmerized by the floating globs.

"Dude," Lou said, looking alarmed. "What are you doing?"

"I wanted to try them out," Jacob answered. "They're cool."

Lou joined him. "I know, right?"

Summer and Casey exchanged puzzled looks. Apparently Summer didn't see their value either.

"Ask me first next time, okay?" Lou said. "Some of them are practically antiques."

"I could use these for my band," Jacob remarked.

"Casey, this is Jacob," Summer said.

As the kid turned around, Casey gaped at the long, narrow face full of piercings in his brows, nose, and lips.

Making a V sign, he said, "Peace."

"Back at ya." His blue eye shadow matched the tips of his mohawk. "I guess you two don't need lunch?" She had no idea how Jacob could eat cheese and crackers without trapping food in those horseshoes piercing his lips.

"We're eating light," Summer replied. "Jacob has band practice in an hour."

"What do you play?" Lou asked.

Casey bet it wasn't the trumpet.

"Base guitar."

Her cell phone rang. It was Denver. She'd half expected his call. Yesterday, she'd left him a message with the new license plate numbers and Richie's name.

"Thanks for the info about Richard Kim," he said. "How did you manage it?"

Casey was afraid he'd ask. Denver was big on whys and hows. She told him everything that had occurred at Winnie's Donuts: the argument between Richie and Liam MacKenna in the bathroom, Richie's fight with Danielle, and Danielle's plans to go out with Mancuso last night. After Casey had finished talking, the line was silent for so long she thought they'd been disconnected.

"Denver?"

"I'm here." He didn't sound pleased. "What's Miss Carpenter up to now?"

"I don't know. We haven't spoken in a couple of days."

"If I can't reach her, I'll contact her parents. Maybe they can talk some sense into their daughter. Did you know there was another race on southwest Marine Drive last night?"

"No. Was anyone hurt?"

"Not this time, but they got away. If Carpenter's been monitoring these guys, she might have seen something."

"I'm surprised she didn't tell me, unless she was afraid I'd start lecturing again. Were the racers Roadkill members?"

"It appears so."

Why hadn't Danielle called? Where the hell was she?

FOURTEEN

"TWO PEOPLE WERE KILLED BY a hit-and-run vehicle at approx-imately nine-thirty last night," the radio newscaster announced with the same voice he used for weather reports and lost pet sto-ries. "The incident occurred at Vancouver's Hastings and Carrall intersection. The victims' names are being withheld pending noti-fication of family members."

Casey stopped rinsing her cereal bowl and darted to the TV remote. She turned on the morning news, which showed two covered bodies on the road, partly illuminated by street lights. Casey looked for familiar faces among the authorities and onlookers visible in the background.

The camera zeroed in on a disheveled woman with wisps of unruly hair fluttering in the wind. She swept one long strand across her toothless mouth. "Guy just bombed right through." The woman waved her hand in the air. "Didn't even try to stop."

A journalist peered into the camera. "This isn't the first hit and run to devastate the city this month, which raises two important questions." The journalist paused. "Why have there been so many hit-and-run deaths lately, and is more than one person responsible?"

Casey plunked onto the sofa. Anger surged and her heart beat faster. Had Danielle heard about this? Casey had finally gotten a hold of her late Saturday afternoon, but Danielle had been too busy working on an article to talk for long. She hadn't known about Friday night's Marine Drive race and was furious that Richie hadn't told her. Also, her date with Mancuso had been a waste of time, as he hadn't told her a damn thing about the racing scene. She'd promised to call Stan. When Casey spoke to Stan earlier, he confirmed that Danielle had followed through. Stan then mentioned that a meeting with the Wieczs had been arranged for later in the day. This was Tuesday; about bloody time.

Casey dialed Danielle's number and got a breathless, "Hello!"

"Are you okay?" Casey heard voices in the background. "Where are you?"

"At the airport. Eagle's getting on a plane for Hong Kong in twenty minutes."

"Have you called the police?"

"I was about to, but it'd be better if you called. They take you more seriously."

"Give me his flight number." After Danielle did so, Casey said, "Is he traveling alone?"

"Seems so. His mom's still here and she looks upset."

"Stay on the phone. I'll use my landline." Casey tried Denver's cell, but it went to voice mail. She called 911 and, after explaining the situation, was assured they'd handle it. She returned to Danielle. "Curious for him to leave in the middle of a semester. You scared him off, didn't you?"

"I think Liam MacKenna did. He showed up at Eagle's house last night, and now the kid's taking off."

"Damn it, Danielle. Were you staking out Eagle again? Were you there all night?"

"I fell asleep in the car, then woke when I heard a vehicle pull out of the garage at 5:00 AM. I recognized Eagle and the lady from the Regency right away, so I followed them."

Casey shook her head. "Was MacKenna in uniform? Did he approach you?"

"No to both. If he'd seen me, I'm sure jerk-face would have told me to take off. Did you hear about the hit and run last night?"

"Two minutes ago."

"I bet the vehicle was stolen. Anyhow, Eagle wasn't the driver. He was home when those people were hit. MacKenna swung by a half hour before the crash, and Mancuso showed up at the house an hour after MacKenna left. Neither of them stayed more than five minutes."

"Why is the kid so popular?"

"He knows who mowed down Beatrice Dunning, so he has one

hell of a secret to protect. That's probably why he's leaving town."
Danielle paused. "There's something else the cops should know. I
think the hit-and-run killer could belong to Roadkill after all."

"What changed your mind?"

"The buzz on all the forums, though no one's saying if the killer's
an A-team driver or one of the others. This time I'll press Dominic
for info."

Casey watched her guinea pig, Ralphie, munch on pellets. "Bad
plan."

"No, it isn't. He asked me out again for tonight, even though
he's broke."

"Mancuso told you that?"

"He implied it. Said he's holding down two jobs, as a mechanic
and an electrician. And he only bought us one beer each. Spent the
whole time going on about movies and kickboxing. Dom loves to
talk. If I buy a few rounds, he may open up about racing."

Casey dropped her feet onto one of Lou's boxes. "Sounds risky, what
with all that beer, and he is pretty hot. Things could get out of hand."

"I don't swing that way, so no worries there."

"What if Dominic doesn't handle rejection well? For all we know,
he could be the killer."

"My gut tells me he isn't. Besides, I'll only see him in public."

"Danielle, no—"

"I'll call tomorrow and let you know how things went. I might try
talking to Harvey and Bashir Kumar too."

"Who is Bashir Kumar?"

"The guy who owns the red Imprezza. He goes by the name Speed
Demon, and I know where he lives. Cool, huh?"

No, not cool at all. "How did you find out all that? I thought
Richie wasn't helping you anymore."

"With the leverage I have on him, he doesn't have a choice."

"What kind of leverage?" She waited, but Danielle didn't respond.
This was going from bad to worse. "Come on, Danielle."

"Richie's parents would freak if they knew about his relationship with Roadkill. After the accident, they didn't want him to have anything to do with racing or racers. They already keep a tight leash on him because of the head injuries. All I have to do is threaten him with his parents and he tells me what I need to know, sort of."

"Why did Richie go see the racers at the donut shop?"

"To complete a business transaction."

"What kind of transaction?"

Danielle took a few seconds to answer. "I saw him give Kumar a wad of cash at the table. He finally admitted that he's an errand boy for the bookie who pays the racers."

The kid was in deep. "Did you talk to Richie about last night?"

"No, but I will. I also need to find out if he thinks Liam MacKenna might be racing again."

"You honestly think that's possible?" Casey wasn't overly impressed with MacKenna, but she couldn't picture him stooping that low.

"Racing's an addiction that doesn't go away easily."

"It nearly killed him, and now he has a great job with a pension."

"Yet he knew about the meeting at Winnie's Donuts, which only insiders would've known."

"Couldn't he have a source too?" Casey asked. "MacKenna might have showed up to let Roadkill know he was around. Make them think twice about racing again."

"Maybe. We should still watch Kumar and Mueller, though."

"No. Too many of them know what we drive."

"I'm using Ginny's Jeep now."

"Ginny?"

"My girlfriend, Virginia."

"Your dad won't let you have the car, huh?"

"That's not it." She paused again. "His tires were slashed in our driveway two nights ago, so I've changed cars. Before you start lecturing, yes, I'm watching my back."

Casey remembered the powerful engine she'd heard at work and the dark car speeding past Mainland's entrance. "Have you heard any souped-up engines on your street?"

"Once, and I thought I saw a black, sporty car behind me the other day, but it took off in another direction."

Casey told her about the incident outside Mainland. After that there wasn't much else to say. Danielle was so bent on stopping Roadkill that nothing could throw her off track. The only thing to do was monitor her closely and try to keep the overzealous girl-reporter safe.

Casey pulled up a list of cars and drivers she'd compiled on her laptop, then typed Bashir Kumar's name next to the red Imprezza. Hellhound Harvey owned the purple Camry. Dominic owned the gray Dodge Neon. Eagle's car was a gold Mitsubishi. Her fingertip paused at the black BMW. Morris Mueller's car was the only black vehicle among the hardcore drivers. Was his the vehicle she'd spotted racing past Mainland? The car might not have been black, though. It could have been the purple Camry. Liam MacKenna drove a dark Mazda, and he seemed to show up at interesting times.

Casey logged into one of the racing forums Danielle had told her about. Members were speculating about whether Roadkill was responsible for last night's hit and run. Hastings and Carrall skirted the Downtown Eastside, an area populated by drug addicts, alcoholics, and the homeless, including some with mental illness. Someone wrote about the victims: *Probably a couple of losers so drunk they stepped into the street without looking up.* Others agreed. Only one person thought it outrageous that no one had stopped to help them.

Ralphie stood on his hind legs and whistled. Casey picked up the black and white guinea pig, then sat in her rocking chair and placed him on a towel. The moment she stroked him, he began cooing. Her phone rang.

"Got your message," Denver said. "Airport authorities have been alerted. If they're on the ball, Eagle will be detained."

"Has anyone questioned him?"

"No, but I will soon."

"Did you find last night's hit-and-run vehicle?"

"It was an old Celica torched in Stanley Park at the Third Beach parking lot," he answered. "Do you know if any of your team were working in that area?"

"Not that I know of, but I can ask Stan."

Stanley Park was only a few minutes away from Hastings and Carrall. "Who were the victims?"

"One was a social worker named Chantel Green. She was with her client, Jason Charlie, an eighteen-year-old who'd just landed his first job."

Casey felt like a rock had rolled through her stomach. Denver needed to know everything. "Danielle says that Richard Kim is not only gambling on Roadkill races, but also working for the bookie who pays racers their winnings. She saw him hand money to a guy named Bashir Kumar Wednesday night. He drives a red Subaru Imprezza."

"Kumar, huh?"

"You know him?"

"Yes. She isn't planning to approach him, is she?"

"She wants me to help her watch him and Morris Mueller, the fifth Roadkill member."

Denver uttered a couple of profanities. "Kumar's bad news. Violent and, considering the three assault complaints against him, misogynistic."

"Any convictions?"

"He hires good lawyers," Denver replied. "Danielle Carpenter needs to stay far away from him."

"I'll make sure she knows, but there's something else." Casey didn't really want to say this, but Denver needed to know. "While Danielle was staking out Eagle's place last night, Liam MacKenna showed up and had a quick talk with Eagle. She's wondering if his appearance might have something to do with Eagle's sudden departure."

"Maybe, maybe not." He paused. "That stays between us, okay?"

"Sure." As much as she wanted to know what was going on with MacKenna and Roadkill, she knew Denver wouldn't tell her. "There's one more bit of news." She took a deep breath. "Danielle has a date with another Roadkill member, Dominic Mancuso. They're going to a pub in Richmond called the River's End tonight, and, short of tying her to a chair, I see no way to stop it. Do you know Mancuso as well?"

"He's been on the racing circuit a while. Calls himself the Dominator. Other than a handful of speeding tickets, he's managed to stay out of serious trouble so far."

After their conversation ended, Casey put Ralphie back in his cage. She was about to return to the dishes when her buzzer rang. She looked at the intercom. Who would show up at this time of morning? She pressed the button. "Hello?"

"It's Greg. Got a minute?"

What the hell was he doing here? Thoughts of Tina's confrontation made her want to say something nasty. Better yet, why not tell him to his face?

"Be down in a minute."

Casey jogged down the two flights of stairs, eager to get this over with. On the main floor, she unbolted the front door and cringed at Greg's hangdog stare.

"Can I come in?" he asked.

She opened the door wider.

"The place hasn't changed," he remarked.

The last time Greg stood in this hallway, they were still married. They'd come here nearly every Sunday for Rhonda's roast beef dinners. That seemed like a long time ago. Greg didn't belong here anymore, and she'd never let him see her cozy third-floor refuge.

"I heard about the suspension," he said, "and gave Stan my statement. Hope it helps."

How humiliating. "Thanks."

He glanced at Rhonda's collection of pen-and-ink landscapes on the wall. "Tina told me about your chat."

Right, here it came. "Is that what she called it?"

He blinked a couple times, looking confused. "Tina said she asked you for help, and you refused."

"She wanted me to reduce the rent, then got pissed off when I wouldn't. Called me the selfish bitch you think I am."

"She said that?" Greg's mouth fell open. "Seriously?"

"Damn right. Guess she skipped that last bit, huh?"

He rubbed his hands on his jeans. "I'm real sorry, Casey. Tina made up that shit about you being selfish. I've never said that and never would."

She didn't like the way his expression was softening. "She thought I wanted to evict you. Did you set her straight?"

"Uh, could I sit down a minute?"

Might as well get this over with. She headed into the living room. While Casey sat, Greg zeroed in on the Christmas village spread over the fireplace hearth, down a makeshift step, and onto the cotton batting on the floor.

"Christmas already?"

"Summer's idea."

He smiled. "How's she doing?"

"Fine."

"It must be hard without Rhonda."

Summer and Rhonda weren't open for discussion. "Did you set Tina straight or not?"

Greg rested his elbows on his knees and lowered his head. God, he looked terrible with all those extra pounds and major hair loss. He'd just turned thirty-two.

"I was trying to avoid another fight, so I didn't tell her about giving notice," he replied. "She knows now, and if I'd known what she'd said to you, I would have made her apologize in person, like I'm here to do."

"I don't care what your wife thinks of me, and I'm not interested in an apology."

Greg's gaze drifted to the lava lamps. Of course, he'd remember them. Greg gave Lou the big purple one for Christmas a few years ago, when they were still friends.

"So, it's true." He sat upright. "Lou's moved in?"

Was that why he hadn't apologized by phone? Because he wanted to see for himself? "My personal life isn't your business."

Greg huffed. "The wait for you finally paid off," he remarked. "I take it you got over your intimacy issues?"

The jab stung. After she'd found out about Tina, she and Greg had their worst fight ever. He'd wanted to know if there was someone else. In the heat of the moment, she'd blurted that she didn't feel close to any man and probably never would. That's when he accused her of being incapable of genuine intimacy.

Casey stood. "Time for you to leave." She marched out of the room and opened the front door.

"Look, I'm sorry, but the truth is Lou was always hovering around, waiting for a chance to steal you away."

"He was best man at our wedding, Greg. You invited him over all the time, and you were the one who screwed around, not me." She hadn't expected to feel this calm. A good sign that none of this mattered anymore.

"You're right." He looked uncertain. "It's just that . . . well, losing you was a mistake I'll always regret."

Casey had no regrets; not anymore. She opened the door. "You don't belong here."

"I don't blame you for still hating me."

"I don't hate you," she said. "You're just not part of my life now."

Greg's jaw grew slack. He stepped onto the porch. "What will you do with the house?"

"Sell it, I suppose."

"You loved that place. It's where you grew up."

"I've moved on, Greg. So should you."

His hangdog face was back. "I'll leave it in good shape."

Casey shut the front door, leaned against it, and exhaled slowly. She'd loved him once, yet sometimes she thought she'd only married Greg to prove to herself—maybe even to her father—that marriage and monogamy could work, that she could handle intimacy and loyalty far better than Mother had. In some ways, she hadn't. Now there was a new opportunity to build a fully committed relationship, one that might even involve having a baby some day. After all, she was only thirty-one. Still, Lou had only suggested moving in. Maybe he wanted to see how things went before they talked marriage. Was part of him unsure about her? Casey closed her eyes. Given the past, he had every right to be.

FIFTEEN

CASEY TRIED TO SHOVE HER thong, bikini, low-rise, and high-cut underwear to the back of the drawer, but the crush merely expanded back into place. She wished she'd tackled this drawer sooner, but the term paper, house cleaning, and other chores had taken too much time. She'd assured Lou he wouldn't need to move his bureau in, and unless she wanted a really crowded bedroom, she had better be right. Besides, after Greg's cheap shot about her intimacy issues, Casey was more determined than ever to accommodate Lou. She just wished she hadn't told him about Greg's visit.

"It was bad enough that he broke your heart by screwing around with Tina," Lou had said. "Now he's telling you it was a big mistake? I knew it! That asshole wants you back."

She'd left out Greg's crack about her intimacy issues. How could she admit that he'd exposed her deepest fear? Should she tell Lou that her heart hadn't been all that broken when her marriage ended? Everyone at work had said how remarkably well she'd taken their split and how mature she'd been to let Greg stay in her house. The gesture had been neither difficult nor generous. His affair had made her realize that she hadn't enjoyed living with Greg even before Tina came on the scene and that part of her—a small part—had been almost glad to be rid of him, although it had taken a couple of years to admit that to herself. Allowing him to rent the house at a reasonable price was compensation for her guilt.

Casey shut the drawer. If she wasn't suspended, maybe she wouldn't be wallowing in so much negative thinking. Yesterday, Stan phoned to say that the twins and their mother missed the second meeting with Gwyn, without explanation this time. Stan had wanted to lift her suspension right away, but Gwyn didn't want the family accusing Mainland Public Transport of brushing them off, so he'd given the Wieczs a third chance. The meeting was to have taken place at 5:00 PM yesterday. At seven, a frustrated Stan had called to say that the family had bailed again.

"I pressed Gwyn to lift the suspension," Stan had said. "He wants me to drive out to their place and see what's going on. If the Wieczs refuse to see him tomorrow, the suspension ends."

Tomorrow had become today. It was now just after 9:00 PM, and Stan still hadn't called. Casey was trying not to let it upset her, but hell, one week of suspension was more than enough. If he didn't call . . . She shoved the ugly thoughts from her mind and opened another dresser drawer, just as her phone rang. She barely had a chance to say, "Hello."

"I'm at the fitness center and need help!" Danielle shouted. "Come get me!"

"What's going on?" No response. "Danielle?"

The line went dead. Fear wriggled down Casey's spine. She dialed Danielle's number. No answer. Casey grabbed her purse and jacket. On her way downstairs, she dialed 911 and told them about the call.

"I don't know if someone's threatened her or what," she told the dispatcher. "Danielle wouldn't have asked for help if she didn't need it. She thought someone had been following her."

After being assured they'd send someone out, Casey hurried into Rhonda's living room, where Summer, Jacob, and Lou were painting a Christmas scene on the large picture window. Jacob, dressed in black and wearing a studded choke collar, was outlining a red bow on a Christmas present. The little twit stopped and placed a hand on Summer's back.

Lou was working on a reindeer when Casey said, "I've got to go out for a bit."

He turned around. "Where?"

"Regency Fitness Center. Danielle needs some help."

"With what?"

"She didn't say."

Lou looked concerned. "Want some company?"

"Actually, it'd be better if you stayed here." She nodded toward Jacob, who'd resumed his work. Much as she'd love to have Lou come along, she didn't want Summer left alone with Goth Boy.

"Any idea how long you'll be?" Lou asked.

"Not really."

"It's just that I was hoping to unpack a couple of boxes tonight, and I need to know where to put my stuff."

"We'll do it when I get back."

Seeing the doubt in his eyes, Casey hurried up to Lou and gave him a quick kiss. "I'll let you know what's going on as soon as I know."

She dashed outside and into her car. She could smell the damp in the air and feel the heavy clouds bearing down. The rain would start soon. Speeding south on Commercial Drive, she wondered if Danielle had tried to talk to Harvey. Casey had read her latest piece in the *Vancouver Contrarian*: an essay about what motivates a racer's desire to break rules—the need for speed and thrills, to compete for cash, or to control something more powerful than themselves. Most important of all, Danielle had concluded, was the need to win, to be king of the road.

Casey had memorized the last sentence. *Only someone decided that they needed to kill people. It doesn't get any riskier, or sicker, than that.*

Had Danielle's comment provoked the killer? At a red light, Casey called Danielle. A recorded voice again told her the number wasn't available. Danielle wouldn't have deliberately switched off her phone, would she?

The light turned green. Casey turned left onto Clarke as a call came through.

"It's me, Stan."

Bloody great timing. "Did you see the Wieczs?"

"Only the mother, who told me her life story. Bottom line is she can't work and barely survives on disability checks and the twins' earnings."

"In other words, she'll never be able to pay a fine. What about the complaint against me?"

"I straightened things out. It seems the girls told their mother some whoppers about you, which is why she filed the complaint."

Casey gripped the steering wheel. "What kind of whoppers?"

"It's not important. I assured Mrs. Wiecz that I could collect a stack of witness statements to refute the girls' claims, and that I had over a dozen passenger complaints about Lara's smoking. Mrs. Wiecz dropped the complaint; you're officially back on duty."

"Thank you."

"There are conditions, though, and—before you get mad—they were Gwyn's idea, not mine."

"What are they?"

"No issuing fines or following the twins off the bus. If they break the rules you can tell them to stop, but if they give you a hard time, the driver handles it. Understand?"

A lousy way to treat his second-in-command. "You're making it sound like I'm on probation."

"Only for a month."

Casey pressed harder on the gas and glanced around. "How about you let Marie keep the assignment? I really don't need the aggravation."

"Marie's having babysitter problems, so you're it, kiddo."

"I don't—"

"I thought you wanted to see this through."

Casey choked back her disappointment in Stan for letting Gwyn do this. "Yeah, I do."

The vehicle in front of her was too slow. She pulled into the fast lane, and a horn blasted behind her. The headlights were practically riding her bumper.

"If the girls break any rules, call me right away," Stan said. "I don't want to read about it in a report first. By the way, you can email reports in, but I want them within two hours of each shift."

"Sure. See ya." Fine. Whatever. She had more immediate worries than being treated like a rookie.

Minutes later, Casey pulled into the Regency Fitness Center's empty parking lot and stopped in front of the entrance. Two lights exposed the empty counter through vertical windows on either side of the double doors. The rest of the lobby was dark. She checked her watch. Nine-thirty. Danielle was probably here when the place closed at nine. Twenty-five minutes had passed since Danielle's call, so where was she, and where were the RCMP?

Casey's fingers ached from gripping the wheel as she cruised farther into the lot, turned left, and spotted a dark green Jeep. Danielle had said she was driving her friend's Jeep. Had the vehicle broken down? She dialed Danielle's number again and got the same message. Harvey's purple Camry was parked on the other side of the Jeep. Casey pulled up beside Danielle's vehicle but didn't see her.

Floodlights illuminated the corners of the building, casting shadows among the trees and shrubs that lined the fence at the back of the property. Casey fidgeted. She could wait for the cops to show up, but what if Danielle was in danger or hurt?

Casey grabbed her flashlight and stepped out of her Tercel. Wind rustled through the bushes and sent a chill through her. She flipped up her jacket hood and peered through the Jeep's windows. No Danielle. Harvey wasn't in his Camry either. Where in hell *were* they?

Squinting through the wind and darkness, Casey headed toward the Japanese garden at back of the building; a quiet, tranquil spot where people could talk without being noticed. The farther she walked, the darker it became. Her left shoulder grazed the building as she shone her light along the treeline, glimpsing the wooden fence through the foliage.

"Danielle?" she called.

The wind blew her jacket hood back down. She heard the garden's mini waterfall ahead, the traffic behind her.

Casey slowed her steps. "Harvey?"

The gravel footpath crunched under her runners. Through the vertical windows on her left, she glimpsed a row of treadmills and stationary bikes in the dark room. Another floodlight illuminated the corner at the far end of the building. As Casey started toward it, a boulder in the garden's tiny pond caught her attention. She stopped.

There hadn't been a boulder that size the last time she was here. Oh lord, it appeared to be floating. Casey shone her flashlight on the object and tried to comprehend what she was looking at . . . and then she knew.

She jumped back. Oh god, someone was face down in the water. Her flashlight illuminated arms and a torso, bundled in a puffy black jacket. Danielle's ski jacket was plum-colored, wasn't it? Taking a deep breath, she turned her flashlight toward the head and saw a baseball cap on backward. Oh, no. Harvey.

Wait, was he alive? Casey scanned the area, hoping for help or at least someone who could tell her what had happened. No one was around. She placed the flashlight by the water's edge and knelt on the pebbles. She reached for his jacket and pulled him closer. Casey lifted his head—blood spilled from the wide gash across Harvey's throat.

"Oh!" She let go and fell back on her butt.

Casey scrambled backward, her palms stinging from the pebbles and grit. She stopped when she bumped against a wall. Gasping for breath, she watched in horror as the flashlight she'd left by the pond shone on his body. Casey hugged herself and shivered in the cold, damp air. Think, she ordered, and reached for her phone. Her hand shook so much she could barely press the digits. She'd almost finished dialing when a bright light appeared on her right.

SIXTEEN

"POLICE! STOP RIGHT THERE!"

A blazing light forced Casey to squint and look down. Her butt was on the ground and her back was still pressed against the brick wall. Where on god's earth did they think she would go?

"I'm the one who called 911," she said. "My name's Casey Holland."

"Face down on the ground, *now*!"

Right. Cops were trained not to trust anyone. She started to comply, when movement on the other side of the pond caught her attention. Casey's heart leapt and she pointed toward the fence. "There's someone in the bushes!"

"Don't move." The officer radioed for assistance, then shone his light across the pond.

A figure darted down the fence. Another flashlight appeared at the other end of the building, and an officer moved forward.

The officer with Casey turned to her. "I *said*, face down on the ground!"

Heat rushed through her body as raindrops began sprinkling her face. "Sure. No problem." Asshole. "You might want to take a look at the body in the pond." She flattened herself on the pebbles. "His throat's been slashed."

"Hands behind your head!"

Voices shouted from both ends of the building. Footsteps crunched the gravel. A third cop knelt by the pond and reached for Harvey.

Casey looked up. "I asked you guys to meet me here," she said. "My friend's in trouble!"

"No shit," the third cop said, quickly lowering Harvey's head.

"Not him. That's Harvey Haberkorn. My friend is Danielle Carpenter. She was supposed to meet Harvey, but she called me, asking for help. Now she's disappeared, though her car's still in the lot. We have to find her!"

A man yelled, "No! Let go!"

The voice was familiar, yet Casey couldn't place it. More voices came from the parking lot. She leaned forward. The guy shouted again, angry and panicky. She needed to see him, but the cop was too busy asking dumb questions and restraining her hands behind her back. Thoughts swirled while she was patted down. Where the hell had she heard that voice? *Think.*

"The guy who's yelling could have killed Harvey!" she shouted. "Can you find out who he is?" The cop didn't answer. "For god's sake, he might know where Danielle is! What if he's done something to her?" No response. "Come on!"

"Calm down, ma'am," he replied. "How do you know the deceased?"

She realized she wouldn't get anywhere until she first answered his questions. "We met briefly. I worked out here two weeks ago, and we talked for a couple of minutes."

"What did you talk about?"

"Job openings. Harvey worked here."

"When did Miss Carpenter call you?"

"About thirty minutes ago." The wind and rain blew into her face, forcing her to squint. The shouting had stopped. "When I got here, she wasn't around, so I called her cell phone. She didn't answer."

"Did Miss Carpenter say if she'd seen or spoken with Mr. Haberkorn?"

"No. All she said was that she needed help and to come right away, and then the line went dead." She wished she could see what was happening with the shouting man. "Maybe she saw Harvey's body and took off."

"You have no idea what her problem was?"

"Correct." This genius was getting on her nerves. "She's been writing articles on street racing for the *Vancouver Contrarian*, and Harvey Haberkorn belonged to a group of racers known as Roadkill. We believe Harvey knew who mowed down Beatrice Dunning last month because he was the other racer that night. Danielle wanted the hit-and-run driver's name." Casey noticed the officer's head move a fraction. Good, she'd caught his attention. Now maybe he'd do something about Danielle. "I'm sure she was also hoping that Harvey would give her a lead about the other hit and runs. Danielle thinks one of the Roadkill racers could be involved. I'm sure you've heard of them."

The officer gave her a blank stare. "What brought you to this particular spot? Strange place for a meeting, isn't it?"

"Not if you don't want to be seen. Harvey wouldn't have wanted to be caught talking to a reporter."

"You headed straight for the back of the building and found the victim?"

This was wasting precious time. "Both of their cars were parked at this end of the building, and I knew a garden was back here. I was expecting to find Danielle, not Harvey."

"If Miss Carpenter saw the body, why did she call you instead of us?"

Good question. "I don't know." The rain began to fall harder. "If you don't believe me, call Constable Denver Davies with the Vancouver Police. He'll vouch for me and my interest in the street-racing deaths. I have his cell number." Although she'd rather not resort to using Denver, there seemed to be little choice.

"Let's talk in the car," the officer said.

"I dropped my flashlight. Could I get it back?"

He put on a pair of latex gloves. "We'll need to take a look at it."

The officer was joined by a colleague, who spoke to him about cordoning off the area. Casey was then escorted into the parking lot, where more police were arriving. Crime scene tape was already going up around the property's perimeter.

"The Camry belongs to Harvey," Casey said, shivering in the downpour. "I think Danielle was driving the Jeep."

The officer opened the back door of the nearest cruiser. "Get in."

She slid awkwardly into the backseat, while he took a seat up front.

"I want more details about the connection between you, Miss Carpenter, and the victim."

Casey blinked raindrops from her eyelashes. Her hair was soaked. She tried to sit comfortably, but it was impossible with her wrists pinned behind her back. "Constable Davies can confirm the connection."

The officer blinked at her. "I want to hear from you first."

As Casey described her first surveillance mission with Danielle at the center, yelling erupted from the back of the building. Officers raced toward the noise, weapons drawn.

"Constable Davies also knows Danielle and why she's so interested in street racers." Her phone rang. "That could be Danielle. My cell's in my left pocket."

The officer stepped out of the vehicle and opened the door. "Lean forward." After she did so, the officer removed her phone and answered the call. "This is Richmond RCMP Constable Prentiss, who's this? . . . Lou who?"

Oh, great. Lou would be really worried now.

"She's fine, Mr. Sheckter. Where are you? . . . I see. Well, we're just having a chat, then she'll be on her way, if all goes well." He ended the call.

"Denver's number is in my phone," Casey said.

Prentiss returned to the front seat and dialed his own phone. Officers emerged from the back of the building, flanking a short man who kept his head lowered.

"It wasn't m-me!"

Casey strained for a better look. Oh good lord, it was Richie. Now she knew where she'd heard that voice. While Prentiss spoke on the phone, Casey leaned out of the partially open door to listen as Richie was escorted toward the cruiser next to the one she was sitting in.

"What brought you here tonight, Mr. Kim?" a constable asked.

Good, they knew who he was.

"To m-meet Danni."

"Who's Danni?"

"Carpenter." His voice cracked. "She was scared."

"Why was she scared?"

"She wouldn't tell." Richie's head began to sway back and forth. "It's not f-fair."

"What exactly did Miss Carpenter say?"

"To come get her." Richie looked from one side to the other, as if searching for Danielle. When he spotted Casey, he stopped. She held her breath, uncertain if being recognized was a good thing.

"Where's your car?" the officer asked him.

"I w-walked."

"Your friend asked you to come get her, so you just walked over?"

"Can't drive." His head was really lolling now. "Where's D-Danni?"

"Where do you live, Mr. Kim?"

Richie looked around the lot before turning back to Casey. His head stopped lolling, and he again stared at her. Maybe he couldn't remember where he'd seen her. He'd only glimpsed her outside the donut shop, and that was eight nights ago.

"Mr. Kim?" the officer asked. "Where were you when Miss Carpenter called?"

"My parents' restaurant."

"What's it called?"

Richie mumbled a name Casey couldn't catch. She glanced at Constable Prentiss as he ended his call and looked at Richie, ignoring her completely.

"What is your relationship to Miss Carpenter?" the officer with Richie asked.

"She's been my friend since she was little."

"Why did Miss Carpenter want you to meet her here?"

"I told you I don't know! Don't you g-get me?" The head loll started again. "I'm talkin' English, you stupid."

"Just calm down," the officer replied. "We're only trying to understand what happened."

Richie lowered his head and the lolling slowed.

"Did you see anyone else here when you arrived?" the constable asked.

Richie looked up. "I c-couldn't find Danni, so I looked around." He paused. "I saw someone in the w-water and heard some lady calling Danni. I tried to hide." He pointed at Casey. "It was her! Maybe she did it. D-Danni could be dead!"

Casey fumed. What the hell was Richie playing at? He knew Harvey, and he sure as hell knew what car Harvey drove, so why not refer to him by name? Maybe Richie's brain wasn't as damaged as he wanted people to think.

"I didn't kill anybody, and Richie knew Harvey," Casey said to Prentiss. "I saw them talking together at Winnie's Donuts a few nights ago."

"Step out of the car so I can free your hands," he replied.

After he did so, Casey massaged her wrists, aware that Richie was still watching her. She and the constable sat back in the vehicle.

"There's something else," she murmured. "Danielle and Richie argued at the donut shop. Richie was furious with her for investigating Roadkill because he's doing business with them."

"What kind of business?"

"The kid's a gopher for the bookie who pays drivers their winnings. Danielle thinks he might also be placing bets on the side. He knows all the racers' names and when the races will take place."

Prentiss looked at her. "You also seem to know a fair amount."

"From Danielle, which reminds me, she's gone out with another Roadkill racer named Dominic Mancuso a couple of times. I don't know where he lives, but I know what he drives and his plate number. The purpose of these dates was to pump him for information about Roadkill. Mancuso might have figured that out and tried to stop her."

A cop emerged through the bushes by the fence, carrying something in a plastic bag. Casey heard him say he found a cell phone. Her heart pounded as she turned to Prentiss. "I know what Danielle's phone looks like."

"Stay here." Prentiss walked toward his colleague.

Casey waited, ignoring Richie's stare. She didn't give a damn what he thought. Why had Danielle called him as well, especially when he didn't drive? Was his parents' restaurant nearby?

After a quick consultation, Prentiss returned and showed Casey the evidence bag.

Casey's stomach flip-flopped. "It's hers." Had Danielle taken off, or had she been abducted?

Another officer approached them, carrying a large black bag. "I found this farther down the fence."

Casey spotted the picture of the hang-gliding woman and the Born to Fly caption. "It's Danielle's." She began to shiver. "God, she really is in trouble."

"We'll find her," Prentiss said. "She's been gone, at most, maybe forty minutes."

It was enough time to die. Guilt curdled Casey's insides. She should have gotten here sooner, and now she had to make things right. The cops would hate the idea of her poking around, asking questions. As far as they were concerned, security officers were civilians with toy badges, not that they'd be too far wrong this time. Mainland didn't train staff to find missing people, but this wasn't job related—this was personal. As Casey's colleagues knew all too well, personal crusades brought out the best, *and* the worst, in her.

SEVENTEEN

AS THE STOPLIGHT TURNED RED, Casey braked and rubbed her bleary eyes. Waiting for her suspension to end had been tough, but waiting for news about Danielle's disappearance was complete agony. Unable to sleep last night and desperate for information, she'd called Denver at 3:00 AM, knowing he'd be at work.

"Any leads?" she'd asked.

"None. Her editor at the *Vancouver Contrarian* said she was supposed to have submitted an article this morning but missed her deadline. Her photo's being circulated, but so far no serious tips have come in."

"I'd like to show Danielle's photo around too. Maybe I'll run into someone you guys missed."

"Fine, but stay away from racers. Let me know if you learn something."

Fifteen hours had elapsed since Danielle's disappearance. Instinct and common sense pointed to someone in Roadkill. Those guys needed questioning, and the safest place to start would be with their most vulnerable contact, Richie Kim. She'd bet a year's pay he knew more than he'd told the cops last night, and she had to figure out a way to get to him. First priority, though, was a visit to Danielle's parents. She'd called the Carpenters an hour ago and spoken to the mother.

"I know who you are, dear," Mrs. Carpenter had said. "I wrote your name on a cinnamon bun."

The woman had sounded shaky, but she'd agreed to let Casey come over to collect a photo of Danielle. Casey pulled up in front of a narrow three-story house and peered through the windshield. The Carpenters' sooty wood-framed home had long passed its prime. Faded gray paint had chipped off the porch steps. Moss had invaded most of the lawn and filled cracks in the cement walkway leading to the steps.

Casey got out of her car and scanned the quiet residential street. She hadn't heard any souped-up engines on the way here, but she wasn't about to let down her guard. Except for a large picture window, all second- and third-floor window blinds had been drawn.

The steps creaked under her feet. She knocked and waited for what felt like a long time before the door opened and a much older and wider version of Danielle appeared, wiping her hands on her apron. Her pale skin and red, puffy eyes made Casey realize that her worry was nothing compared to this woman's anguish.

"Mrs. Carpenter? I'm Casey."

"Come in, dear, and call me Ivy."

Casey stepped onto a dark blue welcome mat and removed her shoes while inhaling the intoxicating scent of cinnamon, yeast, and sugar.

"Let's talk in the kitchen," Ivy murmured. "My rolls are ready." She tiptoed across the worn broadloom, as if worried about making noise.

Casey spotted a large photo of a young man in a high school graduation cap and gown. Tea candles in crystal holders surrounded the portrait. To the right, a narrow silver vase held a single red rose. A wooden crucifix hung above the picture. Ben Carpenter couldn't have been out of high school long before he flew through the windshield and broke his neck. Danielle's grad photo was perched farther down the mantelpiece, without candles or a rose, just a crucifix. Her eyes and broad smile were filled with a mischievous spirit. Had the picture been taken before Ben's crash?

In the bright lemon kitchen, Casey spotted two beautifully decorated cakes on an oak table. A stainless-steel oven, granite countertops, and halogen lights made the room look fifty years newer than the dingy living room. Ivy removed large, puffy rolls from the oven.

"Are you a professional baker?" Casey asked, trying not to salivate.

"Goodness, no. I just like to make things for my church and for the needy. Sometimes, I sell a few treats at craft fairs for pocket money."

Casey glanced at the embroidered words, IN GOD WE TRUST, hanging above a window.

"Would you like some coffee?" Ivy asked. "I was going to make a fresh pot."

"Thanks, but I'd like to start showing the photo around as soon as possible."

Ivy put the rolls down. "I'll get it for you."

Casey wandered around the spacious room and gazed at a display of decorative plates. A glass case held a collection of at least thirty silver spoons. Ceramic animals were perched on top of cupboards. Every one of them gleamed as if new.

Behind her, someone coughed. Casey turned to find a bald, round-faced man in baggy pajamas peering at her.

"Hi, I'm Casey. A friend of Danielle's."

His hunched shoulders straightened. "Do you know where my little girl is?"

"Not yet, but I'll keep looking."

The man, whom she assumed was Danielle's father, pointed a trembling finger at Casey. "You find her." His voice trembled. "She's my little girl."

Ivy reappeared. "Alvin, what are you doing? Go back to bed, dear."

She handed Casey a photo of Danielle standing before a birthday cake adorned with elaborate pink and purple roses and the words HAPPY TWENTY-FIRST. "That was taken a month ago."

Ivy hurried to her husband and placed her hands on his shoulders. "You need your rest."

Their foreheads nearly touched as they whispered together. The couple looked old enough to be Danielle's grandparents, but trauma and grief did that to people.

After Alvin headed upstairs, Ivy's mouth quivered as she said, "He's so upset."

"I understand." Casey slipped the snapshot into her handbag. "I should be going."

"Wait, I want to give you something." Ivy hurried to the counter and placed two fresh rolls in a paper bag.

"It's not necessary," Casey said.

"I know, but I want to anyway." Ivy handed her the bag. "Few people have offered to help search for Danielle."

"Thank you." Casey started for the door. "Are there any particular friends she might try to contact?"

"I used to know her high school friends, but not her college friends, or the people she meets through work." Ivy's dark eyes blinked a couple of times. "She thinks she's all grown up. Comes and goes when she wants. Doesn't tell her mother anything." She paused, glancing at the staircase. "There is someone. A girl who lives not far from here. Her name is Virginia."

The girlfriend. "Do you know her last name?"

"No. She's probably in Danielle's address book."

Which was likely in the Richmond RCMP's possession. If Virginia was listed, they would have called her by now.

Ivy's gaze drifted to the graduation photos. "My beautiful children," she mumbled.

Casey gazed at Ben's photo. His vibrant eyes were filled with humor. "Yes, they are. Danielle doesn't look much different than she does now."

"Her photo was taken four years ago, and Benny's six years ago."

"Danielle told me a little about him."

Ivy nodded, her mouth downcast. "Danielle adored her brother; everyone did. Benny was so full of energy, and smart too." Ivy smiled. "He wanted to be a scientist . . . loved blowing things up." She chuckled. "Friends dropped by all the time. I was always feeding somebody, which drove Alvin crazy."

"You must have known his friend Richie?"

Ivy's face beamed. "Richie practically lived here. He's always loved my baking."

How much should she be told? "I saw him at the Regency Fitness Center last night."

She nodded. "The police told me he was there." The lines between Ivy's brows multiplied. "I don't understand why she called Richie. Danielle hasn't seen him in three years. Not since she visited him in the hospital after the crash."

Danielle's relationship with Richie was work related, and sources had to be kept confidential, even from mothers. Had Danielle called Richie because she thought he could help get answers from Harvey? Had she found Harvey's body after that call, then panicked and contacted Casey?

"Richie misses the old neighborhood," Ivy murmured.

Misses? As in present tense? A minute ago, she had said that "he's always loved her baking." Present tense as well. "Ivy, have you been in touch with Richie?"

Ivy didn't quite meet Casey's gaze. "Let me get you a chocolate pecan cookie to go with the rolls. I made a fresh batch this morning."

Casey usually stayed away from chocolate because it darkened her mood, but she didn't want to offend Ivy, or stop her from talking. She followed her into the kitchen. "I think Richie knows some of the street racers Danielle's been writing about, and I think one of those racers took her." She accepted the cookie Ivy handed her and placed it in her bag. "He could help us find her."

"Richie's not involved with those people."

Casey hesitated, not sure how this would go. "Actually, Ivy, he is."

"*No.* He promised his parents and me that he would never race again."

"He hasn't, as far as I know. But he does keep in contact with a group of them."

Ivy gave her a wary look. "How do you know this?"

"Danielle told me. She's been in touch with Richie for a while now, and we saw him meet with racers the other night."

Ivy took a small step back. Her hands swept down her apron. "Neither of them said anything to me." She glanced around the room, as if searching for answers. "I know why Danielle wouldn't; she's always had her private side. But Richie? He should have told me, that bad boy."

Bad boy? Was she kidding? "Maybe he was afraid you'd be upset if you found out."

Ivy fiddled with the apron's hem. "Danielle shouldn't be writing about such things. There are too many horrible memories."

"She's trying to stop the racing."

"Richie's not even allowed to drive." Ivy scrunched the hem of her apron in her hands. "How can he know those people?"

"That's something I'd very much like to ask him," Casey replied. "Did Danielle know you've kept in touch with Richie?"

Ivy stroked the apron repeatedly. "Richie wanted only me to know. He was afraid his parents would find out. Those people blamed Benny for the accident. They moved all the way to Richmond to get away from us, but it didn't work."

Clearly not. Richie was obviously big on secrets.

"Richie knows the accident wasn't Benny's fault," Ivy went on. "Someone ran them off the road." Anger flashed across her face. "Someone who still isn't man enough to admit what he's done."

"Do you visit Richie in person?"

"It takes me three bus transfers," she answered. "But it's worth it to see Benny again."

"You mean *Richie*."

"Oh, yes. Silly me." She giggled. "Richie, Richie, Richie. I bring him baked goods, you know. His parents never give him any treats. Such cold, unfeeling people."

Good lord, was Ivy all there? Apparently the whole family still had some healing to do.

"When was the last time you saw Richie?"

"Two weeks ago, while his parents were at work." Ivy clicked her tongue. "That poor boy is a prisoner in his own home. They don't understand that Richie only acts out when he's upset. He can't help it." She began to smile. "Our visits are his favorite time of month, he says. Why shouldn't I do what I can to make my boy happy?"

Her boy? This was really getting creepy. "Do his parents' rules make him unhappy, or are there other reasons?"

"He gets frustrated easily, which is such a shame. Richie always used to laugh. Now he's quiet and sad and has trouble speaking when he gets worked up about things."

"Ivy, may I have Richie's phone number and address? Maybe he and I can work together to find Danielle."

Ivy bit her lower lip. "He's allowed to stay home alone on Tuesdays and Fridays."

This was Friday, but would he talk to her? Would he even be home? Casey had stayed around long enough to watch the cops let Richie go, but that didn't mean they were finished with him.

"Poor Richie," Ivy mumbled. "He'll be so worried about Danielle."

Or not. The guy had been pretty angry with her at the donut shop the other night.

Casey retrieved her notebook. "If I could just get his phone number and address."

After Ivy supplied the information, she said, "Be gentle with Richie. He's so emotional these days."

"I will." She didn't dare be anything else with the kid.

"Are you driving there now?" Ivy asked.

"Yes."

"Would you take him some cookies as a special treat? Chocolate pecan are his favorite. He'll welcome you with open arms when he sees them."

Somehow, Casey doubted it.

EIGHTEEN

CASEY PULLED UP IN FRONT of a large home with plenty of windows. The front of the Kims' enormous lot had been paved with cobblestones and landscaped with bark mulch, trees, and shrubs. Clearly nothing was allowed to grow here that didn't fit the plan. No vehicles were in the driveway and the triple-car garage was closed. As far as prisons went, Richie's could be a lot worse.

There were three ways to deal with this guy: appeal to his sense of decency for Danielle's sake, threaten to tell his parents that he was gambling on illegal street races, or vow to tell them about Ivy's visits.

Cookie bag in hand, Casey walked up the tiled path toward the double front doors, which had stained-glass, geometric patterns in the upper halves. Vertical glass panels flanked either side of the doors and ran across the top. Casey was about to ring the bell, when the door opened just enough to reveal a partial look at Richie's wary face. How long had he been watching?

"Hello, Richie. Ivy Carpenter suggested that I come see you today." Casey raised the cookie bag. "She asked me to give you this. Said they're your favorite."

Richie squinted at her. "You're the girl from last night."

"Yes, and I didn't kidnap or hurt Danielle. I'm trying to help the police find her." His blank stare prompted her to go on. "Ivy wouldn't have sent me here if she didn't want me to talk to you."

Richie eyed the bag but still didn't move. Smiling, Casey raised the cookie bag. "Fresh out of the oven."

A glance over his shoulder, more hesitation, and, finally, Richie stepped back. What was he so worried about? Did he have company, or was he in the middle of Roadkill business? Casey entered the foyer and felt the nervousness all around him. She gave Richie the bag.

"Danielle called a few minutes after nine last night and asked me to come get her," Casey said. "Her line went dead before she could tell me what was wrong. Did she say anything to you?"

Richie looked at her feet. "You'll have to take your shoes off. My parents don't like dirt."

It seemed they didn't like untidiness either. Three pairs of slippers were neatly arranged on a black mat, next to the welcome mat she stood on. The burnt sienna ceramic tiles were spotless. Casey slipped off her shoes, then peeked into the living room.

"I'm not allowed in there," Richie said.

Small wonder. Casey counted five porcelain vases depicting mountain landscapes. The two largest sat on the hardwood floor, the other three on polished cherry wood tabletops. Did anyone ever use this room?

She followed Richie toward the back of the house. He opened a door and flicked a light switch. They descended dark, carpeted steps. At the bottom, a sixty-inch TV screen dominated the room. Richie plunked himself onto the brown leather sofa, while Casey took a nearby chair.

"I take it you haven't heard from Danielle?" she asked.

"Nope." He opened the bag of cookies and peered inside.

"What time did she call you last night?"

He pulled out a cookie. "The cops already asked."

"I'm the other person she called, so I'd like to put a timeline together." Casey sat forward. "Everything we say will be our secret, okay?"

Richie hesitated. "You have to promise."

"I promise." For the moment. "Do you know anyone who would want to hurt Danielle? Someone who might have been really mad about her street-racing articles? Or maybe she saw something at the donut shop the other night?"

"Nope." He nibbled on the cookie.

"Isn't it possible that a Roadkill member wants to stop her?"

Richie's eyes narrowed. "She told you about them?"

"She trusts me. The longer it takes to find her abductor, the more danger she's in. What exactly happened at the Regency Fitness Center last night?"

He chewed for a few moments. "Danni didn't call me. I called her."

That explained a lot. "What time did you call?"

"On my break, after eight-thirty."

"Why did you call her?"

Richie paused. "That's private." He took another bite.

Probably not a good idea to piss him off too quickly, so she let it go for now. "How did you know where Danielle was?"

"She said she was gonna talk to Hellhound."

"Why didn't you tell the police about their meeting?"

Richie took a few seconds to swallow. "Because they'd think I killed him and that I didn't want her talking to Hellhound, but I *d-did*."

Oh lord, he was already becoming agitated. "Did you have a special reason for wanting Danielle to talk to him?"

"Hellhound wouldn't run anyone over, but he knew w-who did. Danni would have got him to t-tell."

"And you wanted him to tell Danielle who was responsible for running people over?"

His head bobbed up and down. "If she found the freak, then she'd leave us alone." He shoved the rest of the cookie in his mouth and reached for another.

Wrong. Danielle wouldn't leave any of them alone until Roadkill was dismantled and the racers in jail. "I need to know everything that happened after you talked to Danielle last night." Richie's cookie snapped in half. He shoved both pieces in his mouth and then scrambled to collect the crumbs. "Richie, how did Danielle sound on the phone?"

He chewed with his mouth open. "Hyper."

"But not afraid?"

He hesitated, glanced at Casey, and looked away. "Hyper."

"So, you went to the Regency to find out what was going on?"

"I walked there and saw their cars, but not them." He dabbed a crumb off the gray sweatshirt stretched over his ample stomach and flicked it into in the bag. "Then I heard yelling." Richie blinked at the floor. "H-Harvey was in the w-water."

"Was he still alive when you saw him in the water?"

"Don't think so."

"Where was Danielle when you got there?"

"Dunno."

Casey tried to ignore the crumbs stuck to his lower lip. "I don't want to invade your privacy, but I really need to know why you called her in the first place." He kept staring at that dumb bag. "Please, Richie, this is important."

"You c-can't tell anyone!"

"I promise." Another lie, but she had to find out what this kid knew.

"There's a race coming. Big prize money." Richie wiped his mouth with the back of his hand. "She made me promise to t-tell her when it was as soon as I heard."

"When is the race?" Casey waited with growing impatience while he chewed another cookie. "The person who took Danielle could be there. You want to help find her, don't you?"

When he finally swallowed, he said, "Tomorrow night. Don't know where yet."

"Thank you." Casey sighed. "Do you think one of the Roadkill racers took Danielle?"

Richie's upper lip began to perspire. The cookie bag slipped from his fingers and landed on the carpet. He scooped up the bag and plunked it on his lap. "Dunno."

"I'm especially interested in Dominic Mancuso," Casey said. "He and Danielle had a date three nights ago."

His dark brown eyes bulged. "The jerk-face thinks he's so hot, but he's a l-loser."

Brotherly worry, or something else? "You wouldn't happen to know his phone number or address, would you?"

"I know everything about him."

"Great." Casey smiled. "What can you tell me?"

Richie pressed his lips together, as if afraid the words would slip out.

"I know this is hard, Richie, but we have to help Danielle, don't we? Listen. Harvey's dead and Eagle's just left town in the middle of his semester. Something bad is going on with Roadkill, and if we don't help stop it, more people might die. Do you want that to happen?" The fear in his eyes told her enough. "Tell me how to find Dominic."

His gaze flitted around the room. "I'll show you, but you can't let anyone know."

"Okay."

Richie crossed the room and opened a display cabinet containing dozens of DVDs. Reaching behind the DVDs, he removed a one-inch binder. For the first time since her arrival, he smiled a little. Richie carefully handed her the binder, as if afraid the whole thing would turn to dust if mishandled. Casey opened the binder and gaped at a detailed drawing of the five racers' vehicles she'd seen outside Winnie's Donuts.

"Wow, Richie. Did you draw these?"

"Uh-huh." He looked pleased.

Dividers created seven sections. Casey turned to the first section and found Harvey Haberkorn's name up top and, in brackets, the bold scripted word, HELLHOUND. Beneath was a typewritten, detailed description of Harvey's purple Camry. Richie had also drawn up a personal profile that included address, phone number, height, weight, birth date, and even employment history. Since Harvey was only twenty years old, the list wasn't long. What were lengthy, however, were his racing stats. Turning the page, Casey read line after line of data about races going back eighteen months. Each race was numbered and dated; routes, participants, times, and placings noted. The next four sections showed the same detail for the other A-team members.

"This is amazing, Richie." And disturbingly obsessive.

His smile broadened. How long had Richie been waiting for an opportunity to show off his work? Casey didn't know much about head injuries, except that they were complicated. Other than a few spelling mistakes, Richie apparently had no trouble expressing himself on paper.

Eagle's section came next. His real name was Andrew Wing and he was twenty-one years old. Like Harvey, he hadn't been scheduled to race during any of the hit and runs. The same was true for Dominic Mancuso, AKA "the Dominator." Judging from the number of third- and fourth-place finishes over the past six months, this twenty-seven-year-old hadn't dominated any races lately.

"I see that Mancuso has two jobs, two ex-wives, and three kids."

"He's a puke who thinks every woman wants him."

Sounded like jealousy. Mancuso's entry was followed by "Speed Demon" Bashir Kumar. The twenty-five-year-old had achieved a number of first-place finishes.

Last came Morris Mueller, also known as "M and M"; a twenty-two-year-old third-year university student working on a business degree. He and Kumar had won most of the races over the past six months. Casey started jotting down everyone's addresses and phone numbers.

After Mueller's entry, there was a summary of winners in every race with prize money amounts recorded beside each name. Top prize money seemed to range from ten to fifteen thousand bucks. Second- and third-place finishers earned considerably less. None of the races matched any of the hit-and-run dates.

Behind the A-team racers, a section marked B TEAM listed a half-dozen names, each with their own page and stats. None of the names were familiar. The binder's final section contained a single page listing the wannabes.

"Richie, may I photocopy some of this?"

He shook his head. "No. My mom will be back soon. She doesn't like visitors in the house, so you should go."

Not quite yet. Casey scanned the A team's pages again. "What do the others think about Kumar and Mueller winning most of the races?"

"Lousy. And Demon freaks out when he loses."

Casey jotted down more addresses, hoping Richie wouldn't take the binder before she'd finished. "According to your info, Demon doesn't go to work or school, so what does he do for money?"

"His parents have tons. Gave him his house and car. He's so spoiled."

"Does he live alone?"

"With roommates."

"Are they racers?"

"Wannabes. Real shitheads."

Casey turned the page. "What are their names?"

"Jayden and Ty."

She found them on the list and jotted down their last names and cell phone numbers. "Have you heard from any of the racers since last night?"

"No."

"Do you think Demon is capable of kidnapping?"

Richie's eyes began to bulge. "He could hurt Danni!"

Casey stopped writing. "What makes you say that?"

Richie checked his watch. "You have to go."

She flipped to Morris Mueller's page. He'd only been racing seven months, yet he'd won two-thirds of the races.

"Morris is a good racer, huh?"

"He's a maniac."

"Is he friendly with any of the others, like Eagle, for instance?"

Richie shrugged and glanced at the stairs. Casey flipped to Eagle's page. He too was an SFU student, but in science rather than business. "Who organizes the races?"

He fidgeted. "I already said too much."

"It could be that one of them has taken Danielle. The kidnapper might not be a racer at all, but the organizer."

Richie snatched the binder from her and put it away. "Leo makes them happen."

"My email's on the back of this card." Casey handed him her business card. "Let me know where the race is, okay?" He hesitated, then nodded. "What were you and Liam MacKenna arguing about at Winnie's Donuts the other night?"

Richie's mouth fell open. "You know him?"

"We've met briefly, but we're not friends. Is Liam part of Roadkill?"

"No."

"Then why did he show up at the donut shop?"

Richie's head began lolling from side to side. "He's gonna get himself k-killed."

"By someone from Roadkill?"

"You have to go now."

When he looked about ready to grab her hand, Casey hurried to the stairs. "Can you please just tell me what Liam said to you?"

"No! Go!"

She jogged up the steps, Richie breathing hard behind her.

At the top, Casey said, "What's scaring you, Richie?"

"H-he said he'd kill me."

Whoa. Not the answer she'd expected. "Liam said that?"

"No, stupid!"

At the front door, Casey slipped on her shoes. "Who threatened you, Richie?"

Sweat slid down his left temple. "Get out! N-now!" Clutching his cookie bag, Richie's eyes blazed.

Casey headed outside. Who had this kid so scared?

NINETEEN

CASEY'S JAW CLENCHED AS GREG'S sorrowful eyes watched her board the M7 bus. She should be grateful and happy to be working again, but she'd rather look for Danielle than deal with the twins or her ex. He was already getting on her nerves and they hadn't even left Mainland's depot. Why was he working a Saturday morning shift anyway?

"Isn't this your sixth shift in as many days?" She shifted Vancouver's two daily papers in her arms.

"Somebody called in sick."

Lou would be furious. Greg may have worked for Mainland a few months longer, but Lou had earned seniority because of Greg's many medical leaves. Drivers who'd put in the most time were supposed to have first shot at extra hours, but Mainland wasn't unionized, so management could do whatever they wanted. It was another reason for the escalating rumors about unionization.

"Good to see you back," Greg said. "I knew the she-beasts would lose."

"Thanks." Why tell him the complaint had been dropped because the Wieczs hadn't shown up for meetings?

"What brings you here on a Saturday?" he asked.

"Stan gave Marie time off for some family thing." She started down the aisle.

"Has Tina apologized about the other day?" Greg called out. "I told her to call you."

"As I said, I'm not interested in an apology." Why wouldn't he listen?

"But I am." He stood and walked toward her. "I want this sorted out."

Casey made a point of checking her watch. "Shouldn't we be starting?"

He moved so close to her that she felt his minty breath on her face. "She insulted you. I can't forget that." His jaw tightened. "And I won't forget what we had when we were at our best."

Tension trickled across Casey's shoulders and down her back. "You should."

"Biggest mistake I ever made was letting you go."

What the hell was he talking about? "Greg, you didn't let me go, I walked away because Tina was in your life."

"I wish I could undo what happened."

What a horrible thing to say. "I don't." What on earth had she seen in this guy? "You have your children to think about, so make the best of it, Greg. Now let's get going or we'll be late."

Casey took a seat near the back of the bus, as a powerful-sounding car roared past Mainland's yard. She thought she saw something black and sporty, but it moved too fast for her to be certain. Casey popped a stick of gum in her mouth and began chewing. Gum chewing usually calmed the tension. She hoped it worked fast.

As Greg drove out of the yard, she opened the *Province* and began reading about Danielle's disappearance. Casey had no idea who had told the press about events at the Regency, but this reporter had done his homework. He mentioned Danielle's street-racing pieces and speculated about whether her disappearance was connected to her investigation. He also wondered if the same driver was responsible for all four hit and runs.

The *Vancouver Sun* focused on the latest victims. Single mom Chantel Green had been Jason Charlie's social worker. Jason Charlie, a recovering meth addict, had been working hard to build a new life. A candlelight ceremony would be held tomorrow night, and donations would be accepted to help Chantel's children.

Tragedy just kept spreading. What kind of person cruised the streets looking for people to run down? Vancouverites were growing more outraged every day. She'd heard the anger among her co-workers, in checkout lines, on talk radio shows. Turning to the editorial page, she read, *I hope the maniac flips his car or hits a wall and dies.*

The rants went on. By the time she'd finished reading every article, letter, and editorial in both papers, she was feeling prickly and out of sorts. As the M7 approached Granville and Seventieth Avenue, Casey realized she wasn't looking forward to facing the twins again.

The girls climbed on board and barely flashed their passes at Greg, before heading down the aisle.

Lara spotted Casey and scowled. "Deputy Dog's back."

"I see you've made your pink hair even more brilliant." Paige had also colored her hair a more hideous shade of purple. "Have a seat, girls. I wouldn't want you falling."

The twins grabbed a seat across from her. The bus had barely started moving when Lara's voice rose above the engine. "Aren't you supposed to be suspended?"

Nearby conversations stopped. A couple of people looked up from their phones and other electronic gadgets.

"No." Putting on a compassionate expression, Casey said, "How's your mom, girls? Feeling any better? I heard she had chest pains."

Both girls glared at her. Just as Casey thought, Mom was a taboo topic. Maybe the twins despised her because she'd seen their harsh, invalid mother and shabby home. Was their wrath really about embarrassment, a need for privacy, or the desire to protect their mother from trouble? Maybe it was a combination of all three. Casey looked out the window, until the stench of cigarette smoke grabbed her attention. Crap. She stood as Lara blew a smoke ring.

"Put that out right now, Lara."

Smirking, the girl took another drag on her cigarette. Casey crossed her arms, cursing Gwyn's stupid restrictions.

"Attention," Greg said, using the microphone. "I want the girl at the back to put that cigarette out right now."

The entire bus was quiet. Some passengers turned around to see what was happening.

Lara's smirk barely wavered. "This is your big plan? Rely on drivers to fight your battles?"

"That's his plan. Mine's better." Casey removed her cell phone and a slip of paper from her pocket. "I've been told your phone's working now. I'm supposed to call your mom whenever you two break the rules." A concession from Stan this morning.

"You can't do that!" Paige's horrified face told Casey she'd already won.

A passenger rang the bell and the bus began to slow.

"I totally can." As Casey dialed, Paige's expression contradicted her sister's defiant stare. "It's ringing now."

"Put it out, Lara," Paige said.

As Greg pulled up at the next stop, Lara took another long drag.

On the seventh ring, a voice said, "Yeah?"

"Mrs. Wiecz? This is Casey Holland from Mainland Public Transport." As she explained the situation, she watched Lara mash the cigarette into the floor.

"Lemme talk to my brat," Mrs. Wiecz said.

Casey handed the phone to Lara. The girl hadn't even brought it to her ear when Casey heard Mrs. Wiecz scream, "You stupid bitch!"

Scowling at the floor, Lara held the phone away from her ear. Even from where she stood, Casey could hear Mrs. Wiecz's shouts. Paige turned away from her sister.

"Yeah, I'm listening," Lara muttered. "Fine . . . Bye." Without looking at her, Lara returned the phone to Casey.

Casey went back to her seat and listened to the seconds tick by. There was no mouthing off or foot stomping, only silence. Payback would come eventually. Lara was too spiteful to let it go.

The M7 approached the Granville and Forty-Ninth intersection, which was marked by the roadside shrine to Anna-lee Fujioko. Someone had fastened a large balloon marked MISS YOU on a lamp standard. Conversations that had resumed after the smoking incident lapsed into silence again. Everyone knew what had happened here. Anna-lee's highly publicized funeral was too recent to forget. The reward for information about her killer had risen to forty thousand dollars. According to news reports, little Crystal Fujioko's injuries were no longer life threatening.

Casey prayed that Danielle wouldn't end up another victim. After a visit to Winnie's Donuts and a chat with Regency Fitness Center staff about Danielle, Casey had yet to come up with a single lead. Frustrated, she'd called Denver and learned that the police weren't faring much better. Denver had talked to Eagle twice now, and the kid claimed to know nothing about Danielle's disappearance or Roadkill. Denver had perked up at the news of Richie's binder, though. He'd already known about tonight's race.

"Any idea where the race will be?" she asked.

"United Way Boulevard in Coquitlam."

"That's different."

"They'll go where they think police presence won't be as strong."

"I've worked that route. I'll let my supervisor know and see if we can keep watch."

The M7 cruised past the tribute for Beatrice Dunning at Granville and Forty-First. Three and a half weeks had passed since her death. More flowers than ever covered the lampposts.

At which end of United Way would the race start? Who would be there? If someone from Roadkill's A team had taken Danielle, would that person show up for the race? The quickest way to find answers was also the riskiest, but it was nothing compared with what Danielle might be going through.

TWENTY

DECKED OUT IN HER SLEAZIEST mini-skirt, stilettos, and trusty black leather jacket, Casey stepped out of her Tercel. She gasped as the cold November air hit her thighs and wafted upward. Stan, Denver, and Lou would be ticked if they knew what she was up to, but she couldn't sit back and wait for Danielle to be found. Besides, she'd dealt with knife-wielding drunks, wigged-out addicts, and even a couple of killers. And a macho street racer and self-proclaimed ladies' man would probably rather talk to a civilian in a low-cut top and push-up bra than a cop. As much as she loathed the idea of trading sex appeal for information, desperate times called for desperate measures.

She'd chosen to approach Dominic Mancuso because he'd been out with Danielle and Casey knew where he worked. It was far safer to approach him in a public place than his home, and, thanks to Richie's binder, she knew exactly where to find him. She'd already spotted his Dodge Neon parked in back of the gas station.

Casey had pulled up in front of the air hose, which was next to three open bays, where men in greasy coveralls were working on cars. She recognized Mancuso's goatee and mustache. He was wiping his hands on a rag and talking to a co-worker. Casey didn't have to strut more than a few steps before he noticed her. Wearing her best hey-there-stud expression, enhanced by glossy red lips, she watched Mancuso swagger up to her.

"What can I do for you, pretty lady?"

Since he was zeroing in on the black lace bra peeking out from her top, Casey pulled her shoulders back and smiled. "I was hoping someone could fill my left front tire. It's a little low." Not that she couldn't do it herself, but this was Mancuso's world, where damsels in distress boosted his needy ego.

"Sure, no problem." Dimples appeared on either side of his lop-sided grin.

"My name's Casey." As he knelt in front of the tire, she shivered from the cold.

"Dom." He looked up and winked. "You live around here?"

"No, I'm looking for a friend." She took Danielle's photo from her pocket and held it in front of his face. "I believe you know her." It was fun watching Mancuso's smugness crumple. "She told me you two had a date Tuesday night, and now she's disappeared."

He stood. "If you're a cop, I've already—"

"I'm not. I just want to know where she is."

"No idea, honey. Last time I saw her was Tuesday night. The cops told me she disappeared two days later from some fitness club."

The same club where Casey had seen him cruise through the parking lot two weeks ago. "Do you remember what time it was when you last saw her?"

"Why?"

"I'm trying to figure out when exactly she disappeared."

"Talk to the cops."

"You're much friendlier than the dumb cops, not to mention easier to look at." He looked her over and chuckled. Was Mancuso actually buying this crap? "When did your date end?"

"About eleven. I don't want to bad-mouth the chick, but she wasn't much fun."

"In what way?"

"Talked too much. Asked a lot of questions."

"About the hit-and-run deaths?"

He frowned. "You like to ask a lot of questions too, huh?"

"Yep. So, how about I buy you a couple rounds at the River's End Pub?"

Again, he glanced at her bra. "I'm due for a break. Throw in a meal and we'll talk."

"Fine."

"Fifteen minutes, darlin'. Get ready."

Back to the macho crap. Casey headed for the pub, confident that he'd show up. If Mancuso was innocent, he wasn't likely to pass up free beer and food. If he wasn't, he'd still want to find out what she knew.

The River's End's country decor seemed out of place in a metropolis like Richmond, known for its large Asian population. Yet, two-thirds of the patrons were young Asian adults. A few of them were even sporting cowboy hats. Chatter and laughter nearly drowned out the country music that completed the atmosphere.

At the bar, Casey ordered a beer and showed the female bartender Danielle's picture. "Have you seen this woman?"

The bartender peered at the photo, then at Casey. "Who are you?"

"A friend of hers."

"The cops came around. I told them she was here Tuesday night."

"Did she leave with anyone?"

"She was with one of our regulars. I saw them leave at the same time, but I doubt they stayed together. They were all wrong for each other." The bartender placed the beer in front of Casey, took her money, and went to serve someone else.

When the bartender was finished, Casey said, "Did anyone drop by my friend's table that night?"

"Yeah, and another man was spying on them. I told the cops that, too."

Casey leaned forward. "What did the spy look like?"

"Big and cute. Dark curls, gorgeous blue eyes."

Whoa. That sounded like Liam MacKenna. "Were they aware of him?"

"Don't know." She wiped the counter. "He was sitting at the end of the bar, watching them. When they left, he followed."

A customer waved at the bartender. A couple of minutes passed before she returned.

"What about the guy who approached them?" Casey asked. "Can you describe him?"

"An East Indian creep who hits on all the blondes and treats everyone else like scum. Doesn't take rejection well either."

The bartender was a brunette, Casey noted. "Was he short, tall, young, old?"

"In his twenties. Skinny little runt with a Rolex and a couple of gold chains around his neck." The bartender rolled her eyes. "Like *that's* still in fashion."

The description fit Bashir Kumar. What would he want with Danielle, or had he come to see Mancuso? Now that she thought about it, all of the hit and runs involved women. The only male victim was Jason Charlie, although he'd been walking with the female social worker when he was struck.

Mancuso arrived and took the stool next to Casey. The reek of the sweet, fruity aftershave he must have thrown on nearly knocked her over.

"Hey, Dom," the bartender said coyly. "Your usual, sweetie?"

"You bet, and she's buying." As he nodded toward Casey, the bartender's face dimmed. "You're lucky you caught me today, sweetheart," Mancuso said to Casey. "It was supposed to be my day off."

"Please don't call me sweetheart." She didn't appreciate the lame attempt at honey and charm.

"Here ya go, Dom," the bartender said.

He raised the glass to Casey, who hauled out her wallet once again. "Cheers, darlin'."

"The same goes for darlin'." She sipped her beer. "What did you and Danielle talk about the other night?"

"Sex, love, and rock 'n' roll." He chugged his beer.

"Then she told you she's gay?"

Mancuso sputtered beer all over the counter and onto his lap. Casey covered her mouth to hide her grin.

The bartender was there in a flash with a cloth. "You okay, Dom?"

He was too busy coughing to answer, but he did manage to raise his hand and nod. Casey tapped her foot to a Garth Brooks tune and ignored the bartender's what-did-you-do-to-him? stare.

"What did you really talk about, Dom?" Casey asked.

He wiped his mouth on his shirt sleeve. "Cars. I'm restoring an old Chev, which is partly why I got this second job at a garage."

Danielle wouldn't have let him talk about fixing cars all night. Casey leaned forward until she was inches from his face. "Did Danielle mention that she knows you're part of Roadkill, and that someone from your little club ran down a jogger on October twenty-seventh? It's possible the same person started mowing people down on purpose."

His hazel eyes didn't blink. "I don't know squat about racing."

"Come on, Dom." Casey tilted her head and smirked. "Didn't Danielle mention that she and I saw you meet with racers at Winnie's Donuts the other night?" His jaw tightened as he stared into his beer. "We know you're called the Dominator—very catchy, by the way—and that you drive a metallic gray Dodge Neon with a whole lot of horsepower."

Mancuso drank the beer more slowly this time, apparently in no hurry to respond. "I was having dinner at a friend's the night that jogger was hit, which the cops verified."

"You and your racing buddies must have talked about it."

"The whole city's talking about it." He paused. "Look, the racers could have been just a couple of guys challenging each other at a stoplight. You can't stop that shit."

"Harvey Haberkorn, also known as Hellhound, was racing in his dad's Lexus that night, and now Harvey's dead," Casey said. Mancuso tapped his glass on the counter and refused to make eye contact. "We also know that Eagle was a passenger in the hit-and-run vehicle."

He turned to her, his expression wary. "No way."

"Witnesses described him right down to his gold earring and red bandanna."

Mancuso stroked his goatee. "Not possible."

"Eagle tried to leave on a one-way ticket to Hong Kong but was detained and questioned."

His wariness turned to alarm. "I don't believe it."

He could deny all he wanted, but it wouldn't change the facts. "Do you think Morris Mueller or Bashir Kumar could have been driving the night Beatrice was hit?"

"Ask them, whoever they are."

Really? He was going to play ignorant again? "I'm asking you."

"How the hell should I know? I told you I wasn't there."

This guy was about to stomp on her last nerve. "Okay. Hypothetically speaking, do you think it's possible that one of them abducted Danielle because she knows too much about Roadkill?"

Mancuso glanced at her chest. "You're asking the wrong guy, sweetie."

She wanted to smack him. "Don't call me that either."

Mancuso chuckled and lifted his glass. "I'm not admitting a damn thing, but I've heard that racers like to live on the edge. Most of them aren't normal. In fact, they might actually be insane or maybe high most of the time. A few have tempers that could get them killed."

"Who, specifically?"

"This is only rumor, understand?"

"Whatever you say."

"I've heard stories about that Kumar guy. Seems he's got a nasty temper."

Casey nodded. "What have you heard about Morris Mueller? The truth, please."

"Cards on the table and all that?" Mancuso smiled. "He's a spoiled rich kid who takes crazy risks. Could have a death wish, who knows? Or maybe he really is insane."

A Tim McGraw song came on. "Have you ever heard of someone named Leo?"

He shrugged. "Heard the name, but don't know anything about him. He's kind of a mystery."

"Does Richie Kim organize races? And don't deny knowing him. I saw him at your table the other night."

"Richie can't even organize his own life. Used to be a good driver, though."

"You knew him back then?"

"Sure."

"Then you must have known Ben Carpenter too?"

"Mostly by reputation."

She had a feeling he was holding back again. "What did you hear about him?"

"That he knew how to have fun, didn't have a lot of common sense, and thought he was a better driver than he was."

"Did you hear that Ben died because someone tried to run him off the road?"

"Yeah, but I don't buy it. Any racer worth shit wouldn't do that. It's about skill, baby, not cheating or trying to put one another in the hospital."

"Now it seems to be about killing people."

"I'm telling you," he said, his expression serious, "that real racers wouldn't pull that kind of shit."

Casey had her doubts. "Do you know a former racer named Liam MacKenna?"

Mancuso turned away from the bar and began checking out women. "MacKenna was before my time, but his final crash is legendary. Too bad he chose the dark side and became a cop." He turned to her. "But you already know that, don't ya?"

Casey sipped her beer. "I heard he might be racing again."

"Bullshit," Mancuso replied. "The guy's worse than a reformed smoker. It's like he's on some sort of mission to stop racing, which ain't going to happen. He's delusional if he thinks he can stop it."

"He and Richie Kim were arguing in the men's room at the donut shop that night. Any idea what that was about?"

"No clue." Mancuso's cell phone rang. When he heard the caller's voice he grinned. "I'll see you after work, gorgeous."

He pocketed the phone. "I'd better get back to work, but I'll take a rain check on the meal." He stood and drained his beer glass. "If you find Danielle, tell her to back off, okay? She can write all she wants about racing, but it won't ever stop. And if she keeps pissing people off more bad things could happen."

"When I find her—assuming she's still alive—I'm not sure I'll be able to stop her." Casey also stood. "Ben Carpenter was her brother, and she's on a vendetta to find out who caused his death."

"So I heard." Mancuso stood. "Thanks for the beer, darlin'. If you ever want a real date, give me a call."

Fat bloody chance.

TWENTY-ONE

THE TWINS JOGGED UP THE bus steps and flashed their passes at an exhausted-looking Greg. Casey had no idea why Greg's supervisor had kept him on the road all day. He'd been on duty more than eight hours already and wasn't supposed to work more than nine.

Paige and Lara, on the other hand, looked like they'd breezed through their seven-and-a-half-hour Saturday shift. They each had a bounce in their step and actually looked happy. This time, they carried four bags of food instead of the usual three. Who knew one extra burger could make them so cheerful? The twins spotted Casey and headed for the seat in front of her, which was weird given all the other available seats. She returned the twins' brief nod and looked out the window, her senses alert to whatever crap they might pull.

Once the girls had scarfed down some food, Lara turned around. "Our source said Eagle left the country and the racer called Hellhound got killed."

"The authorities stopped Eagle from leaving." Judging from the twins' baffled expressions, this was news to them. Maybe their source wasn't as reliable as they thought.

"We saw on TV that your reporter friend's missing," Lara said. "Word is the racers know something about it."

Why were these two trying to pique her interest? "The police now know the names and addresses of all the racers. They'll find Danielle."

Lara snorted. "Just like that, huh? Listen up. By the time the cops find the right guy, your friend could be dead," she said. "We know people who could find her faster."

"I doubt it."

The twins looked at each other. No words were spoken, yet they seemed to be communicating.

"We can hook you up with our contacts," Paige told Casey. "They'll help."

"Why would they do that?"

"Like we said the other day," Paige replied. "They're friends with Eagle's sisters, who know a lot of inside shit."

"Why would they rat out their brother or his racing buddies?"

"They hate Eagle. Their parents treat him better than them. Now he doesn't even have to go to school, so the sisters want to get back at him, big time."

Casey recalled the sullen young girls manning the Regency's reception desk. "I still don't understand why your contacts would give me info."

"They owe us, like, this totally big favor," Lara remarked. "They'll do whatever we tell them to."

"I see." Casey smiled. "What's in it for you?"

"A truce," Paige replied.

It was a quick response, as if already planned. "What do you mean by *truce*?"

"Simple," Lara said. "You stay out of our business, and we'll follow the rules."

Casey tried to ignore the dollop of mayonnaise clinging to the corner of Paige's mouth. "I see."

"Give us your cell number, and we'll call you when we hear something," Lara said.

And risk prank calls? Not bloody likely. Still, why not play along to see what the princesses were really up to? Casey handed the girls her business card. "You can contact me through my office."

Lara stared at the card. "What if we arrange a meeting tonight?"

"I have plans all weekend. I'm sure the information will still be relevant on Monday."

Casey caught the twins' pensive glances. Were they planning something more sinister than a prank phone call? Some sort of payback for her trip to their home? Whatever it was, she appeared to have put a dent in their plans. The twins resumed eating.

Interesting that they hadn't mentioned the race on United Boulevard tonight, when they'd known about the previous ones. Obviously Harvey wouldn't be there. And since Denver had questioned Eagle twice, the kid probably wouldn't risk racing tonight. That left Mancuso, Kumar, and Mueller from the A team, and possibly racers from the B team. Despite Dominic Mancuso's many faults, she couldn't picture him kidnapping Danielle. Mueller lived at home and went to school. It would be tough to pull off an abduction without disrupting his routine to the point where someone would notice. Kumar seemed the likeliest candidate. The guy came and went as he pleased, and he didn't like women. He would especially detest a nosy journalist like Danielle, which was why Casey had decided to watch his house tonight.

The M7 eased up to the Seventieth Avenue stop. The twins picked up their bags, empties included, and walked to the center exit. Casey started to relax, until she saw Lou climb on board and glare at Greg.

What was he doing here? She'd arranged to meet Lou at Mainland after work. Judging from the hostile vibes Lou was giving her ex, she knew why he'd changed his mind. She wished she hadn't mentioned Greg's dumb remark about not being able to forget her. Casey held her breath and walked toward them.

"What are you doing here?" Greg asked Lou.

"Meeting my girlfriend. You look like crap. Shouldn't you be home resting your back? Taking care of your wife and kid?"

"Shouldn't you be minding your own damn business?"

"That's the thing," Lou said, his voice low and cold. "Your family is your business, and Casey is mine."

Greg's expression hardened. "Either sit down or get off."

"Hi," Casey said, reaching for Lou's hand.

A second later his mouth was on hers and she could barely breathe. When he finished kissing her, he said, "The twins are gone, so your shift's over, right?"

"Yes."

"Then let's go." He escorted her off the bus.

"See ya Monday, Casey," Greg called out.

She didn't answer. As they walked north down Granville Street, the M7 pulled away.

"How does he rate so much friggin' overtime?" Lou asked. "I should apply to Coast Mountain. I'd make a hell of a lot more money driving for them."

Casey hadn't heard Lou say that before. He'd been with Mainland practically since it opened thirteen years ago, but when layoffs began earlier this year, former colleagues had landed better-paying jobs with the Coast Mountain Bus Company.

Ahead of them, the twins crossed the Seventieth Avenue intersection. Paige dropped one of the paper bags and bent down to retrieve it, while Lara continued toward the curb. A Jeep turned the corner.

"Watch out!" Lara yelled.

Paige looked up as the Jeep screeched to a stop inches from her.

Casey held her breath as she, Lou, and Lara darted toward Paige. Paige lost her balance and landed on her butt. Her second bag fell, spilling french fries.

"Are you okay?" Casey asked.

"Fuck!" Paige looked at the spilled food. "Mom will freak."

Lara helped her pick up the bags.

"The sign said don't walk!" the driver shouted.

"Drop dead, moron!" Lara gave him the finger.

"Up yours!" The driver took off.

Casey and Lou followed the twins to the curb.

"What an asshole," Lara remarked. She then zeroed in on Casey. "I can't believe this! You're following us again?"

"I'm taking her to my car," Lou replied.

Lara studied Lou. "Are you her boyfriend?"

"Does it matter?" he replied.

The twins looked him over again, then continued down Seventieth.

"God, she could have been killed," Lou murmured. "You'd think everyone would be more careful at intersections these days."

"The twins usually act before they think. That's half their problem."

"What's the other half?"

"I'm tempted to say poverty and their mother, but it's probably more complicated than that."

"Families usually are." He glanced at her. "Are you still planning to watch Kumar's place tonight?"

"Yes." She could almost feel the tension sweeping through him.

She had told Lou about Kumar earlier and about her hunch that he was the one who'd taken Danielle. Lou had told her that a stakeout sounded dangerous, and since Summer was sleeping at a friend's place tonight, he had hoped to spend the evening alone with Casey.

"We will the second I get back," she'd assured him.

That was when he had offered to go with her, though he hadn't sounded happy about it. They agreed that Lou would park close to Kumar's house while she parked farther down the street. She'd then wait with Lou in his truck until Kumar left the house, *if* he left the house. If he did, she'd hurry to her car and follow Lou, who would be following Kumar.

"I'm a little surprised you decided to meet me here," Casey said.

"I wanted to talk to you."

And it couldn't wait? She watched with growing trepidation as Lou scanned the Safeway parking lot where he'd left his truck, his eyes looking everywhere but at her. She shivered in the frosty air.

"Casey, I've had second thoughts about moving in, for now."

She stopped walking. "What?"

"There's a lot going on, and you've been kind of paranoid about whether we'll work out. I've realized that now might not be a good time."

Heat rose up Casey's neck and her mouth grew dry. "When did you decide this?"

"A couple of days ago." He shrugged. "I'm just not convinced you're ready. I mean, every time I want to rearrange furniture, you find something else to do."

"I'm sorry. It's just that I've been so distracted by the hit and runs, and Danielle, and everything. I really do want you to move in."

"It's not a good idea right now."

"Yes, it is."

He shook his head. "Why would you rather go on stakeouts and run after street racers than spend one evening figuring out how you're going to make room for me?"

"Because Danielle's life is at stake. Believe me, I don't want to go, Lou; I *have* to. I should have gotten to Danielle sooner." Tears filled her eyes.

"Danielle didn't ask you to come to the Regency until she was already in trouble. It's not your fault."

"It sure feels like it is. God, I'm handling everything so badly." She gripped his hand. "I've let the suspension get to me; even the stupid furniture."

"Furniture?"

"I didn't know how to tell you that I don't like your stuff and don't really want it in the living room. I was hoping you'd realize that it's too big and doesn't work with what's already there." She searched his blank expression for understanding. "That's not even important now. You're what matters, and since you gave notice on your apartment, of course you'll move in."

"Actually, I didn't."

Casey's mouth fell open. "What are you talking about?"

"You didn't seem that thrilled when I first suggested it. I guess I was afraid you'd change your mind."

But she hadn't. He had.

TWENTY-TWO

CASEY SAT NEXT TO LOU in his pickup and tried not to panic over her personal life. They'd barely spoken on the drive back to Mainland. After he took her to her car, she'd headed for Kumar's place and begun to analyze Lou's decision. She'd half expected him to chuck their plan and stop following her to Kumar's, but he'd stuck with her, and for that she was thankful.

Once she and Lou reached Kumar's place, Casey had rejoined him in his truck. Again, she didn't know what to say. While they watched the noisy party taking place in the house, tension wound around her neck and damn near sucked all the air out of the truck.

She tried to focus on the people bouncing up and down to earsplitting music in Kumar's living room. A few people had staggered outside, holding cans and bottles. One guy was vomiting on the front lawn. It wouldn't be long before a neighbor called the cops.

Casey looked at Lou, barely able to cope with the sadness on his face. The seconds ticked by slowly, and still she couldn't find the right words.

"How long do you think we'll have to wait?" Lou asked.

It took Casey a couple of moments to realize he was talking about Kumar. "These guys like to race in traffic, so hopefully it won't be long now. No one's parked behind his car, which is a good sign." She glanced at the red Imprezza in the open garage. "With all those people around, I doubt Danielle's anywhere near the place."

"Maybe he's got a condo or a storage unit."

All the more reason to follow him. Casey shifted her feet and nudged the camcorder she'd brought with her. She'd forgotten that Rhonda owned one, until she remembered a conversation from a few months back. Rhonda wanted Casey to record all the big events in Summer's life, but it had completely slipped her mind. She really needed to work on her domestic skills.

"Lou, I really love you, and I absolutely want you to move in," she blurted. "You can even put the lava lamps in our bedroom and play disco whenever you want. I swear I won't complain."

He kept his gaze on the house. "You need space, Casey. I know you like living on your own."

"It's what I'm used to; not what I want." She fiddled with the camcorder's strap. "As for needing space, well, we're both like that, aren't we? I mean, we've never been clingy people."

Lou turned to her. "Is this about Greg?"

"What?" She frowned. "What do you mean?"

"A couple of guys at work said his marriage is in rough shape, so I'm wondering if you want me around to keep him away."

"He has nothing to do with this, I swear."

"I think he does, whether you realize it or not." Lou paused. "I think you're afraid that if we live together it won't last. Or you think I'll find another woman, like he did."

"You need to know something about me and Greg." Her mouth grew dry. "I wasn't as emotionally committed to our marriage as I should have been."

"You had a lot going on, as I recall," he replied. "Upgrading your security training for transit work, and then your dad dying. Greg could have been a hell of a lot more supportive, instead of trying to persuade you to stay home and be a good little wife."

"But I wasn't giving him what he need—"

A powerful engine started up and the Imprezza's backup lights went on.

"Oh, crap. He's leaving." She opened the pickup's door. "You go. I'll try and catch up, but don't be reckless, okay?"

"Same to you."

Casey darted to her car. By the time she pulled away from the curb, Lou's tail lights were barely visible. She glanced at the house. No one else was leaving.

Casey sped down the quiet residential street, made a couple of turns, and headed east on Curtis. The street appeared to be mainly residential, but it led to the major thoroughfares. Spotting Lou's pickup, she sped faster. Curtis connected with Gaglardi Way, the main route to Simon Fraser University, which was at the top of Burnaby Mountain. Drivers heading down the mountain could connect with routes to Vancouver or turn left and head east toward Coquitlam and the suburbs beyond. If the race was taking place on United Boulevard, Kumar had at least three different routes to choose from to reach his destination.

By the time Casey reached Gaglardi Way, she'd lost sight of Lou. She sped down Burnaby Mountain. Two minutes later, she reached a stoplight as it turned red. Damn. Her foot tapped the floor as she phoned Lou. Four rings . . . five . . . six. "Come on, pick up."

Finally, he answered. "We're flying down Como Lake Road." He sounded excited. "I'm passing the Gatensbury intersection."

"I don't think he's going to Danielle." The light turned green and she floored it. "United's less than ten minutes from there."

"If he has her, he could go see her afterward."

Casey raced through the Como Lake and Clarke Road intersection. "Como Lake's not the only route to United. He could turn off at any street that connects with Austin Avenue. Austin ends at Mariner, and he could get to United Boulevard that way."

"So far, he's staying on this road; there's hardly any traffic. Oh, shit! He's going faster. I'm losing him."

Casey sped up. She hadn't gone far when a police siren went off right behind her. "Crap, I've got to pull over. Call you back."

Kumar was speeding like a mad man, and she was the one caught. Where was the justice? She pulled her registration out of the glove box and took her driver's license from her pocket. She looked at her rearview mirror and tapped her fingers on the steering wheel. Why wasn't he stepping out of the car? How long could it take to run a plate number through the bloody computer?

At last, a hulking officer strolled toward her. The officer bent down and peered at her. "I need to see your driver's license and registration, ma'am." As she handed him the info, he said, "Did you know you were going well above the speed limit?"

"I'm trying to keep up with a street racer who's about to race on United Boulevard."

He stared at her. "How do you know about that?"

"Different sources, including a colleague with the Vancouver Police Department."

The officer took a look at her car and tried not to grin. "You're trying to keep up with street racers in this?"

"Not to race, to record what they're doing for the police. I have reason to believe that one of them has information about the missing journalist, Danielle Carpenter. She's a friend of mine."

He didn't blink. "Is that right? Have you had anything to drink tonight?"

What a moron. "No."

By the time she'd finished bringing Officer Hulk up to speed, she figured the bloody race had probably started. He ordered her to stay put and headed for his patrol car. When he finally returned, he handed her a ticket.

"Slow down, ma'am. The roads will be icy soon."

"No problem." Before she pulled away, she contacted Lou. "What's happening?"

"A bunch of cars turned off United, onto a street called Golden. They've pulled into a parking lot and are standing around talking."

"How many cars are there?"

"Six, including the Imprezza and a gray metallic job."

"Dominic Mancuso." So much for the hot date he'd claimed to have. "Can you see the others?"

"Not really. I'm parked on the side of the road, back a bit. The area looks pretty deserted; mostly industrial and commercial. Wait! They're heading for their cars."

"Stay on the line. I'm on my way."

"I hear engines starting. This is it!"

"Can you record them on your phone?"

"Maybe."

Casey cruised down the road, afraid to speed. Gripping the wheel, she waited.

"Whoa, they're off!" Lou shouted. "Shit, they're fast."

"Are you recording?"

"I got some of them peeling out of the lot, but that's all. I'm going after them."

"Don't! It's not safe." Mariner Way was just ahead.

"I need to see which direction they go." He paused. "They've turned right and are heading down United."

Casey glanced at her rearview mirror, looking for an unmarked police vehicle. It was impossible to tell if one of the four vehicles behind her belonged to the cops.

"This is wild!" Lou yelled. "Three of them are driving side by side! The Imprezza, the gray metallic job, and a black BMW driven by someone with light-colored hair."

"Are you kidding? One of them must be driving into oncoming traffic."

"No, there are more than two lanes—oh shit! The cops! Four cruisers!"

Holding her breath, Casey made a right turn onto Mariner.

"Cars are taking off everywhere," Lou yelled. "Two are taking the Mary Hill Bypass. It's chaos, man!"

"Which way are you heading?"

"Straight through. I'm following Kumar's Imprezza."

Casey couldn't help herself. She floored it.

"Oh my god!" Lou cried.

"What?" Casey's stomach clenched. "Lou?"

"Kumar just lost control making a left turn. The Imprezza's flipping! Oh god, he's upside down! This is bad. Smoke's pouring out of the hood. I'm going to see if I can help."

"What street is he on?"

"Burbidge."

Casey turned left onto United Boulevard. She rolled down her window and listened for souped-up engines. Nothing. Had the others gotten away? She glanced at the cloudy night sky. The roads were wet and side streets would be slippery.

As she passed Golden Street, Casey heard voices coming from Lou's Bluetooth. "What's happening?"

While she waited for a response, Casey passed two police cars stopped in the curb lane. Mancuso's vehicle was parked between them, and he was spread-eagle up against it. Smiling, Casey pulled over and stopped. Two racers were down, but where were the rest? Where was Mueller? Where the hell was Burbidge Street?

"Lou, are you there?"

A loud rap on her window made her jump. Liam MacKenna's angry face was glaring at her. Where in hell had he come from? She'd barely started rolling down the window when he shouted, "What the hell are you doing here?"

"Not racing, if that's what you were wondering, and you're a bit out of your jurisdiction, aren't you?" Was he in plain clothes because he was off duty or undercover?

"Stay away from these losers," he said. "Can't you see how dangerous they are?"

"Look, all I want to do is find Danielle." She glared back at him, grateful for the night air cooling her face. "Time's running out, Liam. She's been gone forty-eight hours, and I think one of these guys has her. I'd especially check out Bashir Kumar, if I were you."

"If you want to help, then stay out of the bloody way. I mean it!"

MacKenna marched toward the patrol cars.

TWENTY-THREE

DESPERATION MADE PEOPLE DO STUPID things. It was the only excuse Casey had for sitting at the back of Morris Mueller's classroom Monday morning. Casey had no idea what following him would accomplish. With Kumar in the hospital and Mancuso in jail, she wanted to know why Mueller was still a free man after Saturday night's race. Based on Lou's description, the BMW's driver had definitely been Morris, the only A-team member left standing. Had he also been the one driving the dark, sporty vehicle she'd glimpsed speeding past Mainland property twice? If the jerk was stalking her, it was time for a little payback.

She had begun her research on Mueller by calling a friend majoring in computer science and, unofficially, hacking. Ten hours later, her friend had emailed her Mueller's bio, complete with high school grad photo and transcript, driver's license number, class itinerary, home address, and phone numbers, as well as his parents' occupations and their employers. Some of it she already had from Richie's binder, but the added info could prove useful.

Mueller had barely shifted in his seat for the past half hour. The guy typed a lot on his laptop, presumably taking notes. After all, he was an honor student on a scholarship. He also happened to live only five minutes from the Granville and Forty-First intersection. Had Danielle found incriminating evidence against him? A kid with lots of money had plenty of options if he wanted to hide someone. Both of his parents had busy careers—the father a surgeon, the mother a real estate agent—so the guy could pretty well come and go as he pleased.

When the class ended, Casey hurried out of the lecture hall and crossed the wide corridor. If Mueller had locked Danielle up somewhere, would he go to her now, or wait until after dark? How long would she have to follow him before she learned the truth?

Mueller shuffled through the exit, head down and books tucked under his arm. Rectangular, black-framed glasses made him look studious.

"Mueller?" a classmate called out. "You still need my notes?"

"Yeah. Thanks."

Borrowed notes? Maybe he was too busy street racing and keeping Danielle hidden to study. Mueller spotted Casey. Oh, damn. She held her breath. Judging from the confused look on his face, he recognized her but couldn't figure out from where. She started to leave.

"Hey, don't I know you?" he said, walking up to her.

So much for the ball cap and rose-colored glasses. "I thought you looked familiar too," she said. "Are you taking that criminology class on justice systems?"

"No." Mueller's eyes widened. "You're the lady from the other night, at the donut place."

She did her best to look surprised. "Really?" The guy had a good memory. It had been dark that night, and they'd only spoken for a few seconds.

"Didn't some guy try to jack your car?"

He damn well knew about the altercation with Richie, but she played along. "Wait a sec. You're the one who asked if we needed help. Wow, small world. So, you're in economics?"

"Yeah, and you? I haven't seen you around."

"A friend begged me to sit in and take notes for him, but most of it was way over my head." Casey noticed a thick gold chain peeking out from his partially unbuttoned shirt. "I should get going. Nice to see you again."

"Just a sec." Mueller took two steps forward. "Isn't the lady you were with that reporter who went missing?"

Casey felt his scrutiny, the realization that this encounter might not be coincidental. "Yes, and she's still missing. I guess you haven't heard anything?"

"I don't see why I would have."

Time to push a little. "Really? Since you hang out with racers, and

Danielle Carpenter's been writing about racers, I thought you might have heard a rumor or two."

He tilted his head slightly, as if puzzled. "I don't understand."

"The police think her kidnapper is connected to Roadkill."

"Dead animals on the road?"

"Dead *people* on the road. Word is that street racers don't like people—especially reporters—snooping into their business. But their business is practically public knowledge now, Morris."

He shrugged. "Nothing to do with me."

"Yes, it is," she replied. "You were the racer in the black Beamer on United Boulevard Saturday night."

"Who told you that?"

"A couple of sources." She didn't like his disinterested expression. "You must know that Bashir Kumar's in the hospital with several broken bones. You've raced him several times, so please don't deny it."

He removed his glasses. "I don't know who's saying this stuff, but you're wrong."

"I don't think so. In fact, I've been told quite a bit about Roadkill's races and your membership in the club, which I really don't care about. I'm more interested in Kumar."

"Why?"

"He's a violent misogynist who could have taken Danielle Carpenter not only to keep her quiet, but also to hurt her. Let's face it, Morris, a lot of money's at stake. Kumar's not about to let a woman stop him from winning cash or bragging rights."

Mueller shifted his textbooks, dropping a notepad. As he bent to pick it up, a pendant swung out from under his shirt: a lion's head the size of a quarter in what looked like twenty-four carat gold. Casey studied the intricately carved piece. According to the info her friend sent, Mueller was born on August fourteenth. His astrological sign was Leo. Leo's animal symbol was the lion. Casey's heartbeat quickened. Was he the Leo who organized Roadkill races?

Mueller straightened up. "I don't know anything about Kumar or the reporter, so I can't help you." He walked away.

Casey headed in the opposite direction, glancing over her shoulder to see if he was following. That guy was too cool and calm. Once she was certain he wasn't returning, she found a quiet place to call Denver.

"Any news on Danielle?" she asked.

"No." His voice was solemn. "You?"

"I wish, but I've just learned something interesting. Morris Mueller could be Leo, the guy who's been organizing Roadkill races. Did you know he wears a gold medallion of a lion's head?"

"So?"

"He was born on August fourteenth. Astrologically speaking, he's a Leo, and Leo's animal sign is the lion."

"You think Mueller might be the mastermind behind the races because of a piece of jewelry? I don't think I can get a search warrant on those grounds, especially if the judge is a Scorpio with a bad moon rising."

"Funny, Denver."

"No, it isn't." His tone became stern. "How do you know about the medallion?"

"I'm at SFU, and we bumped into each other a couple of minutes ago."

"Among thousands of students, you just happened to bump into each other?"

"Weird how that happens, huh?" The silence on the other end of the line was deafening.

"How would he know you?" Denver asked.

"I didn't think it was important to mention this earlier, but when we were at Winnie's Donuts Mueller approached us right after the confrontation with Richie Kim. He wanted to see if we were okay because he thought Richie had tried to steal my car, or so he said. Anyhow, I gather Mueller has alibis for the hit and runs, or he would have been arrested by now."

"There are people who've vouched for his whereabouts."

"What kind of people? Racers?"

"No."

"Who then? Oh . . . family?"

"I'm not saying."

How far would Mueller's family go to protect him? "Have you seen Richie's binder yet?"

"Yes, and it's damn impressive. I imagine he's not too happy with you."

"I'll try to cope," she remarked. "Has Dominic Mancuso told you anything?"

"His lawyer got him out, which is all right. My gut says he doesn't know anything about Danielle's disappearance or the hit and runs."

"Agreed. Have you had any more conversations with Eagle?"

"No. He's got a lawyer now and is keeping a low profile. I'm convinced the kid knows something and is scared of at least one of the other racers. Anyway, didn't I tell you to stay away from Roadkill?"

Damn, she'd gone too far. "Sorry. Just trying to help."

"You've done more than your share, thanks. Now stop it."

She couldn't; not until Danielle was found. She had to try other sources, but who? Eagle's sisters? Would they rat out their brother if it meant sending him to prison? Danielle had told her that Eagle was dating Mueller's sister. Maybe she knew something. The problem was that all of the sisters were minors and approaching them about their brothers' activities could create legal trouble. Was there a way to get to the parents?

Casey mulled it over until an idea formed. The longer she thought about it, the more she liked the idea of putting her house on the market. Wasn't it time to let go of another part of her past? Since Mueller's mother was in real estate, who better to handle things? The mother might not knowingly talk about her son's driving habits, but Casey knew from friends and co-workers that it didn't take much for proud parents to reveal more about their kids than intended.

She headed for the nearest work station cubicle, opened her laptop, and googled Mrs. Mueller's employer. Minutes later, she was speaking with a receptionist.

"I'm thinking about selling my house, and Ellen Mueller was recommended to me." Casey scanned the corridor and work stations to make sure no one was listening. "Is it possible to set up a meeting with her?"

"I'll have Mrs. Mueller call you as soon as she's free. Could you give me a little more information about the property?"

After providing details, Casey decided to catch up on homework here until it was time for work. She wasn't looking forward to another shift with Greg and the twins. Too bad her ex couldn't be as easily banished as a house.

$$\rightarrow \quad \rightarrow \quad \rightarrow$$

BEFORE THE PASSENGERS boarded the M7 bus, Casey told Greg about her decision to sell. "I just talked to a real estate agent, and she's meeting me at ten-thirty tomorrow morning to look through the place. Make sure Tina knows, as we're going in with or without her cooperation."

Greg's lips pursed together. "I'll see if she can get off her ass long enough to clean."

Casey didn't like Tina, but she hated Greg's disrespectful attitude even more.

"Sorry if that sounds bad," he added. "Things have been rough these last few months, and now with a new baby coming and Tina not working . . ."

Yeah, right. As if she cared.

"I want us to be friends, okay?" he went on. "I mean, can't we all get along?"

Was he joking? "Does that mean being friends with Lou as well?"

Greg didn't answer right away. "He wouldn't want to."

"Neither would you."

His barrel chest expanded. "A real man would marry ya, not shack up."

Greg was big on marriage. He'd married Tina right after his and Casey's divorce came through.

"There's nothing wrong with taking things one step at a time, Greg. It makes regret less likely."

Casey took a seat near the back of the bus, then pulled out reading material for class.

When the twins boarded the M7 at Seventieth Avenue, they took the seat in front of Casey. Both of them turned around.

"Good news," Lara said. "Our friend got hold of Eagle, who told him some stuff about the racers and that missing reporter. It's stuff he won't tell the cops. Our friend says he'll give you the info, for a price."

"He should go to the police."

"He hates cops more than we do," Paige replied. "We could arrange a meeting. It won't take more than ten minutes."

Why were the twins so eager to help? "When and where does he want to meet?"

"In front of our house at nine tonight," Lara answered.

Casey raised an eyebrow. "I thought you didn't want me near your place."

"It's okay this time," Lara said with a shrug.

"I'll be there." If she hadn't been watching for it, she would have missed the hint of satisfaction behind the girls' identical blue eyes.

Tributes for Anna-lee Fujioko at the Granville and Forty-Ninth intersection caught Casey's attention, as they always did. Once again, passengers grew quiet. Among the flowers attached to the lamp standard, a new sign said, STOP THE KILLING.

Eight blocks later, at Beatrice Dunning's roadside memorial, there was another sign. This one said, WHO KILLED BEATRICE? Beneath the caption, a notice offered twenty-five thousand dollars for the hit-and-run driver's name. Beatrice had died nearly a month ago. Catching the killer would be like trying to stop a river of mercury: dangerous and toxic. Casey prayed that Danielle hadn't drowned in it.

TWENTY-FOUR

CASEY TURNED OFF SEVENTIETH AVENUE onto East Boulevard and pulled over to study the Wieczs' quiet street. Railway tracks and bushes on the left side of the road offered a number of good hiding spots. Trees and overgrown hedges bordering the yards of the houses on the right made it impossible for residents to see much of the street. East Boulevard was a good place for things to happen without anyone noticing.

Casey eased her Tercel forward. No one appeared to be out, but someone could be hiding in a vehicle or huddling between parked cars. She pulled up in front of the Wieczs' bungalow and turned off the engine. Behind the tattered sheets covering the window, the twins were probably watching and waiting. Casey figured their game plan had nothing to do with a visit inside the house.

Rap music blared from the house next door. Casey checked her rearview mirror and saw Lou park two houses back. Part of her regretted telling him about meeting the twins tonight. Despite her assurance that she'd arranged for backup, he'd refused to stay home and wait to hear how things turned out. At least he still cared enough to ensure she wouldn't be in danger, but would he be safe?

Casey stepped out of the car and breathed in the smell of rotting leaves. The rain had fizzled into a light shower. Pulling up her jacket hood, she strolled to the front of her Tercel. When she reached the sidewalk, three large guys emerged from the bushes across the street and ran straight for her. Before she could move, they had her surrounded.

Casey crossed her arms. "Which one of you has the information from Eagle?"

The boys glared at her.

"Leave Lara and Paige alone, bitch," the tallest guy said.

Her heartbeat quickened. "The girls invited me here."

"Bullshit," the square-faced boy to her left replied.

"Ask them." She turned toward the house and found herself breathing in beer fumes from a pimply third kid.

"What are you gawking at, ugly?" he said.

She was going to enjoy bringing these morons down. Casey raised her voice a little. "I take it you're not the people I'm supposed to meet?"

"You ain't meetin' no one," Tall Boy replied. "You're gonna wish you never came here."

"Wait a damn minute." Casey's voice rose some more. "That sounds like a threat."

"Ya think?" He stepped closer.

She balanced her stance and loosely clasped her hands in front of her belly in a non-threatening gesture that would enable her to defend herself.

Tall Boy whipped out a Swiss army knife.

Adrenaline rushed through her. "You guys are buying a whole lot of trouble." Out of the corner of her eye, Casey glimpsed a crouched figure creeping toward them. "Only fair to warn you." The boys laughed. "This is your last chance to leave before the shit hits the fan."

They were still laughing when Denver and his colleague jumped up with guns drawn. "Police! Drop your weapon and get face down on the ground, now!"

The boy behind Casey took off. Denver's colleague went after him. The knife fell from Tall Boy's hand, and he dropped to his knees. As his friend also complied, Casey smiled. So much for tough thugs. Two more officers joined Denver about the same time Lou rushed up.

He pulled her into a tight embrace. "You okay?"

"Fine, yeah."

"This wasn't my idea, man!" Tall Boy said.

"Whose idea was it?" Denver asked.

"Lara and Paige's."

"They told us to scare her," the square-faced kid blurted. "We weren't gonna hurt her!"

"Why did they want you to scare this lady?" Denver asked.

"So she'd leave them alone," the kid replied. "They said she's been a nasty bitch."

Casey looked at the house and saw the sheet across the window move.

"You called it right," Denver said to Casey. "Let's hear what the girls have to say."

As his colleagues took charge of the boys, he turned to Lou. "I take it you're Casey's friend?"

"Yeah." He shook Denver's hand.

"Would you mind waiting out here?" Denver asked him. "The fewer people on their doorstep, the less intimidated they'll be."

"No problem."

Casey hugged Lou. "I don't know what I'd do without you."

"I didn't do anything. Besides, you know how to handle yourself."

Was he trying to say she didn't need him? Why hadn't she summoned the courage to sort this out yet? "Can you meet me back at the apartment?" she asked. "I won't be long."

"Sure. See you in a bit."

Casey followed Denver up the walkway, curious to see the twins' reaction to him. She hoped he would put them in their place, a place so low they'd have to look way up just to see the sole of her damn running shoe.

She stood behind Denver as he knocked on the door. One of the sheets flickered, but no one answered. Rap music still blared from the neighbor's place. Denver started to knock again, when the door cracked open and revealed Paige's pensive face staring up at him.

"Good evening," Denver said. "Are you Paige or Lara?"

"Paige," she mumbled.

"I'd like to speak with you and your parents."

Paige stepped onto the stoop, quietly shutting the door behind her.

Casey stepped out from behind Denver. "I met your friends." Under the dim porch light, the girl's skin took on a greenish hue. "You invited me here to meet them, remember? Where's Lara? Constable Davies wants to chat with her too."

"Why?" Paige's hushed tone sounded desperate.

"Miss Holland's life was threatened by someone who stated that it was your idea to do so," Denver answered.

"What? Mine? No! That's bullshit."

"I'd like to speak to your sister and parents," Denver said. "Now, please."

"Lara's helping Mom get ready for bed," she answered. "My mom's sick, and Dad's been gone for years."

"What's wrong with her?" Denver asked.

"Parkinson's, and she's gettin' the flu."

"This is important. I won't keep her more than five minutes," he said. "Let's get on with it."

Paige looked as if she'd just swallowed something bitter. "Wait here."

As she stepped inside, a sandpapery voice yelled, "Who the hell's at the door?"

"Constable Davies with the Vancouver Police," Denver called out, holding the door open. "I'd like to speak to you and your daughters a moment, please, Mrs. Wiecz."

"What now?" The obese woman waddled into the living room, wearing the pink robe with the same stain Casey had seen nearly two weeks ago. Mrs. Wiecz's head trembled slightly as she blinked at Denver and Casey, then sat down.

"Lara, get your ass in here and light me a smoke," she called out.

Casey and Denver exchanged glances. The woman didn't look or act like she had the flu. Lara entered the room, her cheeks flushed and her expression defiant as she ignored everyone but her mother. She placed the smoke in Mrs. Wiecz's shaky hand and set a large amber ashtray in her lap. Mrs. Wiecz raised her trembling hand to her lips and took a long drag.

"You were here the other night, right?" she said as smoke whooshed out of her mouth and nose.

"I'm Casey Holland, from Mainland Public Transport. We spoke briefly on the phone."

She peered at her daughters, then at Denver. "This can't be good."

"It isn't," Denver replied. "Someone just threatened Miss Holland with a knife in front of your property. The suspect claims that it was your daughters' idea to scare Miss Holland." He looked at each twin. "I'd like to know what the girls have to say about it."

Mrs. Wiecz looked from Paige to Lara. "Well?" The twins exchanged furtive glances. "*Tell him*, Lara," she ordered.

"We didn't ask him to pull a knife on her," Paige blurted.

"Miss Holland says your daughters invited her to meet their friends at your home," Denver said. "These friends allegedly had information about the recent hit-and-run homicides."

Mrs. Wiecz's narrowing eyes zeroed in on Paige. "What do you know about that? And don't lie, or you know what'll happen."

As Paige's chubby cheeks darkened, Casey almost felt sorry for her.

"W-we just wanted her to leave us alone," Paige said.

"She had no right to come here and spy on us!" Lara yelled.

Mrs. Wiecz grunted. "You were pissed off 'cause she phoned about you smoking, weren't you, Lara?"

"She was supposed to be scared, not hurt. We didn't know about a knife." Lara glared at Casey. "You should have got suspended. It's not fair! Any jerk with a little authority thinks they can get their way."

"Lara, if you don't learn how to deal with authority, you'll be doomed to a life more miserable than what you've got now." Mrs. Wiecz's shaky hand tapped the cigarette. "Scaring and threatening people is stupid. I raised you better than that, so you'd better apologize to this lady."

"Sorry," Paige mumbled.

"Yeah. Sorry." Lara nearly choked on the word.

Mrs. Wiecz released a long, wheezy sigh. "I know you girls are ashamed of me." Her head bobbed. "But I'm way more ashamed of you right now."

The twins looked at the floor.

"Do your contacts really have information from Eagle or not?" Casey asked Lara.

"Who's Eagle?" Mrs. Wiecz asked.

"A possible witness in one of the hit and runs," Denver answered.

"They don't," Paige said.

Denver looked from one twin to the other. "I just want to be clear. You two made up a story to entice Miss Holland here?"

The twins exchanged wary glances.

"Answer him, damn it!" their mother said.

"Yes," Paige mumbled. "Are you going to arrest us?"

Denver turned to Casey. "Do you want to press charges?"

Casey didn't plan to, but she wasn't about to let the twins off that easily. "If the police hadn't been there, I could have been seriously injured or even killed. I need to think this over."

Denver gave the girls a stern look. "I don't want any more trouble from you two, understand?"

Both girls nodded.

Mrs. Wiecz looked at her daughters. "You're both grounded for a month. Now get to bed."

"I have one more question," Casey said. "Do either of you, or your friends, know anything about the disappearance of Danielle Carpenter?"

"No." Paige answered.

"Nothing," Lara agreed and followed her sister out of the room.

"I've tried to raise these girls right but being sick hasn't helped," Mrs. Wiecz said. "Their miserable father poisoned them with his temper. He left when the girls were twelve, which meant no more hitting, thank god. But no more paychecks either." She slid the ashtray off her lap and onto the sofa cushion next to her. "Paige swallowed all the shit her father fed her about being no good till it damn near destroyed her. But Lara, well, she just got mad. Still is."

"Has there been any child support?" Denver asked.

Her laughter was short and harsh. "Don't even know where he is to get it. Too bad, too. Disability checks don't go far."

A little girl, about six years old, peeked around the corner. When she saw Casey, she vanished. No wonder the twins brought food home after every shift.

"Thank you for your time, Mrs. Wiecz," Denver said, heading for the door.

"Please don't arrest my girls," she said to Casey. "I need them."

"I won't press charges," Casey answered. "But they need to respect me and MPT's rules."

"I'll make sure they do."

Somehow that didn't make Casey feel any better.

TWENTY-FIVE

CASEY PARKED IN FRONT OF her childhood home and took a calming breath. She didn't really want to be here, reliving negative memories. Hard as she tried, though, she couldn't stop the images of her parents' arguments or of strangers traipsing out of Mother's bedroom when she thought no one would be home for a while. And then the memories of Greg: learning about Tina from a work colleague and confronting Greg with anger and violence before walking out on her marriage.

At least Greg had kept his word about taking good care of the yard. The bushes had grown full and lush over the past four years, and the steps had been painted. The frilly curtains hanging in the window must have been Tina's idea. Greg had despised what he called "that silly frou-frou shit."

A shiny, blue BMW SUV pulled up behind Casey. The door opened and a tiny woman with wavy, platinum hair stepped out. Dressed in a bright red skirt and matching coat, she looked like one of Santa's helpers. The black umbrella and handbag were a nice touch.

The lady flashed a halogen smile and extended her arm. "Miss Holland?"

"Yes."

"I'm Ellen Mueller." She pumped Casey's hand with surprising strength and turned to the property.

Casey saw little resemblance between mother and son. Morris clearly had some Asian features, like his eyes and nose, but Ellen was Caucasian. Her mouth seemed similar to her son's, though, and Morris had the same slight build.

"This is a great first impression for a forty-five-year-old house," Ellen remarked. "If the interior's as nice it should be an easy sell."

"I'm not sure about the interior. As I mentioned on the phone,

I've been renting to a couple with a toddler and haven't been inside in quite a while."

"You should be doing periodic checks, dear. With all the grow-ops and meth labs around, you can't be too careful. They won't mind if I take a few pictures and measurements?"

"The husband is fine with it, but his wife won't be too welcoming." Casey scanned the windows to see if they were being watched. "She doesn't want to move."

The halogen smile returned. "Trust me, sweetie. I've dealt with all types. You have a key, I presume?"

"Yes."

"Excellent. Are you up for this?"

"Sure." More or less.

Casey followed Ellen up the wooden steps and onto the veranda that stretched the length of the house. Ellen collapsed her umbrella and used the gleaming brass knocker. When deep, angry barks erupted inside, she jumped back.

"You didn't mention a dog."

"I didn't know they had one."

"He sounds big." Ellen bit her lower lip as she glanced at the door. "Do you allow pets?"

"I've never thought about it." Tenant agreement forms hadn't been on her mind when she and Greg split up. She hoped the dog hadn't torn up the place. Casey tried the knocker again.

"Do you think the lady of the house is in?" Ellen asked.

"Probably. She's unemployed, and I doubt she would want me entering the place in her absence."

"A big dog and a little child sound like a dangerous combination."

"Do you have kids or pets?" Casey asked.

"Two kids, but I would never have anything that carries fleas in my home."

On the other side of the door, a woman yelled, "Quiet, Bear!"

Ellen retreated behind Casey. The deadbolt clicked, and the door opened just enough for an enormous, furry black head to poke through. Ellen gasped. Casey had no idea what breed he was, but "Bear" suited him. Opening the door wider, Tina seemed oblivious to the dog's growl, but intimidation could have been part of her plan.

"Morning, Tina," Casey said. "My real estate agent would like to see the house."

Without makeup, Tina looked haggard and her complexion mottled. "Whatever." Her voice was two degrees below frosty. She shuffled backward in bunny slippers that apparently doubled as Bear's chew toys. An eye was missing from the left slipper. On the right, a torn ear barely held together.

Stepping inside, Casey grimaced at the stink of dirty diapers, curry, and wet dog. Ellen choked a bit, then cleared her throat.

As the dog moved closer to them, Tina grabbed his collar. "Sit, Bear." She turned to Ellen. "I haven't had time to clean." She shrugged as if she couldn't care less.

"That's fine. I just need a quick peek to assess room size and features."

"Do you want us to remove our shoes?" Casey asked.

"Suit yourself."

Casey kept hers on, noting that Ellen did the same.

"Let's start with the living room, shall we?" Ellen stepped through the entryway on their left and nearly tripped over a rubber duck.

Casey grimaced when she saw the badly scratched hardwood floor. Even before she'd married Greg, he'd warned her that, except for leaky plumbing and other fix-it jobs, the inside of the house would be her domain. She had done most of the cleaning and cooking for her father anyway, so the arrangement hadn't been a big deal.

Obviously Tina didn't take the same care.

More toys were scattered over the floor and furniture. Lego cluttered the yellow and orange area rug. A rolled up diaper sat under the coffee table. Had Tina left it there on purpose? Bear jogged through the room and picked up what was left of a mangled rawhide bone.

"How many kids do you have?" Ellen asked.

"One, and another on the way."

Surprise flashed across Ellen's face. "Your little one's lucky to have so many toys."

"All of his grandparents spoil him." Tina glanced at Casey, who ignored the jab.

Greg's parents had been desperate for grandkids from the moment Casey walked down the aisle. They eventually concluded that the absence of grandchildren was her fault.

"This is a nice, large room," Ellen remarked. "Plenty of light. Very lively."

Casey thought she heard a hint of sarcasm, but the chunky, bright blue sofa and red chair probably didn't suit Ellen's taste. It definitely wasn't Casey's idea of style. Although she had agreed to let Greg rent the house, she hadn't let him keep the furniture. She'd wanted to show everyone at work that she had no hard feelings about their split-up, but she hadn't felt overly generous toward the two-timing jerk either.

"You painted the walls," Casey remarked. "Is that Dijon yellow?"

"Venetian dawn." Another layer of frost in Tina's tone. "It makes the room much cozier than it was."

Casey looked at the dirty orange rug. God, it was like living in a giant toy box.

"I'd say this room is about twelve by fourteen." Ellen put on a pair of silver-framed glasses, then jotted numbers on her clipboard. "A house this size must have a dining room?"

Tina marched to the door at the far end of the room. Upon entering the dining room, Casey's mouth fell open. The walls and ceiling had been painted ketchup red. Was Tina's color scheme some sort of bizarre tribute to condiments? The clashing pink tablecloth thrown over the oblong table was littered with papers and envelopes. Judging from the familiar logos, most were bills. A newspaper was open at the For Rent page.

"About twelve by twelve," Ellen murmured, writing the numbers down.

A child began to cry.

"Oh, Joshie's awake," Tina said, rushing out of the room.

Bear started to follow her, then stopped.

"Go get your mommy, big boy." Ellen waved him away. "Shoo!"

When the dog trotted out of the room, Ellen shut the door and peered at Casey over the top of her glasses. "Dare we see what she's done to the kitchen?"

"Let's hope it's not relish green."

Ellen snickered as she followed Casey into a room that hadn't changed in fifteen years. Casey remembered when she and Dad tore up the red linoleum. The maple cupboards and ivory walls were still here, though now dull and stained in places. This was where she and Dad had spent most of their time together. It felt like a lifetime ago.

"The lady has some taste, after all," Ellen murmured. "Though the walls need fresh paint."

"My dad and I decorated this room," Casey replied. "We had a lot of talks in here, mostly about how I should try harder at school and date more responsible boys. Of course, I never listened." She smiled. "Do your kids listen to you?"

"My son does, but my daughter's another story. She's obsessed with ridiculously overpriced clothes and immature wimps."

Like Eagle? "Don't boys obsess about girls and cars?"

"My son's interests are broader than that." Ellen opened a closet, causing two brooms and a chest-high pile of plastic grocery bags to tumble out. "Oh look, an indoor dumpster."

"You must have a well-rounded son."

"Absolutely. Morris has always been mad about sports and chess." Ellen shoved the bags and brooms back, then shut the closet door. "His bedroom's filled with awards."

Now he was mad about street racing, which was a whole lot more thrilling than chess. How badly did Morris Mueller need to win, and how did he take it when he lost?

"I have a teenager at home, and she has a lot of trouble managing her time," Casey said. "How does your son cope with so many activities?"

"He's a born organizer."

"Must be nice."

"Pardon me for saying this, but you look far too young to have a teenager," Ellen said.

"Thanks, but I'm just her legal guardian, and I wish she had your son's organizational skills."

"I trained him well." Ellen wandered to the window above the kitchen sink and looked at the backyard. "That water fountain's a liability."

"What water fountain?" Casey opened the back door and gaped at a round cement monstrosity with two peeing cherubs. "Holy crap."

"I should have known it wasn't yours."

Bear entered the room first, followed by Tina, who was carrying a fat, pouting toddler with Greg's big jowls and eyes. When Casey smiled at the little boy, he turned his head away.

"You're taking the fountain with you, right?" Casey asked.

"Of course, it was a present from my parents." Tina kept her gaze on Casey. "This is our son, Josh." The smug look on her face said, *See what Greg and I made?*

"My, isn't he a chubby one," Ellen remarked.

Casey smiled, truly grateful she wasn't bound to Greg by kids. It was hard enough keeping him out of her life.

"Are there any more rooms on this floor?" Ellen asked, ignoring the toddler.

"My father's office was just off the kitchen."

Casey crossed the room, opened another door, and stepped into laundry chaos. Heaping baskets of clothes sat next to a card table. More clothes were piled on folding chairs. A sewing machine sat in a corner of the room. Next to it, bolts of fabric leaned out of plastic bins. Apparently Josh didn't like the mess either because he started to scream.

"Come on, angel. Mommy will get you a cookie." Tina carried him back to the kitchen.

Ellen shut the door after Tina and Bear left, then strolled farther into the room and turned a slow circle. "Great space, but the lazy housewife look will have to go. I can't take photos until the clutter's gone."

"I'll let Greg know."

Ellen examined the blue and white tiles around the fireplace. "The crayon marks will have to go too. How much is his damage deposit?"

"There isn't one."

Ellen nearly dropped her clipboard. "Why not?"

"Greg assured me he'd take care of the place." At the time, haggling over money was more than she could cope with.

"The guy must be some friend."

"Not really. He's my ex, and the lady of the house is the one he screwed around with."

Ellen's mouth fell open. "And you took his word about the house?"

"At the time I wasn't thinking clearly, then I tried not to think about him at all." Sharing this info was probably petty, but since Ellen would be showing the house, it would help if she understood the reason for Tina's hostility.

"I can't believe that little piece has the gall to throw bitchy looks and their baby in your face."

"It's okay. I definitely got the better deal." Casey watched to see if the kitchen door opened.

"Why didn't you kick him out and stay here?"

"Too many memories. Anyway, I'll see that Greg gets things in shape."

"Tell him to paint the place in neutral tones." Ellen flipped a page on her clipboard. "Good for you for moving on, sweetie. There's nothing wrong with making some decent money in the process. Are you planning to buy something new?"

"No, I have a place."

Disappointment flashed across Ellen's face. "Let's go see what atrocity waits for us upstairs."

Casey wasn't sure she wanted to know. As they headed for the staircase, she said, "Do you live in this area, Ellen?"

"Just off Granville."

In the ultra-expensive area of Shaughnessy, according to the info her friend sent. Many of those homes were mansions with separate cottages for housekeepers and other staff.

"Granville?" Casey asked. "Near where the first two hit and runs happened?" She already knew that the Muellers' home was only a short drive from both intersections.

"Hit and runs?" Ellen started up the stairs.

"One at Forty-First last month and the other at Forty-Ninth a few days later. Two women were killed and a little girl seriously injured."

"Oh yes, I heard about that. Horrible." She scanned the hallway and bedroom doors. "Drivers really should be more careful."

Casey fought the urge to roll her eyes. "Hopefully you and your family weren't on the road either night. I heard traffic was backed up for miles."

"The kids were home and I missed the carnage completely. I work most evenings."

Denver had implied that the parents vouched for Morris's whereabouts the night Beatrice Dunning died. If Ellen had been working that night, how could she have known where her kids were? Or had the father been home?

Casey heard an angry scream from Josh downstairs. "You're lucky," she said. "Kids rarely stay home anymore."

"My mother-in-law lives with us and is afraid to be alone at night, so either they or the housekeeper stay home if we can't."

Had the housekeeper vouched for Morris's whereabouts? Maybe they would know more about Morris's comings and goings than the parents.

Ellen stepped inside the first bedroom. "Oh my, how interesting," she murmured. "The trashy campsite look, complete with crushed beer cans."

Casey's cell phone rang. She didn't recognize the anxious voice on the line.

"My name's Virginia, I'm a friend of Danielle's."

The girlfriend Danielle had mentioned. As Casey moved toward the staircase, her pulse started to race. "Any news about Danielle?"

"No, and I've tried talking to the police about Richie Kim, but they're buying whatever bull he's told them."

Tina, with Josh on her hip and Bear in tow, was climbing the steps and glaring at Casey.

The second Tina reached the top, Casey headed downstairs. "Listen, I'm just finishing a meeting. Can you call me back in ten minutes?"

"Sure, I'm on my way to the Kims' place."

That couldn't be good. "Why?"

"To ask that bastard Richie a few questions."

"Bad idea, Virginia."

"It's my only option."

"Don't do anything until we talk about this, okay? I'll call you back shortly."

"I won't wait long."

Fifteen minutes later, Casey was back in her car, trying to calm Virginia down.

"I really believe Richie's got her," Virginia said. "He told the cops that Danni called him for help, but he had to have been lying. After that joy ride in your car the other night, Danni didn't trust the guy. I want to know what he was really doing at the Regency."

What made Virginia think Richie would tell her anything? "Richie and Danielle have known each other for years, and he was nearby," Casey said. "Maybe he'd intended to help her out somehow but found that she was already missing."

"I doubt it. The little creep wanted to stop Danni from investigating Roadkill. He didn't mind giving her info about racing at first, but when he realized she wanted to destroy Roadkill he got mad." Virginia paused. "Just before she disappeared, I heard them fighting on the phone. Apparently Richie warned her to stop writing about racing."

Casey recalled her visit with Richie, the way he had become more agitated the longer she stayed.

"I don't think he wants to hurt Danni," Virginia added. "In fact, part of me believes he's trying to protect her from getting killed as well as protecting his interests. But Danni said he has bursts of rage. If he's provoked, who knows what he'll do. His parents are well respected restaurateurs who donate to a lot of charities. The father sits on a couple of boards, so I doubt the RCMP will be smashing down their door. Besides, they don't believe a kid with brain damage could pull off a kidnapping, but I do."

Casey had seen the methodical order of Richie's binder. Had Richie gone out of his way to hide his cognitive skills from his parents and the public? Something else about the guy worried her. Richie had walked to Winnie's Donuts. He'd told the RCMP he'd also walked to the Regency Fitness Center. The businesses weren't close to each other, unless his parents' restaurant was between the two locations. How had he reached the fitness center so quickly?

"Virginia, do you know where his parents' restaurant is located?"

"No, but my guess is he's at home right now. Danni said he gets Tuesdays and Fridays off from the restaurant and that his mother checks up on him a lot, so he doesn't go out much. Today's Tuesday."

"Did Danielle call you that night too?"

"No." Virginia paused. "We argued before she left for the Regency. I didn't want her to go, but Danni's stubborn as hell. She was convinced that one of the Regency's employees had information about the hit and runs." Another pause. "I need your help finding her. Danni said you're one of the few people in the world who's come through for her."

"I'm not sure what I can do."

"Actually, now that I think about it, could you keep Richie busy at the front door, while I check out the property in back? See, I think he's stashed her in the basement or in a shed or something."

"Richie chatted with me in the basement four days ago, so I doubt she's down there." Casey fidgeted. "Since he has rage issues, wouldn't it be safer to check out the property while he's at work?"

"I can't wait any longer. He's probably drugged Danni to keep her quiet, and she has allergies. The idiot could be killing her." Virginia choked back a sob. "She's the only person on this whole damn planet who means anything to me."

The woman was as headstrong as Danielle. "There are safer ways to do this."

"Too late. I'm almost at his house now. All you need to do is keep Richie talking for five minutes."

"I don't feel comfortable doing that without backup."

"If you can get the cops to come, then go for it, but I'm doing this with or without you. Danni says you're a trained security officer. You know something about conflict resolution and self-defense, right?"

"Yes, but the protocol for this sort of situation would be to stand down and call the police. Richie isn't too happy with me because of what happened after our last chat. I told the police I'd seen incriminating evidence about his involvement with Roadkill, so they went to his place and took it."

"And yet the little puke wasn't busted."

"Nor was Danielle located."

"It probably didn't occur to them to search the property of a head-injured kid who can't drive."

"Maybe not."

"It must be nice to have rich parents. We have to make people see this guy for who he is."

"No argument here, but I'm not sure Richie will even open the door for me."

"Can you at least hold his attention by banging on the door? If I don't do something now, it could be too late for her." Virginia hung up.

Now what? If Richie had Danielle, he'd gone to a lot of trouble and taken a huge risk. Why would he give her up just like that?

TWENTY-SIX

A FAMILIAR JEEP SCREECHED TO a halt behind Casey's Tercel. Through the rearview mirror, Casey watched a tall woman in camouflage step out of the vehicle. If she had conjured up an image of Virginia at all, it wouldn't have been this. Virginia's waist-length black ponytail looked damp, as if she'd already spent time in the rain. The woman marched toward her. Casey rolled down her window and tried not to look at the pink crystal stud piercing Virginia's nose; an identical match to the one Danielle wore.

"You must be Casey. Thanks so much for doing this."

"I still don't think it's a good idea, but I managed to convince the RCMP to send someone." After talking to Virginia, Casey had phoned Denver for advice. He hadn't been thrilled to hear about Virginia's plan, but he had agreed to ask the Richmond detachment to visit the house.

"I haven't seen a cop," Virginia said, "and I've killed a lot of time cruising the neighborhood, checking things out, including the Kims' backyard." She nodded toward the house five doors down. "There's a lane behind their house, and they have a padlocked garden shed near the fence that borders the yard to the left."

"That was risky. Richie could have seen you."

"I made sure he didn't."

How could she be so certain? "If he has Danielle, he'll be watching for cops and strangers."

"We're here now, so what the hell can the guy do?" Virginia replied, bouncing up and down on her heels. "I should be able to get in that shed pretty quick with bolt cutters."

"You honestly think Danielle's in there?"

"Where else could a guy who doesn't have a car take her?"

"He might have friends."

"Danni said he's a loner. Besides, when I was watching the shed, I felt her." Virginia's expression softened.

"Excuse me?"

"Sensed her presence." Her light hazel eyes peered at Casey. "When you're really connected to someone, you always know when they're nearby or when they're in trouble. You can practically feel the air change."

Casey felt a frantic energy swirling around Virginia now. "You need to go slowly and be careful."

"Too late for slow. I'll park in front of the neighbor's on the left and call you when Danni's free."

"Richie might not let her go without a fight. Let's wait for the police."

"I'm ready for a fight. I've got pepper spray and a brown belt in tae kwon do."

And far more bravado than common sense. "What if he has a gun?"

"I'm bettin' he doesn't. Roadkill's about cars, not guns."

"They weren't supposed to be about kidnapping or murder either."

"Park in Richie's driveway," Virginia said. "If he's looking out his window, I want him focusing on you."

"If he's looking right now, he could already be taking off for that shed."

"Another reason not to wait for the bloody cavalry." She jogged back to her Jeep.

Casey cruised into Richie's driveway and wondered how on god's earth she was supposed to hold his attention. There were no signs of life in the windows. By the time she rang the doorbell, the adrenaline was surging and her heart pounding. She counted to ten and rang the bell again, hoping to capture Richie's attention. Had he heard movement out back and gone to check it out? Casey rang the bell a third time, then leaned close to the door and listened. She thought she heard something.

"Richie? It's Casey Holland. I have some important information for you. It'll only take a second."

"You b-broke your promise!"

"I'm really sorry about that, but there've been way too many deaths, Richie."

"Y-you've ruined everything! I hate you!"

"The police think someone from Roadkill's responsible for all the hit and runs."

"Go away!"

"Did you hear about the race Saturday night? Bashir Kumar had a bad crash and he's in serious condition in the hospital. You should also know that Dominic Mancuso was arrested. Roadkill's in trouble, and the police are coming after everyone connected to them, Richie." Casey rubbed her hands together in the chilly air. "I thought you should know because they might show up here." In about two minutes.

The deadbolt turned, and Richie opened the door a crack. "D-Demon needs to die."

That was harsh. "Why?"

"Just does. And Dom should stay in jail."

She waited for more, but he added nothing. "Dominic's already out, Richie. Maybe he made a deal with the cops. Told them what they wanted to know about Roadkill."

Richie's chubby cheeks darkened. "You have to go." He started to shut the door.

"Have you heard anything about Danielle?"

The door halted. Wary eyes blinked at her. "Why?"

"You've known her a long time, so I thought she might have tried to call you." She scrambled for something else to say. "Have you talked to her mom lately?"

Richie's eyes widened as he looked past Casey's shoulder. She turned to find an RCMP cruiser heading toward them. A second later, Richie slammed the door.

Casey dashed along the front of the house, turned the corner, and raced down the side. Five-foot-high vertical boards fenced in the backyard. She tried the gate, but it was padlocked.

From the backyard, Richie shouted, "Get away!"

Casey gripped the two-by-four capping the fence. Having scaled her share of fences over the years, she jumped up and swung her leg over. Richie stood in front of the open shed door, a raised baseball bat in his hands. Casey could hear sirens approaching now.

"Virginia!" Casey jumped down from the fence. "Are you okay?"

"Danni's here!" she yelled.

"I told you to g-get away!" Richie's gaze shifted from Casey to Virginia.

He stepped forward. Casey slowly moved toward him and said, "If the police see that bat, they'll be upset, Richie."

"I have to p-protect Danni!" His head began to sway back and forth.

"From whom?"

"The killer."

"Who is he, Richie?" The kid kept swaying his head. "Did you see who killed Harvey?"

"No."

"Do you know who ran down all those people?"

"G-go away!"

"I bet you know who struck the first woman, Beatrice Dunning, don't you?"

Casey took two more steps to get a closer look at the shed's door but stayed near the house to give Richie a wide berth. His gaze darted from her to whatever was happening in the shed. Rain slid down Casey's face. Why weren't the police joining her? Once she had a partial view of the inside of the shed, Casey stopped. She could see Virginia kneeling in front of a sleeping bag.

"You treated her like an animal, you freak!" Virginia glowered at Richie.

"I'm her f-friend!" Tears rolled down his cheeks. "C-couldn't let them hurt her. S-she's all Ivy's got."

Casey recalled Ivy's compassion for Richie. It seemed the feeling was mutual.

"Don't take her!" Richie raised the bat higher and stepped closer to the shed. "She'll get k-killed!"

"Freeze!" a cop shouted from the back lane. He and his partner had their weapons drawn.

"My name's Casey Holland! I called you guys about the missing woman. We just found her in that shed."

"Is she all right?" one of the officers asked.

"She's alive. Her friend's checking on her."

His partner radioed for an ambulance.

"You with the bat!" the first officer yelled. "Drop it and get on the ground, now!"

Richie didn't move.

"Can somebody help me in here?" Virginia called out.

The same officer hopped the fence and again pointed his weapon at Richie. "Drop that bat! *Now!*"

Casey took swift, shallow breaths; her skin felt hot under the cold rain. "Come on, Richie," she said, keeping calm. "No one needs to get hurt. Just do what they say."

Richie whimpered. His head swayed, and the bat wavered. "Y-you don't get it."

"This is your last warning," the officer said.

Richie began to sob, yet made no move to comply. It felt as if the whole neighborhood was holding its breath. The officer fired a shot into the grass, not far from Richie's foot. Casey flinched as Richie dropped the bat and fell to his knees. The second officer jumped the fence and hurried toward them. Two more cops, their weapons drawn, emerged from the back door of the house. Casey wondered whether Richie had forgotten to lock the front door, or whether they'd kicked it in.

"I was p-protecting her!" Richie said.

"Down!" the first officer shouted.

Richie lay face first on the soggy grass, turned away from Casey.

"What's your name?" the officer asked Richie.

After Richie stammered his reply, he was handcuffed and read his rights.

"ID, please, ma'am," another officer asked Casey.

She handed him her driver's license, while Virginia and the second officer emerged with Danielle between them. She looked too weak to stand on her own.

"Everything will be fine, honey," Virginia said to Danielle.

Danielle's hair was a disheveled mess, her eyes sleepy. When she saw Casey, a weak smile formed. "Hey."

"Hey, yourself." The lump in Casey's throat kept her from saying more.

"God knows what kind of drugs the bastard's given her," Virginia said.

"Richie didn't kill Harvey." Danielle's voice sounded raspy.

"Any idea who did?" Casey asked.

"No." Danielle closed her eyes and leaned into Virginia.

"What the hell did you give her?" Virginia yelled at Richie.

When he didn't answer, the officer hauled him to his feet. "Answer the question."

"S-sleeping pills." Richie's head swayed again. His clothes were wet from head to foot.

"What kind of sleeping pills?"

"D-don't know."

"Anything else?" the officer asked.

"Chloro-f-form."

"Where'd you get the pills and chloroform?" the officer asked.

"The Net."

"We need to see those pills. Where are they?"

"You can't go in. My parents don't like dirty shoes."

Casey held back a smile. Apparently Richie hadn't twigged on to the fact that they'd already traipsed through the house to reach the backyard.

"If you don't want the house tossed top to bottom, then get those pills now," the officer said.

As Richie was escorted toward the house, he looked back over his shoulder and yelled, "I was trying to help for your own good, s-stupid."

"Asshole," Danielle mumbled.

"Did you get to talk to Harvey?" Casey asked her.

"No." She paused. "Richie told me what happened to him."

"This can wait," Virginia said. "You need medical attention."

Great, a new protector. "Do you want me to phone your mom?" Casey asked.

"Yeah. Thanks."

As the rain finally stopped, Casey heard an ambulance siren. Once they reached the front of the house, she spotted Liam MacKenna, again not in uniform, talking to one of the constables. Denver must have told him what was happening. The moment MacKenna spotted them, he headed their way. The guy didn't look happy. Casey crossed her arms and braced herself for another verbal tirade.

"Is Danielle okay?" he asked Casey.

"A little groggy, but she seems fine."

He plunked his hands on his hips. "So, what part of *stay out of the way* didn't you understand?"

"I asked her to come," Virginia answered, "because you guys wouldn't."

"Who the hell are you?" MacKenna asked.

"Danni's girlfriend."

He looked Virginia up and down and shook his head.

As the ambulance arrived, Richie and the constables re-emerged from the house. Tears still trickled down Richie's chubby cheeks. MacKenna marched toward him, while paramedics took charge of Danielle, who looked like she was having a hard time staying awake. Curious about what MacKenna would say to Richie, Casey edged closer.

"The suspect and I have old business to discuss," MacKenna told the officers. "Isn't that right, Richie?"

Richie blubbered.

"I told you I'd never let this go," MacKenna added. "By the way, I saw your binder. Nice work. You're a smart guy, after all. Enterprising too. Do your parents know you're a messenger boy for a bookie? Would they be impressed with your binder?"

"You c-can't tell them!" Richie twitched and whimpered.

MacKenna smirked. "Your memory's not so bad either, is it, Richie?"

"I keep telling ya, I don't r-remember everything."

"You do remember who you were racing the night you crashed. I see fear every time I bring it up, Richie. Isn't it time I got a name?"

Tears dripped from Richie's chin as his head began to loll once more.

"This has to end," MacKenna said. "Here and now."

None of the officers moved.

"Is D-Demon gonna live?"

"Yep."

Richie's head stopped lolling. "Too bad."

The officers exchanged glances.

"Why's that?" MacKenna asked.

"He cut B-Bennie off. It was his fault!"

"Bashir Kumar was racing you and Ben that night?"

"He s-said he'd kill me and my family if I told."

Danielle was being eased into the ambulance. Casey figured she was probably too groggy and far away to hear Richie's revelation.

"We know that Kumar hasn't owned his current vehicle long," MacKenna said. "What was he driving that night?"

"I only remember red. He's always liked r-red."

Casey jogged to the ambulance, tempted to tell Danielle what she'd heard. But what if Richie was lying? She poked her head inside. "I'll come see you."

"My notebook," Danielle mumbled. "Get it."

"Was it in your bag?"

"Yes." She closed her eyes.

The police had Danielle's bag. A paramedic closed the ambulance door.

"I'm going to the hospital," Virginia said.

"Hold it," one of the officers replied. "We need to talk to you and your cohort here."

Virginia muttered something under her breath.

"Danielle asked me to get a notebook from her bag," Casey said to him. "Someone from your detachment picked up the bag the night she was taken. Will I be able to get the book?"

"We'll let you know."

Sure. At a quarter past never.

TWENTY-SEVEN

CASEY PEEKED IN DANIELLE'S HOSPITAL room and found her sitting cross-legged on her bed, putting on makeup. The three other beds in the room were occupied by gray-haired women with pasty faces and closed eyes. Two of them were snoring.

Casey approached Danielle's bed, which was nearest the door. "You look a lot better than you did yesterday."

"Thanks." Danielle smiled. "So, it took you five days to find me? Really? I thought you'd be faster."

"You didn't exactly leave a trail of crumbs." Casey hugged her. "You're all right then?"

"Yep. I'm outta here this morning. Despite the drugs, Richie took fairly good care of me. Supplied food and water and a porta-potty. Even allowed me to use the bathroom when his parents were out." She zipped her makeup bag. "The asshole."

"Are you sure you're allowed to leave this soon?"

"They need beds for sick people." Danielle tossed the makeup bag into a backpack someone must have brought her. "I'm good to go."

How much had Danielle learned about yesterday's events? Did she know that Richie had ratted out Bashir Kumar? Should Casey tell her?

"Richie claimed he was trying to keep you from getting killed," Casey said, "and part of me believes him. Even that night at the donut shop, he wanted you to stop investigating."

"Not just for my protection, though. He was afraid I'd tell his parents about him and Roadkill. How long did the idiot think he could keep me locked up?"

"Probably until the killer was caught."

"I bet his secrets are out now."

"He's not a killer, though, right?"

"No. Just a sneaky little dweeb. I'd already verified that he was at work during two of the hit and runs, but I was shocked when he told me he'd been sneaking out in his parents' car now and then. Richie doesn't even have a driver's license," Danielle said. "It's how he got me to his place. Took their bloody car, then returned it to the restaurant without anyone noticing."

The patient in the bed next to Danielle moaned a couple of times.

"The RCMP have your bag and won't let me look at your notebook, let alone take it," Casey said.

"I'm not surprised. There's info about Roadkill in it—dates and places of races. Alibis for some racers, but question marks for others."

"Actually, the police have learned a lot more." Casey smiled. "It turns out that Richie compiled a detailed binder full of racing stats and bios on everyone."

"Awesome!" Danielle's eyes sparkled. "I'd love to see it."

"Maybe Denver can arrange something after this is all over."

"I doubt it." Danielle put on a jean jacket. "Cops aren't eager to cooperate with me."

"That's because diplomacy's not your strong suit. If you ask nicely, maybe he'll agree."

Danielle stuck out her tongue.

"See?" Casey laughed.

Danielle fiddled with the cuff of her shirt sleeve, her expression becoming increasingly solemn. "If it wasn't for me, Harvey might still be alive."

"You don't know that."

Danielle glanced at her roommates, one of whom was starting to stir. "Remember that second date I had with Dom?"

"Yeah. You never did tell me what happened."

"There wasn't much to tell. He wouldn't talk about racing, except to say that he had a date the night Beatrice Dunning was killed and was working at the garage when Anna-lee Fujioko was mowed down." Danielle rummaged through her backpack. "I was so frustrated that I phoned Harvey and told him I knew he was part of Roadkill."

"Oh, Danielle."

"I know. It was stupid." She stopped rummaging. "I also said I knew he'd been racing his dad's Lexus the night Beatrice was struck."

"Did Harvey admit it?"

"No. That's when I threatened to tell the cops unless I got some information from him. Harvey agreed to meet me at the Regency after work." She shook her head. "We never got the chance to talk."

"What happened?"

Danielle ran her hand through her short black hair. "I parked next to Harvey's car and waited for his shift to end. After all the other cars had left the lot, there was still no sign of him, so I went looking." She paused. "I heard voices at the back and saw two people fighting by the pond. I couldn't see faces, but one of them fell and I heard a splash. The second person took off toward the far side of the building."

"Why didn't you call the police?"

"I thought it was just an ordinary fight. I also wanted some support, so I called you."

"When did Richie show up?"

"It must have been while I was talking to you. I remember ending our call and then nothing. The jerk probably came up from behind and chloroformed me like in some dumb movie."

"He had planned to take you?"

Danielle nodded. "Despite the brain damage, it's become pretty damn clear that Richie's more than capable of planning things."

"How did he know you were meeting Harvey?"

"He'd called earlier and insisted I come see him on his break at work. I told him where I was, and why, then said I'd be over right after." Danielle zipped up her bag. "Ginny figures he parked at the strip mall on the other side of the fence. None of the shops were open."

"It turns out there's a hole in the fence big enough for a person to slip through," Casey replied. "He must have known the area fairly well."

"He did. While I was captive, Richie told me the racers had met in back of the Regency a few times. He apparently liked to listen in without being seen." Danielle fetched her ski jacket from a tiny closet. "The cops should have searched all vehicles in the area. I was probably in the bloody trunk."

"We now know how calculating Richie is," Casey replied. "He could have moved the vehicle farther away before coming back to look for your bag, which I assume is what he tried to do."

"He probably panicked when you showed up."

"Even more when the RCMP caught him hiding in the bushes in front of the fence."

Danielle flung the jacket over her pack. "He would have freaked at the thought of being arrested and me being left in the trunk."

"He was pretty stressed, all right."

A nurse appeared and headed for one of the patients. Within seconds the patient began moaning. Casey wanted to leave, but there were still things to say. "I wish I'd spotted Richie from the get-go," she whispered. "He said he didn't know who Harvey fought with, but I wonder if that's true. Did he say how long he'd been lurking before he caught you off guard?"

"No, but it's an interesting question." She frowned. "How much did he see that night?"

The nurse finished with the patient and left the room.

Casey supposed this was as good a time as any to tell Danielle about Kumar. "Did you hear what Richie told Liam MacKenna yesterday?"

"No, what?"

"He said Bashir Kumar was the one who ran your brother off the road. Kumar apparently threatened to kill Richie and his family if he told anyone."

Danielle's mouth fell open. "You're joking."

"She's not." Danielle's mother entered the room, clutching a big brown purse with both hands. "Just after I got home from seeing you yesterday, Mr. MacKenna showed up."

"It really was Kumar?" Danielle asked, her eyes filling with tears.

"It seems so," Ivy answered. "Mr. MacKenna needs more proof before he can charge him."

Danielle embraced Ivy before dabbing her eyes with a tissue. "Kumar doesn't have solid alibis for any of the hit and runs. Guy's quite the freak." She scowled. "A natural-born killer who has to be stopped."

"Let the police worry about that," Ivy replied. "You've been through enough."

"How can I, Mom?" Danielle stepped back. "Four people are dead and a child was badly injured because some sick freak's targeting pedestrians!"

Ivy frowned. "I told you, that is police business, young lady; *not* yours."

"Kumar won't be driving anywhere for a while," Casey said. "He flipped his car while racing Saturday night. Broke a few bones."

"How ironic," Danielle remarked and turned back to her mother. "Good to see you again, Mom, but remember what I said about moving in with Ginny?"

Ivy fiddled with her purse strap. "Can't I see my own daughter before she goes? Heaven knows when I'll see you again."

"I'll only be fifteen minutes away."

Ivy clicked her tongue. "That doesn't mean I'll see you much."

Danielle sighed, then turned to Casey. "Do you know if MacKenna's talked to Kumar about sideswiping Ben's car?"

"I've heard that Kumar's been too out of it to talk to anyone. They'll try as soon as he's lucid."

Ivy walked up to Casey with her hand extended. "Thank you for helping free my daughter from that naughty boy."

Naughty boy? Was she joking? "Have you talked to Richie since his arrest, Mrs. Carpenter?"

"Absolutely not. I'm still mad at him for not telling me he'd been talking to Danielle, never mind holding her captive, for heaven's sake. No more treats for some time, I promise you that."

Casey and Danielle exchanged baffled glances.

"Mom, how long have you been keeping in touch with Richie?"

"Since Ben's funeral, and don't look at me like I've done something wrong. You know better than anyone that Richie's been family since he was five years old. I couldn't let him go just because his parents wanted to separate us."

"Why didn't you tell me?"

"He asked me not to."

"I bet," Danielle muttered. "And why did you go along with it?"

"Why didn't you tell me you'd been talking to him too, Miss Fancy Pants?"

"Journalists aren't supposed to reveal their sources, not even to their mothers."

"Hi, everyone." Virginia strolled into the room, looking relaxed and happy.

Casey noticed Ivy's disapproving expression and the way she avoided looking at Virginia.

"Ready to go?" Virginia asked.

"In a sec," Danielle replied.

"Are you sure you can't come home first?" Ivy asked. "I made cinnamon buns, and your father would love to see you."

"I'll come over later today."

"For supper?"

"If it includes Ginny."

Ivy hesitated. "Your father's not up for company."

The pink crystal stud in Danielle's nose sparkled as she tilted her head slightly and bit her lower lip. "When Dad's ready for company, give me a call."

"May I at least have Virginia's phone number in case we need to get in touch?"

"Sure, but you know my cell number."

"The cops still have your phone," Virginia said, handing Ivy a business card.

"I'll have to do something about that. Let's swing by the cop shop, and does anyone know which hospital Kumar is in?"

"Does it matter?" Casey had been relieved that Danielle was here at Richmond General and not near Kumar in New Westminster's

Royal Columbian Hospital. Knowing Danielle, she'd want to confront the guy.

"I'm not interested in interrogating him," Danielle replied. "But I want to say something, and it'd probably be better if he just lies there, or I might have to kill him."

"Danielle!" Ivy clutched her purse to her chest. "Hasn't there been enough death?"

"Sorry." She put her arms around her mother. "Listen, I'll pop by later today. Promise."

"Please don't make trouble," Ivy said.

"I won't." Danielle gave her mother a tight hug, whispered something in her ear, and then escorted her to the door. With a brief wave, Ivy left the room.

"Why don't you come see Kumar with me?" Danielle said to Casey.

"Is there any way I can talk you out of this?"

"Probably not."

Casey sighed. "Fine, I'll go." Someone had to keep Danielle from doing something stupid, and Casey didn't have confidence that Virginia would take on that role. Besides, she was curious to see how Kumar responded to Danielle.

"Any word on what Morris Mueller's been up to, or Eagle?" Danielle asked.

After Casey updated her on recent developments, Danielle smiled. "One by one, these losers are going down. Let's go see the shithead who killed my brother."

TWENTY-EIGHT

WITH GROWING TREPIDATION, CASEY FOLLOWED Danielle and Virginia down the hospital corridor. She didn't like the way Danielle's fingers twitched, or her apparent hostility. It was like watching a hungry dog hunt for food. When they reached the nurse's station, Danielle smiled and asked for directions to Kumar's room.

The nurse peered at all three of them over the top of her glasses. "Mr. Kumar's due for some tests in a few minutes. Are you family?"

"Friends, and we'll only be two minutes. I just want to say hi and let him know I've been thinking about him," Danielle replied.

Casey glanced at Virginia, who stood on the other side of Danielle. Back straight and hands at her sides, Virginia kept her expressionless face toward the nurse.

"If you can get past the officer posted at the door, then you can have five minutes," the nurse said. "The man never stops drinking coffee and takes a lot of bathroom breaks, so it shouldn't be hard."

"Is Bashir awake?" Danielle asked.

"The painkillers make him groggy and a bit incoherent, but he seems to understand what we're saying."

Danielle beamed. "Good."

They headed down the hall, passing a tall metal cart filled with trays of food. Casey smelled chicken and overcooked broccoli.

"Why a cop?" Virginia muttered. "It isn't as if Kumar can jump up and run away."

"Maybe they're worried that someone will help him bust out." Danielle scanned the room numbers. "Let's face it, the loser will be charged with something, and he has enough money to hire guys to watch his back."

Casey spotted an empty chair opposite a closed door.

Danielle charged ahead and read the room number. "This is it." She peeked inside. "He's alone. Come on."

Casey and Virginia exchanged cautious glances as they followed Danielle into a private room. Virginia closed the door behind them. Kumar was on his back, attached to an IV and a heart-rate monitor. God, the man was all casts, tubes, and machines. His face and fingertips were the only parts of him exposed to the air. When he heard their footsteps, his eyelids flickered.

"How sweet is this?" Danielle remarked. "Roadkill almost became roadkill."

Casey stood on one side of Danielle, while Virginia took the other. Kumar slowly opened his eyes and turned his head just enough to see Danielle.

"Hello, Speed Demon." She gave him a chilly smile. "You're done, you murdering freak."

He blinked at her. "Who're you?"

"I'm the one who's going to make sure you rot in jail."

He closed his eyes and turned his head toward the window.

"The cops know you ran Ben Carpenter off the road three years ago," Danielle went on. "Richie Kim told them." Kumar didn't respond. "Are you listening, you piece of shit?" Danielle stepped close enough to touch the cast on his arm. "You raced Ben on Georgia Street toward the Stanley Park causeway. You swerved into Ben, forcing him off the road. He and Richie went through the windshield, and I bet you didn't even bother to slow down because winning was all that mattered, right?" Rage swirled around Danielle like an electrical charge. She leaned forward until she was within a hair's breadth of Kumar's head. "Don't try to deny it, asshole."

"Fuck off," Kumar mumbled.

"You're a killer, you *pathetic* loser, and I'm going to make sure you pay." Danielle raised her arm, but Virginia gripped it before she could strike Kumar.

"It doesn't matter what he says," a familiar voice said from behind them.

Casey turned to find Liam MacKenna, in uniform, standing in the doorway. That he was the one posted outside the door didn't surprise her. The guy probably couldn't wait to extract a confession from Kumar. MacKenna gave Casey an icy stare before zeroing in on Danielle. "What are you doing here?"

"Back at ya," she replied. "Babysitting's a bit beneath you, isn't it?"

"This is a special situation." MacKenna strolled into the room. "It looks like our boy's more alert."

"He's the one who ran Ben off the road that night, right?" Danielle asked.

"It appears so." MacKenna glanced at Kumar. "We located the car Kumar was driving when your brother crashed."

"Awesome!" Danielle said, gripping Virginia's arm. "How did you find it?"

Casey spotted Kumar watching MacKenna.

"Our friend here's racked up a mess of driving infractions over the past five years," MacKenna replied. "Six months before your brother's crash, we impounded Kumar's car for a few days."

Casey smiled as the digits on Kumar's heart-rate monitor began to jump.

"We just learned that a week after the crash, Kumar sold his shiny red Corvette for dirt cheap because the right fender was damaged."

Danielle looked at MacKenna with disdain. "What took you so long to find this out?"

"We were led to believe that the vehicle had been sold before the crash to a buyer in the States. The paper trail was fake." He shook his head. "All I can say is that I was a rookie who had no say in how things were handled."

"You mean investigating officers dropped the ball," Virginia remarked.

"I'm just sayin' that we're not frigging psychics. The point is, we've got him now, and here comes the good part," MacKenna replied. "The new owner was T-boned several weeks after he bought the car. Adjusters took pictures of the vehicle, including the damaged fender, which the owner couldn't afford to fix when he bought it. The guy swears he had no idea the car had been involved in a fatal crash."

Kumar closed his eyes, while the digits on his heart monitor kept rising.

"After your brother's crash, red paint chips were taken off his car, analyzed, and the info entered into a database, which brings me to the big finale." He winked at Danielle. "It matches the Corvette. The adjusters' photos show exactly where paint was missing from the fender."

"That still doesn't put this jerk behind the wheel," Virginia said.

Kumar's jaw tightened, but his eyes remained shut.

"Richie's statement does," Danielle said. "Maybe he's not the only one who knows the truth." She glared at Kumar. "I bet Speed Demon's made a few enemies who might be willing to talk."

Kumar opened his eyes and returned her hate-filled stare.

"This guy could be facing a few murder charges," Virginia remarked.

Kumar lifted his head as far as he could. "He hit my car . . . lost control."

"Then why did you threaten to kill Richie and his family if he told anyone about it?"

"Didn't." Kumar collapsed back on his pillow.

"Okay, ladies." MacKenna clapped his hands and stepped in front of them. "Time to go."

"Make him tell the truth!" Danielle's eyes blazed. "I bet he mowed down those other people, too."

"Come on, Danni. Chill." Virginia put her arm around Danielle. "They've got him, and he's not going anywhere."

"Didn't kill anyone," Kumar said, licking his lips.

"Yeah, right." Danielle glared at him. "It's just a big coincidence that there've been no hit and runs since you've been in the hospital."

"Garage," he mumbled.

Danielle frowned. "You mean Dominic's garage?"

"M and M's." Kumar winced, as if hit with a spasm of pain. "His uncle's."

Danielle leaned closer. "What about it?"

Kumar's IV started beeping. The smaller bag was nearly empty, but the larger bag was still half full.

MacKenna moved closer to him. "What's the garage called?"

Kumar's eyelids fluttered and he groaned. "Clint."

Most cops didn't reveal much in their faces or body language, but Casey had worked with enough of them to recognize subtle changes. MacKenna stood a tiny bit straighter.

"What about the garage?" Danielle asked.

Before Kumar could answer, the nurse came in, carrying a fresh IV bag. "You were supposed to be five minutes. I need everyone to leave now, please."

Virginia took Danielle by the arm and pulled her into the corridor. Casey followed, aware that MacKenna was close behind.

"Any idea what's up with the garage?" Casey asked him.

MacKenna put his hands on his hips. "How many times do I have to tell you people that this isn't your concern?"

"I'm not leaving without answers," Danielle shot back. "So please, just tell me what made you so sure that Richie knew who ran him and Ben off the road, or had you just hoped he did?"

MacKenna let out a long sigh. "The kid got nervous whenever I asked him about it. When I heard about his connection to Roadkill, I figured he knew others who remembered that night."

"And you decided to make your presence known." Danielle nodded. "Thanks for not giving up."

He shrugged. "I told your folks I'd find out what happened that night, and I don't quit, ever."

Danielle's expression softened. "Thank you."

"You're welcome. Now go home." He headed back inside Kumar's room.

Danielle gazed at the closed door for a few moments before heading down the hall. She said nothing until she reached elevator. "Good cop." She pressed the button. "But still an A-hole."

"You're going home now, aren't you?" Casey asked.

"As soon as I look up an address."

Oh, no. Hadn't this girl learned anything?

"Danni, I have to be at work soon," Virginia said.

"We have time."

No one spoke as they rode to the main floor, but Casey again felt the tension. This time it came from Virginia. They stepped onto the main floor. Danielle marched toward the information desk and asked for the phone book.

"Danni, we are *not* going there," Virginia said.

Danielle took the book from the receptionist and flipped through it until she found what she was looking for. "Clint's Collision." She read the address aloud. "We'll just drive by. The place is practically on the way home."

"No, Danni."

"I promise I won't go in. I just want to see if they do body work." Danielle turned to Casey. "Want to tag along?"

"Sure." Casey was curious, and until an arrest was made for the hit and runs, Danielle needed to be watched more than ever.

Virginia said, "The place might not have anything to do with Kumar's Corvette. He might not have anything to do with the pedestrians getting hit at all."

"I know," Danielle murmured. "The black car that hit Beatrice Dunning was never reported stolen and never found. Which means, it could have been fixed right away by someone friendly with racers. Mueller drives a black BMW."

"As far as I know, the make of the first hit-and-run vehicle has never been established, and Mueller's car was never confiscated by police. There's no evidence pointing to him," Casey said.

"Mueller could have been driving something else that night," Danielle replied. "Harvey was using his dad's car."

Casey shook her head. "If the uncle's covering for his nephew, he sure as hell won't talk, and he'll be suspicious of strangers loitering near his shop."

"Like I said, I'll only take a quick look," Danielle replied. "If Mueller's there, we'll leave right away."

Casey and Virginia exchanged suspicious glances. If Mueller was there, they'd all be in trouble.

TWENTY-NINE

THROUGH THE DRIZZLE MISTING HER windshield, Casey studied Clint's Collision. She'd pulled into the parking lot of a tattoo parlor across the street from the body shop, while Virginia had parallel parked on the road in front of a motorcycle retailer. Beside the retailer were a pawnshop and a tool repair place, both looking a little run down.

The headlights of Virginia's Jeep were off, but the wipers were on. They'd all been watching the place for ten minutes, but nothing interesting had happened, and probably wouldn't; not in the middle of the day with customers coming and going. Casey wanted to leave but wouldn't until Virginia left first.

She studied the four open bays. Between bays two and three, a metal door remained shut. A small brick building marked PAINT SHOP stood to the far right of the main structure. Based on what she'd seen so far, Clint's Collision specialized in repairing high-end vehicles. Her cell phone rang. It was Denver.

"I just heard that you saw Kumar," he said.

Before Denver could lecture her for going there in the first place, Casey said, "Did MacKenna tell you about Mueller's connection to a body shop called Clint's Collision?"

"I knew about it. Why?"

He wouldn't be happy if he knew she was staring at the place. "Just wondering if it's involved with what's been going on."

Denver didn't answer right away. "The media's picked it up, so you might as well know that the Carrall Street victims were hit by a car stolen from Clint's Collision."

"Oh my god. It's Mueller, isn't it? He's the one mowing people down."

"That's too big of a leap without more evidence. The killer could be an employee or a friend of the racers."

Casey counted five mechanics, three of them young enough to be racers. Nearby, a tall, lanky man carrying a clipboard approached one of the mechanics. Was he Mueller's uncle? The white hair plastered to his head made him look old enough.

"Now that Kumar's been arrested, do you think Eagle will say more about the hit and runs?" she asked.

"His lawyer says the kid will talk under certain conditions."

The Jeep's headlights came on. "Will you tell me what he says?"

"That depends on what it is. Listen, I've got to go. Stay out of trouble, okay? MacKenna hates that you keep showing up."

"I'm not crazy about it either. Talk to you later."

Casey was about to call Virginia's cell when her phone rang again.

"We're taking off," Danielle said.

"Good. What's next for you?"

Danielle paused. "I'm going to write about my brother."

"I look forward to reading it."

Casey didn't have to be on the M7 bus for another three hours, but there was a term paper due and other chores to be done. Maybe she should call Lou. They hadn't talked much since he'd changed his mind about moving in. She could invite him over for a late supper after work and try to put things right. She'd thought about asking Lou to reconsider his decision, but life had gotten crazy, or so she kept telling herself. The truth was, she'd been afraid he'd turn her down. Maybe if she was more forthcoming about how she'd lost interest in her marriage. She needed to share her deepest fears and hope Lou wouldn't think less of her afterward.

OH, NO. *Now* what? She'd finally mustered up some courage and asked Lou to meet her after work, so why was he boarding the bus here? Had he changed his mind about her dinner invitation?

Greg swiveled in his seat and scowled at Lou, who ignored him as he waved to Casey. Lou's tentative smile made her stomach muscles clench and her heart begin to pound. He wasn't going to break up with her, was he? Not in front of her ex.

"This is a surprise." She tried to sound cheerful.

Lou sat down beside her. "I didn't want to wait till dinner to see you."

Casey squeezed his hand, noticing the dark circles under his eyes. "You look exhausted."

"Haven't slept well lately. Lots on my mind."

Casey kept her grip on his hand, afraid to ask what he'd been thinking about. The twins would be boarding soon, and she needed to focus on them.

Lou glanced at the other passengers before his pensive eyes turned to her. "I've been worried that you're furious with me for changing my mind and was wondering if you invited me to dinner to break up?"

"God no!" She squeezed his hand harder. "The dinner was to persuade you to reconsider your decision."

"Really?" Lou started to smile. "That's great, but could you ease up on my hand? It's starting to bruise."

Casey let go as Greg pulled up to the Granville and Sixteenth Avenue stop. Paige and Lara boarded, flashing their passes at Greg. Casey wished the girls would sit reasonably far away, but when they spotted her and Lou, they took the nearest available seat, three rows up and across the aisle.

"Have they been behaving?" he murmured.

"Yes, but I'm not sure it'll last." She turned to him. "Listen, I'm so sorry for screwing up. I was too involved with the street-racing mess and Danielle. I need to tell you something about Greg and I—about our past—but it's too complicated to discuss now."

"Can you give me a condensed version?"

Since Casey wanted this resolved too, she whispered, "When Greg and I broke up, I wasn't all that upset."

Lou gave her a puzzled look. "I was there, Casey. You were hurt."

"You saw hurt pride. The truth is, I didn't love Greg enough by then to be that upset about him and Tina." Casey returned Lara's stare until the girl looked away. "I scarcely paid attention to him those last two or three years. Letting Greg stay in the house after I ended our marriage was to ease my guilt as much as anything. It's something I've barely admitted to myself, let alone anyone else."

"What does that have to do with us?"

She hesitated. "Mother left, Dad's gone, Greg found Tina, and now Rhonda's away for years. All the people I've loved and depended on aren't here anymore. It's a pattern I've pretty much come to expect."

Lou gazed at her for what felt like a long time. "You think everyone you love will leave you sooner or later?"

She lowered her head. "Uh-huh."

"And you believe Greg wouldn't have hooked up with Tina if you'd been more attentive?"

"My behavior helped push him away, and yes, I know he was still in the wrong, but I just didn't care about our relationship as much as I should have."

Lou slumped back in his seat, a dazed look in his eyes. "I promised him I wouldn't say anything. Even after we weren't friends anymore, it seemed right to keep the promise. But if it affects our future, then screw it." He sighed. "Tina wasn't Greg's first affair. There were at least two others."

Casey wasn't quite sure she'd heard right. "What?"

"The first was a one-night stand in Vegas; the second was here and lasted a couple of months, I think."

Casey's mouth fell open. "When?"

"The Vegas thing was about eight months after your wedding. The second was two years after that. Greg knew I wasn't happy about what he was doing, so he stopped confiding in me. I wouldn't be surprised if there were more."

"Eight months?" Casey stared at Greg's back. "I wish you'd have told me a lot sooner."

"He was my best bud, and I'd promised. Besides, I thought the truth would crush you."

"It would have in the early days. Now it merely validates what I already knew. Leaving him was one of the best decisions I ever made."

She turned to Lou. "Now you know why I worry about putting all of my trust in one person. Things unravel, secrets come out, and people leave one way or the other."

Lou peered into her eyes. "I get it, Casey . . . The truth about your parents, the tragedy of their deaths, and Rhonda, of course. It explains why I felt you were holding me at arm's length sometimes."

"I didn't mean to."

Lou nodded. "I wish I'd realized it sooner." He paused. "You've been afraid I'll bail because you think you're incapable of truly committing."

Casey nodded. "If that happened—" The words caught in her throat. "I'd be lost for good." The tenderness in his gray eyes had her on the edge.

Lou slipped his arm around her shoulder. "It won't happen."

Aware that the twins were watching her again, Casey looked down. She hated feeling this vulnerable in front of them.

Lou kissed the back of her hand. "Even before this conversation, I realized I made a mistake and was going to ask, over dinner, if I could move in after all."

Casey smiled. Relief surged through her. "You know you can."

"How about I bring a bunch of stuff over tomorrow?"

"Absolutely. I'll help."

After the twins disembarked, Casey and Lou spent the trip back to Mainland's yard discussing furniture arrangements. She no longer cared if her apartment would be a crowded mess. She wanted him there—ugly furniture, disco music, lava lamps, and all. It would work. She would make it work. Casey nestled against Lou, oblivious to everything except his lips on her cheek, until Greg hit the brakes hard when they pulled into the yard.

As she and Lou headed for the exit, Greg stood and said, "We're moving out on December twentieth. Place will be clean by the thirty-first. That real estate lady put a sign on the lawn."

"Okay, thanks."

Ignoring Lou, Greg exited the bus. Lou gave Casey a long, passionate kiss.

"Let's continue this at home," she said. Casey flipped up her jacket hood to keep the rainy drizzle at bay.

"Do you need to write a report for Stan before we go?" Lou asked.

"Nothing happened tonight, so it can wait till the morning."

While they strolled toward their vehicles, Casey yakked about moving plans until they stopped behind her Tercel. Lou's pickup was parked four stalls down.

"Meet you at home," she said, embracing him.

"Can't wait." Lou started toward his truck, then stopped abruptly. "What the hell?"

Casey's car key hovered near her lock. "What?" She watched Lou edge toward her passenger door. "What is it?"

Casey hurried around the car and gasped at the sight of someone lying motionless on the ground.

THIRTY

CASEY'S STOMACH CLENCHED. THE PERSON, a man, was on his right side, face pushed up against the front tire, the lower half of his legs hidden under her car. In the greenish hue of the parking lot lights, the dark blotches on his jaw looked horrific. A gust of wind blew hair into Casey's eyes.

"Who is he?" she asked. "Is he alive?"

"No." Lou bent over and peered at the head. "His throat's been cut. I've never seen this guy before. He's not staff. Call 911." He straightened up. "Oh shit! I've stepped in blood!"

Casey gaped at the motionless jean-clad legs, dark socks, and runners. His familiar haircut sent dread slithering down her back and made the air feel thinner, tougher to breathe.

"I need to see his face."

She fetched her flashlight from the glove box. By the time she rejoined Lou, her lower back was clammy. When she shone the light on the victim's head, the dark slit across his throat became alarmingly clear. The vacant eyes and bloodied chin made him look like a horror movie mannequin. She thought she knew who the victim was, yet she wanted more confirmation.

"Can you tell if he has a small gold hoop in his right ear?" she asked.

"Shine the light on his face a bit more," Lou said, leaning over the body.

Casey held her breath until she heard Lou say, "Yeah, there's an earring."

She swallowed the bile rising in her throat and leaned against the rear fender. "It's Eagle."

"The Roadkill guy?"

"Yeah." She looked away. "His real name was Andrew Wing."

"Do you think another racer did this?"

"Maybe."

Dominic Mancuso and Morris Mueller were the only hardcore members left. Casey tried to calm down and not jump to conclusions. Air. She needed more air. As she looked up and breathed deeply, her hood fell back. Rain sprinkled her face.

"Want me to make the call?" Lou asked.

"No, I'll do it." She removed her phone from her pocket but dropped it on the ground. As she picked it up, her arms felt heavy. Casey gazed at the six parked buses in the yard. At the far end of the yard, the garage was closed. No one was around, except for a few staff in the admin building.

"Maybe you should sit down," Lou said, joining her.

"I'll be okay." She just needed to get a grip. It wasn't like she hadn't seen a dead body before. Still, how had he ended up next to her damn vehicle?

The rain grew heavier, and another gust of wind swooshed through the lot. She listened to the traffic coming from Lougheed as it passed on the other side of the building. Everything sounded so ordinary. The depot looked as it did on any normal night, except nothing felt normal or safe.

"Casey, the killer knows what you drive and where you work; maybe where you live. I'm calling Summer," Lou said.

"She's having dinner at a friend's. I told her I'd pick her up around nine."

"It's starting to pour. I'll get the tarp and tape from my truck and cover this guy before the evidence is washed away."

Casey called 911 and wiped the rain from her eyes as she spoke to a dispatcher. Too bad MPT headquarters was located in Burnaby, which was RCMP jurisdiction. She'd rather deal with the Vancouver Police, given everything that had happened. After she explained the situation to the dispatcher, she called Denver but got his voice mail. She left a message.

Casey again glanced around the lot. A prickly sensation ran up her spine, and she hurried over to Lou. With the wind and the rain, she wouldn't be able to hear footsteps until an assailant was almost on them.

"What if the killer's still here, watching us?"

Lou scanned the lot. "I'm almost done."

He duct taped the tarp to the roof of Casey's vehicle. The tarp sloped down, creating a tent that didn't touch the body. Once the bottom of the tarp was taped to the ground, Lou and Casey jogged toward the building entrance.

Casey glanced over her shoulder, half expecting a knife to come soaring at her. She tried to listen for footsteps and unusual sounds, but the rain was pounding too hard to hear much else. Once inside the admin building, Casey huddled against Lou and tried not to shake. He rubbed her back, but the shaking wouldn't stop; probably wouldn't any time soon. Eagle's body had been left by her car for a reason.

The sound of heavy footsteps made her and Lou turn around.

"Why are you two still here?" Greg asked. He'd changed back into street clothes and was carrying a lunch pail.

"We're leaving soon," Lou answered. "Have a nice night."

Scowling, Greg stomped outside, heading away from the Tercel.

"Do you think we should have told him?" Casey asked.

"No. He's not parked near you and was with us when it happened."

"What if the killer's still nearby?"

"He's not interested in Greg."

No, not Greg. Casey's cell phone rang. It was Denver.

"What's this about a murder?" he asked.

After she told him, there was silence at the other end of the line. It made her feel even more on edge.

"Why was your vehicle targeted when Danielle's the one on a vendetta?" Denver asked.

"Roadkill's seen her in my car at least once, and Danielle doesn't own a vehicle. Hell, she doesn't even have a regular workplace." Rain dripped from Casey's bangs onto her face. "She's moved out of her parent's home, so I guess I'm easier to find."

"Not good."

No kidding. "You know what's really bad?" She didn't wait for a response. "Both of the guys who could have identified the driver who struck Beatrice Dunning have been murdered. Makes you wonder about the driver, doesn't it? Maybe he's taken to killing other racers with knives and pedestrians with cars. The guy's a real psycho, Denver."

"No argument here."

"Because of Mueller's connection to Clint's Collision, my money's on him."

"Like I said before, don't jump too far ahead. We still have other leads to follow."

Two RCMP cruisers—lights flashing but without sirens—turned into the depot.

Casey's rigid shoulders began to relax. "Did you or anyone else get anything useful from Eagle before this happened?"

"No."

"Crap." Did he die because he was going to talk? "The RCMP just showed up."

"I'm en route. Will be there shortly."

As Casey slipped the phone into her pocket, Lou's eyes narrowed. "How did the killer know you'd be here tonight?"

"Good question." Wiping raindrops from her forehead, she thought of her chat with Morris Mueller at the university two days ago. Had he decided to monitor her? Do a little investigating of his own?

One of Mainland's newest and youngest drivers approached. Tall, skinny, and still plagued with acne, the kid looked like he should be heading for a high school basketball game rather than the driver's seat of a bus.

The kid started to head outside when he spotted the cruisers. "What's going on?"

"Hey, Avery. Are you starting or finishing a shift?" Lou asked.

"Just finished break. Why?"

"Did you happen to see or hear anything unusual in the parking lot before you went for your break?" Casey asked.

The kid looked from her to Lou and back again. "Did somebody key your car?"

"Nothing like that," Casey replied, pointing toward her vehicle. "My Tercel's over there, and I was just wondering if you saw anyone, or another vehicle, near it."

Avery craned his neck and peered through the glass. "Sorry. Didn't see anything."

"Are you sure?" Casey replied. "A vehicle would have pulled up near my car within the past hour. It might have had a powerful engine."

His eyes widened. "Wait, I heard something loud pull into the lot just after I stepped inside. I looked back and saw a pair of headlights, but that was all. Didn't think much about it."

"Could you tell if the vehicle was light or dark?" Lou asked.

Avery's forehead crinkled, as if he was trying to remember. "Only saw the headlights."

"Did you see it stop near my car?"

"Nope. What's this about, anyway?"

Casey spotted two police officers lifting the tarp. A third officer circled her car. "Avery, what time did you start your break?"

He checked his watch. "Thirty-five minutes ago, and I'm late. Gotta roll, but if you're looking for witnesses or something, you should talk to Benny Lee." Avery pushed the door open. "When I was coming in, he was going home."

Casey looked around. Benny's SUV wasn't in the lot. "Thanks, Avery."

"No problem." He stepped outside.

"Avery would have gone inside at about ten to eight," Casey said to Lou. "You wouldn't happen to know Benny's home number, by any chance?"

"I'll get it from dispatch."

Lou hurried down the corridor as a Vancouver patrol car pulled into the lot. Denver stepped out and walked toward the tarp. Casey went outside to meet him. She flipped up her hood, but a wind gust blew it off. As she approached her car, an officer moved in front of her.

"Who are you?" he asked.

"Casey Holland. I own the Tercel next to the victim."

"Did you know the deceased?"

"Not really. We spoke briefly at a funeral about a month ago." As Denver joined them, she said, "I do know Officer Denver Davies, here. In fact, I asked him to come by because this man's death is likely connected to a series of hit and runs he's been investigating."

Denver nodded to the constable. The two men chatted privately for a moment, then the constable returned to Casey and said, "When did you discover the body?"

After providing a timeline, she told him what Avery had seen and mentioned that Benny Lee might have seen more. "We're getting Benny's phone number now," she added.

The officer nodded and looked around. "Who else is on site?"

"A dispatcher, supervisor, and cleaners, plus a few drivers," Casey answered. "Admin staff start leaving around four. Management would have left a couple of hours later, though sometimes one or two will stay late."

The officer turned to his colleague. "We'll need a list of everyone who was here from 7:00 PM until now, especially those scheduled to either arrive or leave during that time. We'll also need to talk to the person in charge tonight."

Lou jogged up beside Casey. "I called Benny. He was walking past your car on the way to his and saw a gray Dodge Neon idling behind the Tercel."

Casey gripped Lou's arm and looked at Denver. "Dominic Mancuso's car."

"Did he get a plate number?" Denver asked.

"No, but he thinks the driver was alone and didn't see him get out of the vehicle. Benny was in a hurry to get home, so he didn't pay much attention."

"Did he tell you what time this would have been?" the RCMP officer asked.

"Ten to eight."

As Lou gave the officer Benny's phone number, Casey stepped closer to Denver.

"I don't understand this," she said. "Danielle confirmed that Mancuso had alibis for at least two of the hit and runs."

Denver moved away and spoke into his radio. In less than a minute, every cop in the Lower Mainland would be watching for Mancuso's vehicle. Casey shook her head. That silly arrogant womanizer was a killer?

She approached an RCMP officer. "I know my car will have to stay, but my boyfriend's truck is parked four stalls down. Is there any chance that we can go home soon?"

"Wait here and I'll check."

BY THE TIME she and Lou were allowed to leave, Casey was exhausted. She'd written her shift report and talked to the supervisor in charge. She'd also phoned Summer, who'd been invited to stay the night at her friend's. Normally Casey would have said no on a school night, but keeping Summer away from the house was a safer option. When she and Lou finally left the depot, they were too drained to talk.

Once they arrived home, Casey made sure the alarm was on and all the windows and doors were secure. After a maniac had come into the house and tried to shoot her last year, she'd had the system installed. But she'd gotten lazy and kept it turned off most of the time.

Casey and Lou had just stepped into her apartment when her cell phone rang.

"Dominic Mancuso wants to meet me at Clint's Collision!" Danielle blurted.

"*What?* He called you?"

"His friend, who works at Clint's, did. Dom told him to call me."

"Why?"

"I don't know. Maybe he thought I'd hang up the second I heard his voice. Anyway, he said Dom knows who the hit-and-run killer is."

Casey didn't like this. "Why doesn't Dom or his friend phone the police?"

"He's afraid the cops will throw him back in jail without hearing his side of things first."

Casey caught Lou's pensive stare. "I thought you said Dom had alibis for two of the hit and runs."

"A couple of mechanics verified his whereabouts, but he could have paid them to lie."

"Danielle, you can't go there. The police have a bloody good reason to go after Dom themselves now."

After Casey highlighted events at Mainland, Danielle said, "No wonder this sounds like a setup. I can't wait to see the police take the bastard down."

"You aren't still going there, are you?"

"Already on my way."

"Danielle, do you have any idea how stupid that is?"

"I've already phoned the cops and told them what's happening. Now that Dom's wanted for murder, they'll show up pretty damn quick. I won't even have to get out of the Jeep."

Casey sighed. "I'm calling Denver."

"Can you meet me at Clint's? You live close by, right? You could take the back while I watch the front until help arrives. I'm almost at the body shop now."

"Damn it, Danielle. Are you alone? Where's Virginia?"

"At work. See you soon."

Casey prayed the police showed up before Danielle because the odds of that girl staying in her vehicle were slim to none.

"Lou, don't take your coat off," she said, rushing through an explanation while ushering him out the door. "We're going to get Danielle away from that place if we have to kidnap her ourselves."

THIRTY-ONE

CASEY AND LOU SPED NORTH, zipping past familiar cafés, markets, and shops. Speed and apprehension blurred the shapes of Commercial Drive, making the world feel risky and beyond her grasp. She looked at the side mirror for signs of flashing police lights and tried to slow her breathing, but the worry was too big.

Lou braked for the red light at Hastings, while Casey called Danielle. After four rings she started to panic. Why wasn't Danielle answering? Had Mancuso spotted her? Maybe the police had arrived and Danielle was talking to them. Casey listened to the continuous rings. Her call to Denver had prompted a string of curses and rude remarks about Danielle's sanity, but he'd promised to get there as soon as he could and assured her that other officers were on their way. Danielle finally answered.

"Where the hell are you?" Casey asked. "And why didn't you answer the phone?"

"It fell on the floor. I've just parked across the street from Clint's. All's quiet. There's no sign of anyone."

Casey's shoulders sagged with relief. The light changed and Lou turned left onto Hastings. "Is Mancuso's car there?"

"No. I was going to take a look at the back of the building, but it looks pretty dark. Wait a sec. A Smart car's pulling up in front of the shop. A chick's behind the wheel and there's a passenger. Oh. Now they're driving around back."

"Do *not* follow them, understand?" She thought she heard a door close. "Danielle?"

"Wait," Danielle replied.

Casey strained against her seatbelt. Clint's Collision was on a side street three blocks ahead. Traffic forced Lou to slow down. "Danielle, talk to me!"

"I'm on foot," she murmured, "behind some bins next to the building."

"Get out of there!"

"Dom's car is behind the body shop. Shit, he's getting out of the Smart car!"

Two patrol cars sped in opposite directions on Hastings. One turned onto the street in front of Clint's. The other turned into the lane running behind the shop.

"Danielle, the police are pulling up. Let them take over."

"Dom's in his car and heading north down the lane." She sounded breathless. "The Smart car's heading south. One cop car's after her and the other's going after Dom. I want to see them bust the jerk. I'll call you back."

"Danielle!" It was too late. She'd hung up.

By the time Lou turned off Hastings, Virginia's Jeep was disappearing behind the garage. Lou sped up to follow her. They reached the back of the building in time to see Danielle's tail lights.

"Should we follow her?" he asked.

"With the cops there, all she can do is watch from a distance."

Lou pulled up to the body shop and parked in front of the door. Everything looked shut tight.

"What now?" he asked.

"Don't know. I'm not sure if we should wait and update Denver or just leave."

"You could do it from home. He's probably listening to all the cop talk, anyway."

"What about the person who made the call for Mancuso?" She gazed at the building. "Do you think he's still inside?"

"I don't think we should be the ones to find out."

"You're probably right. Let's go."

As Lou shifted into reverse, a crash inside the building made Casey jump.

"Help!" a man shouted from inside. "Somebody help!"

It sounded like he was just behind the door. Was he an employee, the owner, or an intruder? To their right, a dim light shone through narrow windows set higher than the doorframe.

"Think we should go in?" she asked.

"Let's wait for Denver."

Casey couldn't see any parked vehicles near the building. "What if someone's badly hurt?"

"What if he's not alone?" Lou replied. "What if there's a fight? They could have weapons."

Casey dialed 911, described the situation, and was told to stay on the line.

"I can't move!" the man yelled. "Is someone out there? Help!"

"He just called for help again," she said to the dispatcher. "The guy could be crushed under something, and I know first aid."

"I understand, ma'am, but you need to think of your safety first."

"I'm aware of that, but if this is real and the guy's bleeding badly or having breathing problems, the ambulance could be too late. The window's fairly high. If I stand on the hood, I might be able to see."

"I'll do it," Lou said.

"Help! Please!" the man called out. "Oh god, it hurts!"

Casey cringed. It sounded bad, or did someone just want her to think so? Someone who'd been expecting Danielle. "He just cried out again," she said to the dispatcher. "Listen, I'm here with my boyfriend, who also has first aid. He'll look through the window, and I'll check out the door. If it's unlocked, I'll stay on the threshold and see what's up." She fetched the flashlight Lou kept under the passenger seat.

"Help!"

"He just called out again." Casey gripped the phone. "I'll stay on the line, and if I sense a trap I'm out of there."

Lou eased the truck close to the wall, directly beneath a window. "Don't go in till I get a look. I'll need that flashlight."

Casey handed it to him, then got out of the truck.

"Take the crowbar I keep in back," he added, climbing onto the hood. "I'll be right there."

"Help!" the man shouted. "Don't leave! I can't move!"

Casey put her phone in her pocket, then picked up the crowbar, while Lou shone the light through the window. "I can't see anything."

"Give me the light," she said.

Lou hesitated before handing it to her.

"Help me! *Please!*" the voice screamed.

As Lou got down from the hood, Casey walked up to the door and slowly turned the handle, afraid to make any noise. The door was unlocked, which was no surprise since someone had been expecting Danielle. Her heart bounced against her chest. Sirens approached. Bolstered by the arrival of help, she opened the heavy metal door and poked her head inside. The smell of oil and gasoline was strong. Casey saw a light switch on her right. As she reached for it, a hand clamped around her wrist and yanked her inside so fast her shoulder hit the door and she lost her balance. The door slammed shut. A bolt turned.

"Hey!" Lou shouted, banging on the door.

Casey dropped to her right knee, losing the flashlight. As she started to stand, a sharp kick to her lower back made her double over and drop the crowbar. It clanged on the cement floor and started to roll away. Casey grabbed it. Desperate to get away, she stumbled forward into the garage.

"Casey!" Lou yelled and banged on the door. "Casey!" It sounded like he was jiggling the handle, then there was a thud—he must have kicked the door.

Aware of someone close behind her, Casey turned and swung the crowbar as hard as she could. A voice cried out in pain and her assailant fell. The only light, coming from another room, was too dim for her to be able to identify her attacker.

In the shadows, she thought she saw the door between the bay entrances that she'd noticed the other day. Two cars were on her right. A toppled cart was in front of her, tools scattered everywhere.

"*Casey!*" Lou again banged on the door.

If she responded, the nut would find her. Sweat trickled down

Casey's sides and coated her back. She had to get out of there.

The sirens stopped. A strong beam of light blinded her, and a kick to her right hip sent her reeling against a car. The glaring light lowered. She saw eyeglasses on a familiar face and a long, shiny blade in Morris Mueller's hand. Casey's legs shook so hard she worried they'd give out.

"Police!" a man yelled. "Open the door or we'll break it down!"

"He has a knife!" Casey yelled. "Help!" Mueller stared at her as if oblivious to the commotion outside. "You've got one chance to get away, Morris. Just open a door and take off. I won't stop you."

"Why not?" For someone about to be arrested, his voice was unnervingly calm. "That's what you've been trying to do all along."

She needed to keep him talking. "You're the one who ran down Beatrice Dunning and all the others, aren't you? Harvey and Eagle were with you that night. They died because you thought they'd eventually tell the police."

Another bang on the door made her flinch. Morris still seemed unconcerned.

"The driver was a friend of Eagle's from high school," he said. "It had nothing to do with me."

He didn't even ask how or when Eagle died. Suddenly Casey heard a tinny voice call her name; she had no idea how long the dispatcher had been shouting to her. She'd forgotten she had left the line connected. She pulled the phone from her jacket pocket.

"I'm here," Casey said, "with a man named Morris Mueller. He has a knife!"

"Can you get out of there?" the dispatcher asked.

"No."

"Can you hide somewhere?"

"Too late. He's right in front of me." Why wasn't Mueller leaving? Didn't he realize it was over, or didn't he care? Nausea swirled faster. A huge crash against the door sent her jumping backward. "If you didn't kill anyone, then put the knife down and open the door."

Mueller didn't move. "Why should I trust you?"

"Because I'm just trying to figure out what's going on. Why did you yell for help?"

"I thought someone else was in here, but then I heard a car pull up."

"Why did you kick me?" Casey asked.

Another attempt to bash down the door made her flinch. It wouldn't be long before they were in. Mueller was eerily still.

"I couldn't see clearly and was a bit freaked out," he replied. "For all I knew, you were the killer."

"Why did you come here in the first place?"

"Dominic Mancuso called and said he was in trouble. He begged me to meet him here."

"Where did you get the knife, Morris?"

He looked down and appeared to study the thing. "I found it on the floor when I got here."

This was his plan? To make things up as he went? Fine, she'd play along. "Is Dom the one who's been killing people?"

The door started to give way.

"All I know is that I'm not the one running people down, and if I wanted to kill you, wouldn't I have done it by now?"

He still might try. His hand had begun to shake. "Why don't you drop the knife?"

Another bang. Help would be through any second.

"Can't. I don't know where Dom is," Morris replied. "But I think he brought me here to kill me."

The door came crashing down.

THIRTY-TWO

"SEE YA, CASEY," PAIGE SAID, following her sister toward the bus exit.

Casey looked up from the *Contrarian*. "Actually, you won't. I'll be on a new assignment."

Since the twins had obeyed the rules for a couple of weeks, and Stan needed her elsewhere, this was her last run on the M7 for now.

"Try not to piss people off," Lara said, sweeping her pink bangs to the side.

"Back at ya."

Casey returned to Danielle's piece about the demise of Roadkill. She'd written about the gamblers who had waved big bucks in front of these guys, enticing racers to push harder and risk their lives. The gamblers weren't just thugs and criminals, but also doctors, lawyers, dentists, and stockbrokers. *People who depend on the recklessness of others for thrills. People who are born cowards and will be until the day they die.* Richie must have told her about the gamblers.

Danielle had gone on to write that money hadn't been the sole reason for Roadkill's recklessness; there was also the competition, thrill-seeking, and bragging rights. *Among them was a sociopath who'd discovered a new thrill: deciding who would live and who would die.* She mentioned Morris Mueller's arrest for the murders of Eagle and Harvey and for the hit-and-run deaths of Beatrice Dunning and Anna-lee Fujioko. Charges were still pending over the deaths of the last two victims, Jason Charlie and Chantel Green.

Casey looked up at the clear night sky. She was grateful to Denver for sharing information, for telling her how Morris had phoned his uncle the night Beatrice died and begged him to fix the black Miata he'd claimed to have hit a tree with. He'd taken his father's car for a joy ride, just as Harvey had taken his dad's Lexus. Casey had no idea if the uncle had mentioned anything about seeing blood on the vehicle, but if Morris was smart he would have washed it off before taking it to the body shop.

Casey had distanced herself from Ellen Mueller, who was vehemently denying her son's involvement in any hit and run, according to last night's news clip. Casey had phoned Ellen's office to say she'd decided to take her house off the market. She hoped she'd never hear from that woman again, although she had a feeling they'd meet in court.

Taking a deep breath, Casey inhaled the slight odor of mothballs coming from the passenger beside her. She scanned the passengers, many of whom were absorbed with paperbacks or electronic gadgets, then returned to Danielle's article.

While gamblers profited, mothers, fathers, brothers, sisters, and friends mourned for those killed by a motor vehicle. I'm one of them. Three years ago, my brother, Benjamin Carpenter, was killed while racing on Georgia Street. He made a huge mistake and it cost him his life. I remember the funny, athletic guy who brought home stray cats and tons of friends. I remember how proud he was when he passed his driver's test and how he took my parents and me to the Dairy Queen to celebrate. They often told Ben to be careful, and he always promised them that he would. He was twenty years old when he died. I still miss him. I'm still furious with him for breaking his promise.

Casey looked up and wondered if the Carpenters could finally begin to heal. By the time she'd finished reading the rest of the paper, the bus was only ten minutes from the depot. Greg pulled up to the next stop, watched the last passenger disembark, then strolled toward her. Terrific. Just what she needed.

"Casey?"

"Shouldn't we be heading back?"

"I'm five minutes ahead of schedule. Traffic's light for a change."

Based on the way Greg shifted his feet and blew out little puffs of air, something was on his mind. "What is it, Greg?"

"I'm quitting Mainland. Handing in my notice as soon as we get back."

This was a surprise, but a welcome one. "Did you find another job?"

"Yep. Coast Mountain hired me."

A union job. The jump in Greg's salary would annoy the hell out of Lou. "Congratulations."

"I noticed that the real estate sign was taken down," he said. "Now that I'll be able to afford the rent, I'd like to stay."

No way in hell. Time to sever this tie once and for all. "I'm still selling, just changing agents."

When her phone rang, Greg trudged back to his seat. Casey smiled at the sound of Danielle's cheerful voice.

"Good news, my series is being picked up by other papers. My byline's going to be everywhere. I'm so stoked."

"I'm not surprised. I just read your latest column and it's wonderful."

"Thanks. Listen, I wanted you to know that Richie's story about Kumar running him and Ben off the road held up. Another witness came forward. One of Kumar's roommates ratted him out."

"How did you learn this?"

"A source. New ones do pop up now and then."

"Speaking of sources, how's Richie doing?"

"Miserable. If he isn't sent to jail, his parents are shipping him to Ottawa to live with his grandparents. Richie says they're even more strict than his folks, but they also know nothing about computers, so he figures he can stay in touch."

"Do you want that?"

Danielle didn't answer right away. "I'm not sure. Anyhow, I got hold of Mancuso and he said the blonde in the Smart car came on to him at the River's End Pub, promising all sorts of goodies."

"And since Dom is so predictable . . ."

Danielle laughed. "His lawyer found out that Mueller paid the girl to keep him busy."

"How did Dom wind up at the shop?"

"An anonymous caller said his car had been stolen and taken to Clint's Collision."

"Morris made the call, right? He arranged the whole thing."

"Looks that way. I think his plan was to kill me for getting too close to the truth about him and frame Dom for it."

"Did Dom know that Morris's uncle owns the place?" Casey asked.

"He claims he didn't, but who knows? Yesterday, on Facebook, Morris's sister said her brother had been afraid for his life and thought Dom was going to kill him. I'm guessing Morris gave his family quite a sob story, so they're doing damage control. Can't wait to see it fall apart on the witness stand."

"And it will." Although Casey despised courtrooms, she looked forward to bringing Mueller down.

"The cops told me that the reward money will be split between you and me," Danielle said. "I'm buying a good secondhand car and a laptop. What about you? Isn't it about time you bought a rust-free car?"

"I still like mine."

Danielle laughed again. "Hey, thanks so much for all your help. If it wasn't for you, Mueller might still be running people down."

"You're welcome, but don't take any more risks, okay? No story is worth your life."

"It wasn't about my life." She paused. "It was about Ben's. Keep in touch."

"Count on it."

Casey pocketed her phone, then picked up the *Contrarian* and found herself again drawn to the last paragraph of Danielle's article.

Although Roadkill's hardcore racers have been sidelined, street racing hasn't stopped. More idiots could form clubs, and more greedy cowards might pay to watch the carnage. Whether vehicles are racing or not, pedestrians are struck down every day by speed, recklessness, sleep deprivation, substance abuse, and other careless acts. Don't let your guard down any time soon. I won't.

Casey folded the paper and looked out the window. The evening reminded her of the night Beatrice was killed, just over a month ago, but without the looming Halloween madness. Instead, Christmas was coming . . . good times with Summer, a deepening love for Lou. Life was just fine.

A powerful car engine behind the bus broke Casey's reverie. She looked out the window as a Jetta zoomed past, its red lights shrinking into the distance.

Acknowledgments

Once again, many thanks and much gratitude to the members of Port Moody's Kyle Centre Writers' Group. They patiently critiqued every chapter in this book and offered many insights and more enthusiasm than I could have hoped for.

Another huge thank you to Ruth Linka for continuing to believe in my work and for her collaborative approach to publishing. Also, huge thanks to Frances Thorsen and Cailey Cavallin for their amazing editing skills and to talented cover designer Pete Kohut and publicist Emily Shorthouse, who work so hard.

Endless thanks and much love to my family for their support and patience during my daily retreat into the world of fiction. Thank heaven everyone in my house knows how to cook and do laundry.

Although many settings in this book are real, others are not. Monty's Diner, River's End Pub, Regency Fitness Center, Winnie's Donuts, and Clint's Collision are all products of my imagination.

DEBRA PURDY KONG's first Casey Holland transit security mystery, *The Opposite of Dark*, was released in 2011, and the second, *Deadly Accusations*, appeared in 2012. She is also the author of the Alex Bellamy white-collar crime mysteries, *Taxed to Death* and *Fatal Encryption*, and has published more than one hundred short stories, essays, and articles for publications such as *Chicken Soup for the Bride's Soul*, *BC Parent Magazine*, the *Vancouver Sun*, *Lynx Eye*, *Orchard Press Mysteries*, *Crimestalker Casebook*, *Futures Magazine*, and *Shred of Evidence*. In 2007, she won an honorable mention at the Surrey International Writers' Conference for her short story "Some Mother's Child." Debra has a diploma of associate in criminology and has worked in security as a patrol and communications officer. She lives in Port Moody, BC, with her family. More information about Debra and her work can be found at debrapurdykong.com. Follow her on Twitter at @DebraPurdyKong.